ROYAL TEASE

NANA MALONE

COPYRIGHT

Cover Art by Najla Qamber

Photography by Wander Aguilar

Edited by Angie Ramey

Published in the United States of America

1

Roone...

ONE RULE. I WOULD NOT SHAG MY BEST FRIEND'S SISTER.
I felt that as rules went, that one bore repeating... over and
over again. As the hip-hop grime music drummed around me,
I watched her. She was no fairy princess. Lean but with curves
in all the right places. Hair piled high in a ponytail with curls
cascading down her back. Wide hazel eyes. Amber skin that
gleamed.

She was beautiful. I probably should have expected that
considering Sebastian and Lucas were both handsome little
shits.

And it doesn't matter if she's beautiful. Because I would not
shag my best friend's little sister. That was a wanker thing
to do.

No, it didn't matter. I had a job to do. Protect her. Keep
her safe. Not ogle.

In my earpiece, I could hear Ariel clearly as if she were
sitting right next to me. "You see her?"

"Yeah I got her."

"So, do you know how to make an approach, or do you need some coaching?" Ariel's voice was sweet, but I heard the sarcasm laced between her words.

"I don't need coaching, thanks very much. I do know how to talk to women."

Ariel chortled at that. "If you say so."

Sure, women I normally chatted up weren't royalty. They also weren't the little sister of my best mates either, so I needed to tread carefully but still get the job done.

"Any day now, Romeo."

"Would you shut it?"

"Is that any way to talk to your mission commander?"

Leave it to Ariel to remind me that, on this job, I reported to her. I was still smarting about that one. Yes, it made sense because she had had more undercover work experience. But generally speaking, I had seniority.

Focus, would you?

I lost Jessa for a moment in the crowd, which I didn't think was possible. She had this way of marching, or maybe it was more of a strut, like no matter what she wanted to do, she was getting there quickly and with verve. There was no slow meandering for her. Everything about her was determined, deliberate. No mistakes. No wishy-washiness. Honest.

"If you keep staring at her like that, you're going to have a problem," Ariel muttered.

"I'm not staring. I'm waiting for my opportunity."

She is not a potential date. She is the *lost princess. Get your shit together.*

The other thing that fascinated me, was that she was completely in charge of everything. No pampering here. When waiters had shift changes, she took up trays. She talked with the clients and worked the room. I had already seen her take on soothing someone whose date apparently hadn't shown up. And she managed client expectations.

From the file, I knew that this was a birthday party for Abena Nartey Chase, the famous photographer. She was married to Alexi Chase, the billionaire startup kid. And she was sister-in-law to Xander Chase, also a renowned photographer. I had studied all of their dossiers. I knew exactly who the players were. I knew exactly who was on her client roster, and who she was courting.

Currently, she was courting Emerson Poole. Poole had financial business interests all over the world. He also had an extensive gambling habit. But, what he lost at the tables, he made back with gambles on new companies. And thanks to Ariel, I knew that the princess's company, Evans PR, hid him on retainer as a client. And Jessa was laying it on thick, but not *too* thick. Professional, but attentive.

As a result, Poole couldn't take his eyes off of her. More like he couldn't take his eyes off her ass. *Twat.*

As she left, she carried one of the trays toward the back where the staging area was. I stood up. "Show time."

"Okay. See if you can get close enough to tag her body. Bug in a jacket or something. If you can get close enough to her purse, do it."

I knew how to do my bloody job. "Yeah, I hear you."

Thanks to our partnership with Blake Security, we had some amazing state-of-the-art technology. Bugs so small, they'd be virtually undetectable. Under the collar of a jacket. Inside a purse. On a credit card. I just had to get close enough.

"You take any longer and you're going to miss your opportunity."

I rolled my eyes and very deliberately took out the tiny earpiece. I didn't need Ariel in my head for this.

Timing was everything. I slid into the staging area right behind Jessa. Luckily a busboy was coming out right after she went in so there was a delay.

I knew exactly where the lockers were. Jessa and her

colleagues apparently didn't know enough to be worried about their safety and security and had left most of their belongings out. I saw her purse behind one of the benches and palmed her wallet before sliding into the shadows.

I pulled the pen light out of my pocket, then the bugs, gently peeling them off of their plastic contact sheet before applying one to her driver's license and one to the inside of her wallet.

Ariel would handle the larger surveillance monitoring jobs like her flat and car. The finesse was my job. With a final deep breathe I stepped out of the shadows… right into the princess and the glass of champagne she was carrying.

She swore and teetered on her heels as she tried to recover the glass.

"Fuck." My arms snapped around her, dragging her to me as champagne spilled down my jacket and the glass shattered.

Her scent wrapped around me like a delicate man-trapping orchid. Light, floral, and flirty. Wholly enticing. It made me want to lean in and breathe deep.

The next thing I registered were her curves. *Lush* curves… pressed up against my muscles. And finally, her hair. Her ponytail flipped up and several curls whipped me in the face.

Zaps of electric current fired all around me. *What the fuck was that about?*

Her hands pressed on my shoulders and reluctantly, I let her go. "Oh Jesus. I'm so sorry," she muttered.

I shoved her wallet into my pocket. "No, it's my bloody fault. I got turned around. Someone told me I'd find the loo over here."

Hazel eyes blinked up at me before she shook her head. "Oh, no. Actually, you're in the staging area. The bathroom is on the other end of the club."

"Bathroom? I sense a yank in my midst." *What the hell is*

wrong with my voice? I sounded like I'd suddenly swallowed a frog.

My dick twitched as if to say, *if I have to tell you... then you're a lost cause.*

I ignored the flare of desire. She was beautiful, but she wasn't the first beautiful girl I'd ever met in my life. I could ignore this. *You have to ignore this.*

Her grin flashed. "Canadian-Brit actually. Don't let my inaccurate colloquialisms and the accent fool you."

Of course, I knew that after her father had gone off the map, he'd moved them to Toronto. "Since you're Canadian, why don't you buy me a glass of champagne to make up for spilling yours all over me? I know how nice your people are."

She laughed then. Not just with her face but with her whole body, tipping back slightly, her head falling back. I couldn't help but smile in return.

She stared at me for a moment then blinked rapidly. "*Or you* could buy me a drink to apologize for bumping into *me* because see, you're bigger than I am. You should make way."

I grinned and tilted my head. "All right, how about this... You buy me the first round while you apologize, *then* I buy you one?"

I'd started to walk and steer her away from the glass, consequently bringing us right back to where the staff had tossed their wallets and purses. I palmed her wallet again as we approached. "In the meantime, let's have a look at you to make sure that you're not hurt by any of that glass."

As she took a seat, I casually dropped her wallet back into her open purse behind the bench. I wished I had time to zip it, but that would be too risky.

"*I* have nothing to apologize for."

I clutched a hand to my heart and rocked back on my heels. "What? You were in such a hurry you nearly plowed me over. I have delicate sensibilities. I was almost hurt."

She giggled as her gaze roamed over my shoulders. "As if. Muscular as you are, I don't even think you felt it."

Score one for me, she'd noticed I was muscular. *You will not fuck your best friend's sister.* I lifted a brow. "Oh, I felt it."

A light flush crept up her neck. "I wish I could get a drink, but I'm working. You know what, next time, you should probably watch where you're standing."

My job was done, so why the hell did I feel like I was losing her? "Nope, I do not concede. I request that the lady apologize with a drink. Or her phone number."

She laughed then. "Oh, slick. You're going to have to work a lot harder than that for my number."

"I'm willing to work harder."

Her tongue peeked out to moisten her lips. Just the simple motion flooded me with heat. "I would love to. But I have to return to work."

"I understand. Are you at least going to tell me your name? That way, when we run into each other again, I can use it. We'll seem like old friends, and then you can buy me the drink you owe me."

Her smile was slow. "Jessa McLean."

"*Jessa McLean.* You know I'll remember that, right? And since I assume you're working the event, I think it's a safe bet to guess that you work at Evans PR."

"Astute. And you are?"

"Roone Ainsley." Lucky for me we were using my actual name. All Ariel had done was scrub out my military stint and change my job title in the islands. Anyone who wanted to look would find the truth… mostly.

I shrugged and helped her to her feet. "So, I'll be seeing you around, Jessa McLean. And whenever you're ready, you can buy me a drink."

I left her in the staging area and let myself back into the club. When I put my earpiece back in, Ariel was right there waiting for me. "Well done, Cassanova. The bugs are live. I might have to start calling you 007."

I sighed. "You were listening?"

"Oh, you know it. Even I couldn't have come up with a better meet cute. Who knew you were so smooth?"

I rolled my eyes as I posted back up at the bar. "Everyone."

"Modest too," she chuckled.

I'd barely had time to order a drink when Ariel's voice came in loud and clear. "Looks like the princess has trouble. On your six."

I whipped around. Sure enough, Jessa was stepping in the middle of a fight between Emerson Poole and Toby Adamson. Toby also worked at Evans and, from the looks of it, was a troublemaker. He'd been quietly supplying party drugs to a couple of the attendees. Not to the Chase's or anyone in the inner circle, but to the periphery guests. So far it didn't appear that Jessa knew what he was doing.

The two idiots seemed like they were getting into over Jessa.

"Come on, Romeo, do your thing, or this is going to get ugly."

"Can you not be such a backseat driver, please?" I grumbled.

"Well, if you need me to show you how this works, I can."

"Anyone ever told you that you're a pain in the ass?"

"Nope. Never," Ariel said as she laughed. "Go on, make a good impression."

Something told me that Jessa was not the kind of girl to be at all impressed with a fight. Which meant I needed to diffuse and get her to safety.

I pushed my way through the crowd and tried to use low, calming tones. "All right? Do you need anything?"

My question was directed at Jessa, but Poole answered. "Piss off, mate. I was here first."

Adamson added his two cents. "What are you, mad, Emerson? Clearly, she isn't feeling your vibe. She can make her own decisions." Toby shoved Emerson in the shoulder.

Emerson shoved back, but Toby, despite being smaller, apparently knew how to handle himself. He evaded the shove and came back with a punch. All the while, Jessa was trying to separate them. "Oh my God, Toby, get it together."

Toby glowered mutinously. "You didn't hear what he said, did you?"

I wasn't sure which one landed a hit on her, but Jessa went flying.

With Ariel cursing in my ear, I dove for Jessa as adrenaline flooded my veins. I couldn't remember the last time I had moved so quickly. I was going to fucking murder those idiots.

Toby, to his credit, did try and reach for Jessa, but he wasn't fast enough. While what I wanted to do was stop and dismember them both, Jessa was more important.

I managed to catch her and drag her to my body just before she hit the ground. Startled, she whipped her head around, hair cascading behind her. "Jesus Christ, I swear to God you're super human. Always there just in the nick of time."

"Are you all right?" I asked through gritted teeth.

Behind us, I could hear the chaos. In my earpiece, Ariel was giving me the blow by blow. "Punches flying, remove the target."

Jessa's eyes were wide, pinned to some spot behind me, and she struggled in my hold. Was she trying to go *back* into it? I didn't really have time for this shit. "Are you okay?" I repeated. She nodded absently and tried to scurry around me, heading right back for the fight. "Are you mad? Those two tossers are throwing blows, the rest of this place is about to go off like a powder keg, and you're running back *into* the fight?"

She glared at me like I was crazy, her bright eyes flashing fire at me. "I need to diffuse this. They'll listen to me."

I laughed. "No, they won't. Both of them are high, in case you missed that memo."

Her mouth fell open. "That is Emerson Poole. I've put a lot of effort into that client. He's not high. Now let me do my job." Her Canadian accent was more pronounced when she was mad.

"No can do. You're going to get hurt, princess." I wasn't sure why I used that particular endearment, but once it was out, it was too hard to recall.

She glowered at me, not intimidated by me in the least. I was six foot three and well aware that I looked intimidating. But it seemed Jessa McLean didn't give two shits and thought she could handle herself.

"I have a job to do, and you are keeping me from doing it. If you don't move aside, you'll find yourself missing your left nut."

I forced myself to strip the aggression out of my voice. *Remember the cover, you eejit.* I couldn't go caveman. "I understand, but you can't go back into that fight."

She laughed then crossed her arms. "Just how do you plan to stop me?"

Fuck it. I wrapped an arm around her waist and gently pulled her back when she tried to break free from me.

"Let me go. I have to stop this, or those idiots are going to undo my months of hard work with Emerson."

"I'm sorry, I can't do that."

Jessa feinted to one side then scurried under my arm. But I was fast and caught her. She struggled as she yelled, "Let me go, you arrogant, overgrown oaf. "

She was so squirmy and slippery, I did the only thing I could think of in the moment. "Sorry, princess." Leaning down, I picked her up, fireman style, and headed for the door just as the bouncer started to weigh in on the fight.

Jessa, as it turned out, was a fighter. She was also an inventive curser. "You douchwaffle asshat. I'm not wearing any underwear! Put me down."

Fucking hell. File that under things to examine later. But being chivalrous, I planted a hand on her ass to keep her skirt down.

All that did was make her scream and wiggle more, which made the skirt shift and adjust. Swear to God, it wasn't my fault. I didn't mean to have my hand on her bare ass, but when my hand came in contact with smooth, bare skin, I cursed under my breath.

She whacked me on the back several times as I carried her through the crowd, out the door, and into the parking lot. Some of her blows would have done damage if she'd had any leverage.

When I gently set her down back on her feet, she laid into me. "What in the world? Are you some kind of psycho with a super hero complex? I have a job to do."

My temper, as it turned out, gave zero fucks. "You've lost the plot, princess. You could have been hurt. Those arseholes in there were brawling. You've already been hit once. I did you a favor."

She blinked up at me. "Let's get something straight; I am *not* a princess. I can handle myself, and I have everything under control." She huffed. "Also, keep your hands off my ass."

"Gladly. I want my hands nowhere near your ass." OK not exactly the truth. "Does your job involve getting hurt because two assholes are too wasted to talk their shit out like normal people?"

"My *job* involves babysitting and keeping crises at bay. All you just did was make my job twenty times more difficult."

She was ridiculous. "Then I'm sorry to say, you are very bad at your job."

She whipped around on me then. "I will have you know, I am *excellent* at my job. I am the best publicist at Evans Public Relations. You just interrupted before I could stop those two idiots."

I couldn't help it, my lips twitched. She was spunky. And to be fair, I couldn't be blamed, because her tits were legitimately bouncing right in front of me. I fought to keep my gaze on her eyes. "I admire your determination, but you have to know when you're beaten."

Her gaze narrowed. "You can feel free to go and self-fornicate."

Oh shite. My cock twitched. I liked this one. I bit back the laugh. She was… something fantastic. Out of the corner of my eye, I saw the bouncers escorting people out. And then I heard the blare of sirens, so she was safe for now. I had to let her by.

She strutted away, and I stared in disbelief. Woe be the kingdom with her as their princess.

After a moment, Ariel joined me in the parking lot. "Smooth. *Real* smooth. Remember the time I said to make a good impression?"

That was probably going to be easier said than done now.

2

Roone…

"SO HOW DO YOU WANT TO PLAY THIS?" LUCAS ASKED over the speaker phone.

I was trying to hunt down one of my new work shirts. If I didn't get a move on, I'd be late. I still had no idea what was in half the boxes. I'd unpacked my surveillance equipment but the clothes, not so much. I searched through another box and muttered, "Come again?"

"My sister. How are you going to do the whole undercover thing?"

Oh boy. "You have the mission brief. What's the problem?"

"Yeah, the mission brief says go undercover to protect her, but you're going to get close, right?"

I sighed. I wasn't sure which question Lucas was asking, so I tried to tread carefully. "Lucas, I've already moved in across the hall from her. I'm in place to have a job at her company. And you know Ariel. She'll have this place wired up tighter than Fort Knox. So she'll have cover."

"Dude, you know what I'm saying. I mean, are you gonna go in as the helpful neighbor like Penny did, or are you gonna go in and maybe make friends, or are you going to try and date her?"

Shit. I really wasn't having this conversation. "Look, mate, you just leave that to me and Ariel. I promise I will keep Jessa safe. It's my number one goal, and you know that. It's literally the only reason I'm here."

There was a pause. "Dude, I know that. Besides being my best bro, you're really fucking good at your job. You know… and that's coming from someone who tried to give you the slip more than once."

"Too soon, mate. I thought we weren't going to talk about that anymore." I'd forgiven him for ditching me as his security detail… mostly.

"Yeah, sorry. But the whole point is I know how good you are. And I know you go all soldier-mode of protect and serve. But I know Ariel is a little faster and looser, so I'm trying to figure you how you guys have laid out the plans. Helpful neighbor? I mean that works. But there probably won't be a lot of instances where she's going to need you."

"I'm aware of that. Which is why I'm also going to be with her at work. Rick Evans will pretty much do anything for status. So the fact that Sebastian called him personally means he's in. Whether she likes it or not, I'm going to be unavoidable. She might be ready to kill me by the end of it." Rick Evans and Evan Millston had started Evans PR ten years ago and had soon established themselves as the premier public relations agency to use in London. Everyone affectionately referred to them as "the Evans."

"You really think antagonism is the way to go?"

"If it were you, what would you do?"

There was another pause on the line from Lucas. "I don't know, if I were you I'd probably date her. But that's weird because she's my sister. Though I have no real connection or feelings about you wanting to date her."

"Oh my God, I do *not* want to date her. I think the whole dating thing is sloppy. Messy. Blurred lines make the job much more difficult."

"There you go again. Sometimes you gotta play in the shades of gray, man."

"Let me just make sure I have this clear; You want me to play in the shades of gray with your sister. All right, I'll see where I put my flogger."

It took Lucas a moment to get the joke. "Oh, hardy har. That's funny. You know what I mean though."

"I *do* know what you mean. But I'm not a shades-of-gray kind of guy, so I'm going to keep this as clean and pristine as possible."

"Have you seen her yet?"

I could still feel the curve of her ass in my hand. Just thinking about the spark of fire that lit her gaze sent an electrical current zapping down my spine.

Yeah, but you're not gonna tell him that. Nope. I was not going to offer up that little tidbit of information. Because this was Lucas, and he'd give me shit for it. But also, she was his sister whether she knew him or not. Not to mention, that just wasn't how I did things.

Penny and Sebastian had crossed the line. And Lucas... Well, Lucas had crossed *all* the lines. I wasn't that guy. Sebastian had given me a mission, and I was going to complete it to the best of my ability without shagging his sister, because I was pretty sure that was the last thing he wanted.

"Look man, all I'm saying is what if Ariel gave you the precise instruction to date her? I mean, isn't that the whole point of the dating app?"

Ariel's role was plan B. To come in as a client hoping to take her exclusive dating app to the next level. Everyone in the company would be required to use it. If I couldn't get enough coverage on Jessa by working with her, Ariel would pair us via the app.

"The whole point of the dating app is plan B. We have several Royal Guards in the system, so she'll match with somebody. The whole point is I won't *really* be dating her. And Ariel's never going to give me the direct instruction to start shagging your sister."

"Whoa, who said anything about *shagging*?"

I laughed. "Mate, when was the last time you went on a date that did not involve shagging?"

A beat of silence. "Yeah, fair enough."

"Besides, Ariel might play fast and loose, but she knows what I'm here to do. She's giving me leeway to play it the way it's most comfortable."

"Okay, if you say so man. I just, I don't know. I want you to be careful with her, I guess."

Oh boy, out comes the big brother conversation. "You don't need to worry about me mate. I'm not that guy. I'm just here to do my job, protect the princess, find out who's behind the conspiracy, and bring her home. Those are my directives, and that is the mission that I have chosen to accept, so don't worry about it. I'm not gonna shag your sister."

Yeah but you sure as hell thought about what it would be like to shag her last night. Yeah, I needed to get that thought the hell out of my head. Either that or bury it deep, behind locks and chains so it wouldn't come back out again. I wasn't that guy.

Jessa was gorgeous, with a pair of tits that could make a grown man cry. An ass worthy of worship. But she was a *princess.* So that meant hands-off for me. Unwanted sons of English Lords didn't end up with the prize. Hell, soldiers didn't end up with the prize.

So, I planned to do whatever was necessary to get the

mission done, even if it meant telling her she was in danger, though I knew Ariel didn't want to go with that protocol.

"How's it going with Ariel, by the way? You okay with her being in charge?"

Nope. "Yeah, she's great."

Ariel was brash and flew by the seat of her pants half the time, always going with her gut instincts. I wasn't saying she wasn't good, because she was. She was a tech genius.

But in terms of being mission command, I didn't know about that. I'd assumed it would be me. But maybe after the whole Marcus thing, Sebastian had lost confidence in me. I'd been really surprised in that mission meeting when Ethan had named her as lead, but I thought I'd hid it well. "It's fine."

"Man, you're all zen about it. I feel like I would've lost my shit. But I mean she's cool, though. Smart. She's not going to do anything that's gonna put Jessa in danger."

The jury was still out about that, but what I said was, "Absolutely. Look, I gotta get going. But I'll check with you later. Give my love to Bryna."

Lucas groaned. "She's saying to send you kisses."

I chuckled. Yeah, that sounded like Bryna. "Well, if your fiancée is willing to give me kisses, I'll take them."

"You take a kiss from my fiancée and I swear to God I will kill you."

God it was fun fucking with Lucas. "You're welcome to try."

I hung up on him and tried the last box, still searching for a shirt.

Success. Now all I had to do was pull off the act of a lifetime.

⚜

Jessa...

I was late. Really late.

I'd been up since five trying to fix the debacle of last night. I'd started with the police, trying to work my contacts to make sure that Emerson's name never appeared on any reports. And then I went to work on Toby.

Last night I'd gotten him a solicitor, even though I was pretty sure he wouldn't need one. But still, because he was part of the company, I did what I needed to do. I hadn't *seen* him with drugs, but better safe than sorry.

The police hadn't found any drugs on him so, it was mostly speculation. Unless they could get someone to corroborate, it wasn't going to be a problem.

As soon as I woke up, I sent breakfast and *I'm so sorry your party was busted by the cops* flowers to Abbie Chase. I'd done more before seven a.m. than most people did all week.

And then I had a disaster morning. I spilled tea all over the front of my favorite blouse and followed that up with a broken heel. By the time I was running out the door, it was 8:15. And I *always* left at 8:00 and walked in the doors of the office at 8:30. Now, I'd be late. And I'd miss the morning status meeting.

I attempted to close my door, send a text Chloe to check her email for all the status notes she would need, and balance my to-go cup of coffee. It wasn't until I finally had my door locked and turned around that I noticed I had a new neighbor across the hall. My unit faced the street. Those inward units had their own gardens and faced the courtyard with direct access to the storage units.

A block of row houses was owed by Evans PR and served as corporate housing, but sometimes they leased their units out. That townhouse unit had been empty for about three months, but someone was running across the kitchen now. Someone tall, with *very* nice back muscles. It was only when he turned his head that I realized that first, I was staring, and second, I knew *exactly* who he was.

"You?"

He looked up as he shook out his shirt and unhooked it from the back of the chair at the kitchen island. "Me. Hello, neighbor. But then, we've met already. Jessa, right?"

No.

This was not happening to me. No, no, no, no. There was no way that guy could be my new flatmate. Okay, not exactly flatmate, but this was too close for comfort.

"Do you always get dressed with the door wide open?"

He flashed a grin that was almost as devastating as the rest of him. "No. I was running something to the garbage and spilled something on my other shirt. I flew back inside in a hurry, hence the open door. Now I'm late for work."

He was still shirtless. And yes, I was still drooling. Apparently eight pack abs were a thing. "Well, fine."

Shit, how was he my neighbor? This wasn't even fair. I could still feel the imprint of his hand on my ass. My *bare* ass. FML.

Oh, there was nothing worse than being helpless, having someone else completely in control. If I could, I would kick him. I hustled to the lift when I heard him say, "Hold the lift for me, would you?"

The hell I would. If he thought it was okay to fondle my ass, then he had another think coming. He could take the stairs. Not that he *fondled* my ass exactly... *You might have enjoyed that.*

I heard his footfall in the hallway as he rushed toward the lift. I, in turn, frantically pushed at the *Close* button.

On a scale of one to petty, yes, this was *Real Housewives* level, but I didn't care. The idiot had manhandled me.

Well, you kind of liked it.

No. I did not like it.

Liar.

Also, he was trying to keep you from getting hurt and from flashing the world your snatch.

The doors to the lift finally slid closed with only an inch left as he skidded to a stop in front of me. Our gazes locked just before the doors closed completely.

I smiled to myself as the lift lowered to the ground floor. I'd pretty much just cemented the two of us *not* being the friendly, borrow-sugar kind of neighbors. But, I was okay with that.

3

Roone...

ON THE WALK TOWARD EVANS PR ON BEAK STREET IN the heart of SoHo, Ariel walked fast and talked even faster. I could've slowed down my pace. But I wasn't really in the mood, because she was busy telling me how to do my job.

"Okay, you had a slight setback last night. It seems Jessa wasn't really in the mood for the caveman thing. But everything about her says she needs someone strong. Her entire psych profile says it. She won't respect anyone who isn't. She's a survivor, so she's going to need someone strong and firm who can coax who she really is out of her. But you need to be really crafty."

I nodded noncommittally. "Uh-huh."

She charged on. "You know how important this is. You've got to get in, get close. Establish trust. You were doing so well at first yesterday and then—well, the whole hand-on-her-ass thing probably did you in."

I stopped. "The hand on her ass was merely to keep her in position because she was fighting me so hard she was going to fall off my shoulder. It's a six-foot drop." It was also because it seemed the princess didn't like to wear underwear. But I kept that to myself.

She waved her hand. "No, I know. But still, someone like her is going to bristle at that. She never lets anyone close. Clearly, she never lets anyone near her ass. Which is a point of note for you."

The laugh tore out of my chest in a sharp bark, making several pedestrians around us turn to stare. I didn't want to laugh. I didn't. But the way she said it, I wasn't even sure Ariel knew what had come out of her mouth.

It was only then that Ariel stopped and turned. "Look, Cassanova, I'm gonna tell you right now, if you want to establish trust, anal isn't going to be the way to do it." And then she turned around and kept walking.

Oh, so at least she understood the ramifications of her joke. "I'm not an idiot. You recognize this isn't my first rodeo, right? I do know how to protect someone. And believe it or not, I do have a way with women."

She scoffed. "With women that you'll never have to see again. In the last two and a half years, I have seen you go through women like Kleenex. Which, if that's your thing, then whatever. But…how you get close to *those* women, will not be how you get close to *this* one. Even when you were doing well, she was wary. Cautious. But you need to move faster. Find something, seize it, and make it stick. Make it work."

"Okay, Tim Gunn, I get it. I've got my Bedazzler out, and I will make it work. Picture me covered in sparkles."

Ariel grinned then. "Actually, that would be hilarious. You think there's a chance she'll like you better if you bedazzle yourself?"

I rolled my eyes and kept marching.

"Okay, you know who the players are. Her right-hand woman is Chloe. She's been at Evans for three years. Jessa's dad died a year ago. Toward the end, he wasn't well. I'm sure she's got daddy issues, so use it to your advantage."

"I know the plan. Get as close to her as I can."

We were two blocks away. She stopped and sighed, forcing me to stop along with her. "What?"

"Look, I know that we haven't really talked about this whole *I'm in charge of the mission and you're not* thing. And with you being His Majesty's close friend and confidant, I know it can be awkward."

I rolled my shoulders. "Now is not really the time to talk about this."

"I know, I know. I'm just saying I'm aware that it's awkward. And I'm not saying that you don't know what you're doing. You've kept him safe for years. That was your job. It's always been your job. And you're good at that. You're an excellent soldier. The difference is that this assignment needs finesse. You have to *lie*. And lie well. Make her believe you. Make her want to be near you. Your open brash honesty, your directness, you have to use it but in a different way. There's a reason I kept your profile as close to the truth as possible. It's so you don't have to lie too often, because it's the little lies that get you caught. But you have to *not* be *you*. I mean even now, you're walking like a soldier. And it's totally sexy, sure. But it's gonna put her off or at least make her suspicious. You need to be strong, but not soldier-bodyguard strong."

I ground my teeth. I didn't want to listen, but I forced myself to because she might have a point. I didn't really know how to do the nice, cajoling thing, the nuances, the lying. I hated to lie. Mostly because of the whole inconvenience. You had to keep track of those things. But my profile was close enough to who I actually was, so I wouldn't have to lie too much. "Okay, I hear you."

She nodded. "With Penny and Sebastian, it was difficult.

Penny had a hard time separating reality from who she had to be for the mission. It worked in her favor then. But for someone like you, that murky line is going to suck. I just want you to be ready."

"I am. And frankly, I didn't know you cared."

She pursed her lips. "I don't. I just don't want you to make me look bad." And then she started walking again.

I chuckled behind her as we approached the building. "Noted. We'll be fine. We started on the right foot yesterday, and then we faltered. But you're right. When the fight started, I went into soldier mode. It was a wrong move for her. Now she thinks she hates me."

"No. She *actually* hates you, and you're starting over from less than ground zero. So I hope you are really, *really* charming when you need to be."

I laughed. "I promise, I've been taking lessons from Lucas. I'm charming."

She eyed me up and down and then blew a strand of hair out of her face. "For both our sakes, I hope so. She nodded at one of the guards that was posted in the front the building. He returned her nod, accepting the signal that we were taking over from this point. She looked at me and gave me a wide-eyed, reassuring nod. "Let's do this."

No way in hell I was telling Ariel, but this assignment was almost more terrifying for me than protecting Sebastian on the battlefield.

That I knew how to do. *This*, not so much. But I had to learn and figure it all out. Jump right in. I just had to convince the princess she didn't actually hate me.

Something told me that would be easier said than done.

♛

Jessa…

"Where have you been?"

I scuttled down the hallway, my jacket draped over my arm, watching Chloe chase after me. "I know. I'm late. You will never believe what happened last night. I'm sorry I left you to handle the client status updates on your own this morning, but you should have had everything you needed."

She handed me my mug with *I could agree with you, but then we'd both be wrong* printed on it. I couldn't help but smile. I loved my sassy mugs.

"I did, but that's not the point." She huffed as she chased after me.

Chloe was shorter than me. Barely five feet. She made me feel tall. Also, I'd replaced my trainers with heels, so my longer stride was probably killing her. I slowed my pace down a little and then took the turn at the end of the hall toward the conference room.

"Toby and Emerson Poole got into a fist fight last night. Can you imagine? Then some idiot picked me up and stopped me from diffusing it right away. The police were called. It was a mess. I got the Chase's out of there. Then I got Toby into a cab. Emerson required some fast talking, but he's out of the nik." All in all, I'd gotten about three hours of sleep.

We all lived to fight another day. Crisis managed. I'd sent a status update to Evan and Rick. In the end, my pride was hurt more than anything else when that asshole swung me over his shoulder, caveman style, but I'd come out of it unscathed.

Chloe stopped short right in the doorway, bracketing herself between the door jam. "Are you serious right now? The police?"

"It's fine. I dealt with it. I just need to touch base with the Chases and make sure they had a good time and were happy... before the brawl. I have it all under control."

She huffed. "Actually, I was chasing you down because of last night."

I groaned as I finally managed to slide into my jacket. "Oh God, what now?"

She shook her head. "No, it's not entirely bad. Emerson called the Evans and raved about you. Seems he wants to renew his contract but only with you on the account."

I bit back my grimace.

Chloe frowned. "What?"

He was an important client for Evans PR, but I really didn't care for him. Or his tendency to stare at my ass like he'd never seen a woman who had one before. "Nothing. That's great news." I forced a smile

She hesitated. "But, uh, Toby has been fired."

My mouth fell open. "You wait until now to tell me?"

"I was getting there. Evan stopped the status meeting and called him. Fired him on speaker."

"Shit." There was no love lost between us, but I didn't want the kid fired.

"There's more. He got in a wreck after he left the club and is in the hospital."

"What the hell?" My mind raced. He'd been on the clock but off premises, so technically we weren't responsible for him. And I'd made it a point to put him in a hired car so he wouldn't have to drive, so that removed liability from Evans. I hated where my mind went, but I was a fixer by nature. And it was my job to fix it so the Evans didn't have to.

"Okay, call around and verify that. If it's true, then send flowers. Make sure his expenses are covered."

She nodded as she took notes. Now I was going to have to go see the kid. What the hell had happened? I paused to check I had no lipstick on my teeth and took a deep breath. I could do this. No one knew I was a fraud. *Nobody knows.*

Evans PR was one of the most exclusive PR firms in

London. They were selective about their clientele and they always got results. *I* always got results.

Chloe bumped into me. "Sorry. Also, I think we have new clients."

Perfect. *Just* perfect.

"And…"

God this was just getting worse. I sighed. "What?"

Chloe fiddled with the hem of her blouse. "I know you didn't want to talk about it, but your father's former facility called. They'd like to know when you're going to pick up his things."

I clenched my jaw, ignoring the slice of pain through my belly. I'd been avoiding this for six months. He'd been gone for a year and it had taken me this long to go and pick up his things. I'd paid a year in advance, thanks to his savings, so I hadn't had to deal with it until now. I knew I owed it to him to go there, go through everything, but I couldn't make myself do it. I couldn't make myself follow through. After his funeral, I couldn't let him go or process how he died. Now he lingered around refusing to be put to rest.

Only look forward.

"Okay, thanks. I'll deal with it. You ready?"

Chloe grinned at me. "Yep. I love new clients."

"I'm glad one of us is excited."

4

Jessa…

I WALKED INTO THE CONFERENCE ROOM TO FIND MY bosses, Evan Millston and Rick Evans, weren't alone. A pretty redhead sat directly across from them, and she gave me a wide grin when I barged in.

Her hair was a full-on fire engine red. The kind of red you only saw on true redheads. It hung past her shoulders and swung as she talked animatedly. Her wide blue eyes sparkled as she chatted. From the sound of her accent, I assumed she was American.

"Sorry, I didn't mean to interrupt."

Evan had a smile for me. "No, no. Come in, come in. Jessa, I want you to meet Ariel Scott. She is the creator behind the Meet Cute dating app."

I smiled at her and gave her my best squared-shoulder, efficient strut, marched over, and shook her hand. I was careful not to squeeze too hard. Evan said it scared off female clients at times.

Not Ariel, as it turned out. She gave me a warm smile in

return, and her grip was just as strong as mine. "It's nice to meet you. I have heard so many great things about you and am so delighted to work with the best. When I found out that Evans had an opening, I couldn't wait. I'm desperate to take my business to the next level. Oh, and I love your mug."

I grinned at her. "Thank you!" I liked her already.

Rick jumped in. "Jessa is one of the best we've got. You'll have the benefit of working with her and our newest account manager."

I frowned. "What?" *New account manager?* No one had been hired in six months.

A low voice, reminiscent of whiskey and smoke, sounded behind me. "It's nice to see you again, Jessa."

I didn't move. My heart was clattering out of my chest. In the far seat, observing the meeting, was the one person I didn't want to see today. And he was using that voice. The same one from last night... before he'd ticked me off. Deep. Smooth. It made my skin tingle like a rolling orgasm.

Yeah, I knew that voice. I also knew those massively broad shoulders and that ass. After all, I'd been staring at it last night when I was slung over his shoulder.

I turned slowly. He flashed a smile. That stupid smile. It threw me, and I couldn't find my voice. My voice was too caught up in an internal girly giggle.

I was a goddamn professional. I'd done this hundreds of times.

Put on a smile, fake it till you make it. What you don't have in skill you make up in bravado.

Except with him, I couldn't exactly focus. I faltered. "I—uh—"

There was something different about him this time though. It was as if he'd shut off that arrogant, cocky demeanor. Well, not entirely. There was something about his eyes, but the rest of him was unassuming in a way, as if the last thing on earth he wanted to do was intimidate me or anyone else. It wasn't in his shoulders. It was as if… I don't know. I couldn't define it. But it was like he'd shed off that arrogant skin. Maybe it was the smile. It was completely disarming.

He stood and strode over. Confident, but not overdone, less like a prowl and more like a straightforward, direct strut. "It's nice to meet you *officially*. Both Evans have had amazing things to say about your work." Was it me or did the word *work* have a sarcastic slant?

I stared up into his moss-green eyes, surrounded by thick lashes that made me jealous. Up close I could see that his hair was a dark russet.

Say something. Anything other than, *Hey twat-face, what are you doing at my job?*

"You work here?" *Something smarter.*

Roone grinned. "Yeah, guess so."

I turned on Evan and Rick. "He works here?"

Rick grinned. "As of yesterday. You were already prepping for the Chase event, so you missed our introduction. And great news. I know you're a man down with Toby gone, so Roone will partner with you on your accounts. In particular the LL and Meet Cute accounts. The two of you will also plan the annual Tillerman Gala."

My brain tried to sort through all the information.

Partnering on *my* accounts. Last night he hadn't been a guest. He'd been checking on me and how I ran things. *Scoping out the competition.* The corporate housing. Now this. *Shit. Shit. Shit.*

Think. I had to think. "I appreciate it, but Chloe and I can survive without Toby. It won't be too much of an adjustment." Translation: He barely did anything, so I don't need the newb.

"Oh, we know, but you won't have to adjust. Roone comes highly recommended. And you know we need all hands on deck on the LL account. And Meet Cute will need a fast ramp up. We want to show Miss Scott what we can do with an expedited timeline."

The pit dropped out of my stomach. The London Lords account was the biggest account with the firm. Everything I'd worked so hard for the last three years was on the line. I'd come to Evans while I was still at Uni. I'd had to juggle the schedule while looking after my father and generally taking care of life. But the company had given me a stability I'd never had before. Roots I'd always wanted. And now pretty boy was going to encroach on my home? *Hell no*. He could have Meet Cute. I wanted the meaty accounts.

To be fair, I knew nothing about Meet Cute, but why not give the new account to the new kid? London Lords would need a more finessed approach.

All you have to do is show you're better. That was true. I was a veteran. Clients loved me. I could do this. Except everything about the smirk on his face said he knew I was freaking out.

Never let them see you sweat. Oh no. I was in control here. I was fine. I could do this. I slid my hand into his and resisted the urge to snatch it right back.

An electric shock that ran through my body kept me rooted to the spot. And the current that ran through me kept my brain from forming functioning words, but it seemed he was completely unaffected. "I can't wait for us to get started."

Rick spoke up then. "Roone told us he saw your work last night."

The smile Roone gave me was sweet and engaging, and honest to God, it muddled my brain. I was a goddamn expert in all things bullshit. But there was an edge of sincerity to what he said that had me almost believing.

…*Almost.*

Pretty boy was talking. It took my racing mind a moment to focus on what he was saying. "I can learn a lot from Jessa. She was an expert last night. A professional. I think together we can give Miss Scott what she's looking for with Meet Cute and manage the LL account. Obviously, I have to get up to speed."

Ariel Scott didn't look like she was buying his line of bullshit either, but she gave the Evans a beatific smile. "I'm so excited to have your team on this. Meet Cute is ready to revolutionize the market. Everyone is on dating apps now. Everyone. I'm sure even you two have used them before. But what makes Meet Cute different is that we take the guesswork out of some of the things that you'll do. We do the matching for you. We're your virtual blind date. We've taken everything about what you like, as long as you were very specific, and we match you. And not just that, we provided the first five dating experiences. After that point, we hand over the reins. That is, unless you prefer for us to do it, and then we continue to date number ten. Then you're really on your own."

I turned and lifted a brow. "Wait, you plan the dates?"

She nodded. "Yep. Based on the complex questionnaire we have, we tailor the dates to showcase each person's abilities and interests. To really help people find common ground."

I slid my glance back over to Roone, who grinned at me and indicated I should take a seat. I glowered, but I couldn't really avoid it. My bosses were watching me carefully. I sat, and he joined by taking the seat closest to Rick.

Ariel continued. "When I came up with the idea five years ago, we had no idea it would be so successful. People are lazy by nature. So, when they get matched they want someone to take initiative. I've removed that step. Once people are matched, the app provides a place and a time to meet. It's their job to show up. And that's all users have to do. And obviously, be themselves and have a good time. After the date, both people indicate if they want to see each other again, and if so, we plan the next date. We take the guess work out of the equation. If one party doesn't want to see the other person again, a new match is formed for both parties. No more questioning if someone is going to call. And of course, obviously if things are going well, they can exchange phone numbers, and talk, text, and do all of that fun stuff. But this helps the two busy professionals to really get it going."

You could use this.

I ignored that thought. "If it works the way you say it does, that's actually kind of amazing."

Evan was more skeptical. "If this is so great, why have I never heard about it?"

Ariel's smile softened, and she inclined her head toward Roone, who chuckled. "It's extremely exclusive. We do a heavy vetting on our participants because we plan the dates. We would never want to put anyone in an uncomfortable situation."

"So, it's invitation only?"

Ariel nodded. "People refer their friends, and everyone goes on a waiting list until I can have the app vet them. If they pass muster, they get put in the app. Then we find them a good match. We don't match anyone who's not at least seventy-five percent compatible."

I laughed. "Who determines compatibility? You can't determine chemistry with a computer."

Ariel grinned. "Well, that's where I beg to differ."

I tried to ignore the hum of electricity across my skin. I tried to ignore the way the hairs on the back of my neck stirred at attention. I was excited. The idea of working on an app like this was fun and exciting. I already had promo ideas. Our marketing team would love this. They'd have graphic ads done in no time. The press would eat this up. I could probably get placements on several morning television shows. My blood hummed.

The bad thing was Rick noticed it. The way he was grinning at me told me he was about to say the one thing I didn't want him to say.

"I'm so glad you seemed so excited by this Jessa. We'll all be using the app to get acquainted with it."

Say what now? My mouth hung open. I could feel Roone's gaze on me, daring me to quit or to run. Instead, I snapped my mouth shut, tilted my chin up, and met his gaze.

Never going to happen.

⚜

Roone...

"Hey, Jessa, wait up."

I wasn't used to chasing after women. Especially needlessly stubborn women. Annoyingly stubborn. But still, that was the job. "Jessa, please wait."

After the meeting, she'd taken off like her hair was on fire. At the lift, she stopped only because she had to push the button. She turned with a brittle false smile, her hazel eyes shining. "What do you need?"

"Well you walked away before I could even tell you how excited I am to work with you."

Her smile was sweet, and her eyes crinkled at the edges, which told me she was enjoying herself. But there was still a flash of heat in them that told me what she was about to say wasn't going to be good for me. "Oh, you think you're cute, don't you?"

A grin teased my lips. What was it about fighting with her? It was like I was getting ready for a long battle. And I was ready. *More* than ready. "Well, it wouldn't be the first time someone's told me that."

She chuckled softly. "Of course not. You could have told me who you were last night. You didn't have to attempt to embarrass or discredit me or something. All that did was piss me off."

"I wasn't trying to discredit you. I was trying to keep you from getting your arse clocked. You're welcome."

"Oh, that's so funny. You think I need a savior. Clearly you weren't listening last night."

I cocked my head. "You seem upset. Does this have anything to do with me carrying you over my shoulder last night? I promise, no one saw your bare arse."

Her pupils dilated even as her gaze narrowed. When she spoke, her words were biting. "Since we're on the subject, I don't like being man-handled."

I narrowed my gaze in return. "When I man-handle you Jessa, you'll know." I turned and left her standing at the lift.

5

Roone...

I'D HAD NO TIME. THERE WAS NO WAY TO BACK STOP THIS. There was no way to have seen this coming. We'd known LL Hotels were on the Evans roster, but Evan Millston was listed as primary on the account.

How the fuck were we supposed to know he'd transferred it to Jessa?

Back in my office, I pulled out my cellphone and made a call praying I would get through immediately.

But nothing. "Bugger." I forced my brain to run through the possible solutions. I might have a way out of the mess, but that would take relying on a decade-old signal. This was what I got for not calling my cousin and telling him I was here.

My phone rang and I answered on the first ring

"Are we fucked?"

Ariel. Right to the point. "I don't know. I just tried to call my cousin to warn him to go along and nothing."

"What are the odds he'll just go with it? I mean at the end

of the day, your background *is* your background. We didn't change anything, I merely scrubbed out your military history. So it shouldn't come up."

"It shouldn't. But she's so wary of me already."

"Damn it. I should have known she was on the account."

Was this her admitting a fault? "We'll deal with it."

"I'll also try to get in touch with him."

"And tell him what?"

"Let's cross that bridge when we come to it. Please tell me you have a good relationship with your cousin and he doesn't want to dick with you."

"Well…"

"You know what never mind. You go. And try to keep the princess from killing you okay?"

"Roger that." I hung up and tried Ben again. Fuck it. I hated risking the whole mission on a long-ago code we had as kids. But I didn't really have any choice.

Twenty minutes later, we pulled up to the main headquarters of London Lords flagship hotel. LL Westminster was sleek, modern excellence. From the exterior, everything screamed refined luxury. Everything the rich and wealthy could want. There was nothing opulent about it. Nothing gaudy.

I had to give it to my cousin, he'd built something outstanding. The last time I had seen Ben was when Sebastian had popped into London following King Cassius's death for an impromptu state visit.

We'd spoken maybe twice more since then. There was a lot to catch him up on, so I hoped to God he'd remember the signal from when we'd been kids.

Before I had left for Sandhurst, we'd been really close. And it would be good to see him, except not exactly under these circumstances.

"You have all your notes for the meeting? I need someone

with balls of steel, so if you have no balls you need to tell me now."

I forced a grin. "Oh, I think you and I both know I have balls."

Jessa rolled her eyes. "You know what? I can already tell you are going to be a major pain in my ass."

I left that one alone. No way was I going to remind her that I'd already had my hand on her ass. Very nice ass that it was. Right now, my brain space was occupied with trying to keep the mission alive. Without breaking cover, and, without alerting the princess.

Security let us up to the twentieth floor. It was beautifully appointed, with balconies all around and floor-to-ceiling windows. All of West London was on display. Obviously Big Ben, Westminster, the House of Commons. Everywhere the eye could see were panoramic views of the city.

Ben's assistant stood behind the glass desk as we approached. "Mr. Ainsley, Ms. McLean. Mr. Covington will see you now."

Here goes nothing.

She opened up the massive oak door. "Mr. Covington, Ms. McLean and Mr. Ainsley from Evans PR are here."

Ben put his finger up as he finished a call. His tones were hushed, but authoritative. And then he hung up and smiled wide. "Ms. McLean, it is good to see you again. I was wondering when you would grace us with your presence. East and Bridge were disappointed to miss this meeting. We were hoping that you would let us take you to lunch. After all m—" His gaze flickered from Jessa to me, momentarily landing back on Jessa and then stuttering back to me. I could almost hear his brain doing that screeching car tire sound. *Errrrrr.*

Thankfully East and Bridge weren't here. From what I remembered about Ben's partners, neither one of them had a particularly good poker face.

Shit, that meant that Ariel hadn't been able to reach him. I tapped my left temple twice with my index and my middle finger. And I prayed to God he remembered. I had no idea if he did or not until he shook his head momentarily. "Oh, I see you brought someone with you."

Jessa gave me a tight smile. "Yes, I have a new partner on the account. I wanted you to meet him before we went ahead and met with Madison." Jessa was the epitome of cool professional confidence. Her smile was friendly, warm even. But there was something very hands-off about her. She'd clearly ignored the slight flirtation from Ben, which made me excessively happy.

I knew my cousin's reputation with women. Back in school, everyone had called him Big Ben. We all played rugby and cricket, and I knew full well what my cousin was packing downstairs. I didn't need Jessa knowing as well.

Ben met my gaze steadily and gave me a smile. "Mr. Ainsley. It's a pleasure."

Thank fuck. He remembered the code, which meant I would be getting a call later about what the fuck I was doing in town and why I hadn't called him. And why I needed him to pretend he didn't know me. Yeah, fun times. "It is a pleasure to meet you as well. I'm very excited to be working on the account."

That earned me another eyebrow raise. So much to explain.

"Well, the more the merrier, I suppose. I am so glad Evan has been putting a priority on this account. With the new openings of the hotels in New York and Los Angeles and then Paris, you can imagine we want the marketing and publicity to be effortless. Spot on. We're taking things in a new direction, so we are excited to have more hands."

"Well I am excited to work with you. Jessa is obviously more than capable, and I will be playing catch up a little bit.

But I look forward to seeing the portfolio and what we have to work with."

And there it was. We were both faking it. There would be a long conversation later. But at least Jessa was buying it.

Everything seemed to go off without a hitch while we went over the preliminaries. As he was about to hand us off, Jessa gave him a warm smile and a firm handshake. I had to admit she was good at her job.

Ben, though flirtatious, treated her with respect. She was smart, on her game. I had expected her to maybe try and dick with me when it came to the client files. But all the information I needed was there, and it was easy to follow along as they talked.

We were off to meet with Madison, who would be our more day-to-day contact. Ben made eye contact with Jessa, his gaze boring into hers. "Now Jessa, just because Madison is your contact, doesn't mean you get to be a stranger, please. I think we owe you dinner after that amazing engagement party that you ran for Bridge. I've never seen my mate look so happy."

She smiled, and I could see the flush on her cheeks. It made me scowl at my cousin.

"And we will definitely have to get those plans on the books, but I am so swamped. This client I have is opening three multimillion-dollar hotels in major metropolitan cities, so I am going to have my hands full with the plan for him."

Ben laughed… and still held on to her hand. *Twat.* "Well then, we will call it a planning dinner. From the start, I've been looking to get to know you better."

I scowled at him then. His gaze flickered to me, and his wink was so brief that if I didn't know him, I would have sworn that I'd imagined it. He was dicking with me. Fantastic. I would kill him later.

"Well, we will see what we have time for." She turned her

attention to me. "Roone, come on, and I will introduce you to Madison."

I turned to shake Ben's hand. And perhaps my grip was a little firmer than planned, because he grinned. Wide and bright. "Mr. Ainsley. I look forward to hearing more from you."

"Yeah, same."

I had lived to fight another day. But I was certainly going to have to do a bit of explaining to my cousin.

Roone...

I'D LUCKED out just now. Ben had played along.

But I still actually had to pull this job off. At Sandhurst, I'd taken International Studies through the Open University, so I had a good base level business knowledge. But whatever I didn't know, I'd have to fake.

But I couldn't be smug. I had to pull this shit off. I recognized I was acting a little mad. I didn't like how she put me on edge. I grinned, remembering her frustration as I'd been assigned to her clients. Though I had a feeling she'd make me pay.

"I'm glad to see you're so happy," she murmured in the lift. "Madison Jeffries is a tough nut to crack. Game face on. I can't have you running scared."

As if this wasn't my game face. *Don't be a smug asshole. This morning could have been shite.* "What's there to be scared of?"

She didn't answer. Just smirked.

Ten minutes in to the meeting, I understood what there was to be scared of. Madison was on her game. She was smart. Called everything into question and didn't take any shit. No wonder she was VP of operations for my cousin.

But what Jessa had failed to mention was that Madison Jeffries was a man-eater. She was beautiful, a little older, maybe mid-30s, maybe 40, and she was currently sliding her foot up my leg under the conference table.

She leaned forward, hands steepled, her voice sultry as she spoke. "My goodness, Mr. Ainsley, I would love to hear so much more about your past work. I had a look at your résumé, and I was enthralled."

I could hear Ariel cackling in my earpiece as she mimicked, "So enthralled..."

It was Jessa's stiff back that told me how to play it. "Yes, well, it was a great experience. I'd love to tell you about it sometime. And I hope I can do the same level of work here as I did in the islands."

Madison's voice dripped honey, "My God, that must've just been so beautiful working in the Caribbean. However did you get any work done? Honestly, I would just be topless at the beach all the time. You really must take me there. I would love to see the islands from an insider's perspective."

Next to me, Jessa's jaw worked as she tried to redirect the conversation back to the work. "Madison, obviously you and I have worked together before. Roone is new, so he's still getting up to speed, but I look forward to continuing our work together. This afternoon, I wanted to scout some locations for our events. It's a no-brainer to use the hotels, but I'd really like to consider an approach to leverage partnerships. For example, I know that Ian Talbot will have a restaurant in the New York hotel, so hosting an event at one of his restaurants as a 'sneak taste' will really benefit the branding and marketing."

Jessa was saying things. *Smart* things from the sound of it. But Madison wasn't listening. Her foot had found its mark, and I had to swallow the squawk in my throat. "Ms. Jeffries —" I gently adjusted her foot and moved it off my lap. "While you have worked with Jessa for a while, I bring fresh blood and new ideas, I think. I can't wait to dive into your account wholeheartedly."

Ariel cackled. "Dude, it sounds like when you say account, you mean her snatch."

Fuck. Next client meeting, I was taking the stupid earpiece out. It wasn't worth it having Ariel's voice in my head all damn day.

Madison's brows went up, and she grinned. I could practically hear Jessa groaning next to me. She made another last-ditch effort. "If you still have the time this afternoon, I'd love to head down to the restaurant to take a look around and see how it would work for the first event. LL hotels have such an elegant luxury to them, but unfortunately we won't be able to do anything to promote that in the new properties for a while. I think we start with the tease. The amuse bouche, if you will."

Luckily, Madison turned her attention back to work for the moment. "That's a good idea, we can meet the chef and discuss further. Since there will be several retailers in the hotels as well, we could incorporate those flagship venues in the plan."

Jessa took notes in her tabbed notebook. I was surprised she wasn't using her laptop. "Right. I think we should probably head down to the restaurant. I think it might be just the place to announce the new locations. Everyone knew there would be three sites, but revealing the cities can be made into a huge celebration."

"Sounds like a great plan."

"Oh, I was also hoping to see Mr. Hale and check in with him about his engagement party. See if he was happy with the work."

Madison's smile was a little less natural then. "He has asked about you. He was very impressed with the work Evans PR did on the event."

I noticed that little dig there. *Evans PR* had done a great job *not* Jessa. That little dig made me dislike Madison even more. Nonetheless, Jessa took the compliment.

"Thank you. I'll relay the message back to the Evans."

We all stood, heading out for lunch. While Madison went to her office to get her purse, Jessa walked with me to the lift. When we stopped, she pressed a hand to my shoulder and leaned into me. "I see what you're doing."

I grinned. "Pray tell, what am I doing?"

"It's disgusting. You're flirting with her. That's not how we do business at Evans." Her voice was a harsh whisper as she spoke through her teeth. "You might not take this seriously, but I do."

"Oh, I take it seriously. Just a reminder, whether you like it or not, I'm on these accounts with you. *All* of them. So you might as well get used to working with me because I'm not going anywhere."

She stepped back and grinned. "Yeah, you'd actually be right about that."

I frowned. "What—"

Madison came up behind me, her hand stroking my back. "Well, if you're ready."

I cleared my throat. "Actually, I drove, so we'll just meet you at the restaurant. Jessa, we can talk strategy on the way."

Jessa's gaze was all mischief. "If you don't mind, Madison and I haven't had a chance to catch up, so I'll ride with her in the limo."

Bugger. In my ear, I heard Ariel swear.

I could hear her scrambling to get coverage on the limo. During the day, the plan was that since I was on Jessa's accounts, I would be her primary security. But, if she was avoiding me, not much could be done about it.

"Are you sure?" I asked through clenched teeth.

"Yeah, I'll meet you there." She'd made me drive on purpose.

We all rode down in the lift together. The two of them got off at street level, and I was forced to go down to parking. When I was alone, I ran to the car as I mumbled into the earpiece, "Jesus H. Christ, it's like she knows what I'm here for and wants to thwart me at every step."

"I don't want to be the one to say I told you so, but maybe try honey instead of vinegar. It'll work better."

I reached for my keys.

My. Keys.

"Fuck."

Ariel's voice was sharp. "What?"

"The little princess stole my keys."

"What do you mean she *stole* your keys?"

I could almost pinpoint the moment. At the lift, her hand on my shoulder, distracting from where she was taking the keys out of my pocket. "Son of a bitch."

"Wait, Jessa *deliberately* stole your keys?"

"Yes. It would appear that way. All so she can meet with Jeffries on her own."

"I have to respect her hustle."

"Whose fucking side are you on?"

Ariel laughed. "The princess's, of course. Get to street level. I'll get someone to fetch your car. We have to get you to that meeting."

I knew the restaurant they were going to. They already had a head start and were on the road. At best I'd be late. The restaurant was on the other side of town.

"God, I hope you have someone on her. Because right now I don't have her. And I also have to negotiate for an Uber. I'll get to her as soon as I can."

She thought she was cute. Well, she wouldn't find it cute when I tanned her hide.

Dick: *Now we're talking.*

Me: *Shove it. Tanning her hide is not an option.*

Dick: *Bummer.*

But throttling her might actually be something I could get away with. It was all I fantasized about on the way to the restaurant.

6

Roone...

AFTER NEARLY A WEEK OF PRINCESS DUTY, IT SEEMED I'D underestimated Jessa.

She was smart, conniving, and would do just about anything to win. And what I'd done by turning up on her turf was basically poke the dragon with an ice pick. The fire-breathing, scaly, angry kind of dragon. And she was going to defend her territory.

I ran a hand through my hair as I dragged my laptop over to the couch. I missed the islands, but I was getting used to the space. This was the ideal kind of flat for me. It was a town-house with three levels. All the fixtures were modern, steel, but there was still a sense of warmth with the hardwood floors and the orange-yellow hue of the walls.

Back home on the islands, I was one of the few guards that actually lived in the palace. My quarters were beautiful, elegant and pristine, but they *looked* like a palace. Everything was gilded and ornate.

Sebastian, of course, said I could do anything I wanted to

the place. But it never felt like that choice was really mine. I almost would have preferred one of the bungalows because at least then my comings and goings would have been my own.

I knew it was considered an honor to be posted inside the palace, but it always felt like too much. Like I was undeserving somehow. It just wasn't really my style.

And yet it had never even occurred to me to leave.

Sebastian was family. Lucas was family. Hell, Penny and Bryna too, even Ariel and Bryna's best friend Jinx. We all had dinner together about once a month. It was loud and raucous, and we played games and it was fun. It was the kind of family I'd always dreamed of having one day.

But it never felt like I really belonged. Like I was more than just an attachment. And with Penny there, Sebastian needed me less and less, as did Lucas.

Stop being a sentimental twat and focus on your job. As I took a sip of my beer, I turned on the telly. Old episodes of Top Gear were on. I missed the old incarnation of the show. The new version didn't really do it for me. And the original hosts' new seasons just felt off somehow.

It was Friday night and I didn't have to be on duty, but I'd still opted for a night watch so everyone else could rest. Then I'd have tomorrow and likely Sunday off, though I still needed to be hyper-aware and careful on my days off. As far as I was concerned, this was my life. I tried not to balk at the undetermined length of the job. It's not like I had anything else to do, really. I was a soldier; I went where I was commanded.

The red-light indicator went on in the corner of the screen, indicating movement in Jessa's flat. Luckily, she didn't have a pet, so we didn't get a lot of the false-read signals, but she was definitely on the move. "Why aren't you asleep, princess?"

The door to her bedroom opened, and out she strolled... naked.

My beer spewed out of my mouth. Holy fuck. She was

naked. Very fucking naked. I meant to avert my gaze. I really did. That was the plan… any second now.

Me to eyeballs: *Look away.*

Dick: *Don't you dare.*

Eyeballs: *I'm clearly not in charge here.*

Why was she naked? Did she know she was being watched? *No, you idiot. It's her flat. She can walk around naked if she wants.*

Since my eyeballs wouldn't cooperate, I forced myself to shut the laptop. I wasn't here to ogle her. I sat on my hands so that my dick couldn't take control of those too. I was not going to watch.

Problem was just that glimpse had already left an indelible imprint on my cerebral cortex. Long, lean lines of muscles, full breasts, dark nipples, burgundy colored. My mouth watered.

That was knowledge I didn't need. Knowing the exact color of her nipples could in no way be helpful to me. But I'd never forget it now.

You can have another look. You know you want to.

No. Yes. The problem was I was on watch. I had to have my eyes on the monitor.

"Whatever you need to tell yourself to get yourself through the day." I muttered.

I opened the laptop again, teeth locked, jaw tight, ready for the pure torture of it. Sure enough, she was at the fridge. Peering in, still completely starkers.

Jesus, that ass. Tight, firm, rounded like a peach. I was so screwed. I forced my eyes over to her bookshelves until she went back to her bedroom.

As my imagination ran wild, I thanked my lucky stars that I was the only one monitoring surveillance tonight. I had to remind myself that I was not the kind of bloke people wanted for their sisters. I was a soldier. She was a princess. Not going to happen.

I loved Sebastian and Lucas like they were my own brothers. What would happen if I made the mistake of touching their sister?

You'd lose everything that you worked so hard for.

So despite Jessa's attempts to make me crazy, I wasn't going to give in. I couldn't give in. I knew that I was, basically, not good enough, so the little fantasies about the princess needed to stop. Now.

Dick: You can try, but you can't make me. I want her. I'm going to have her.

It was certainly a good thing that my dick wasn't in charge of my life.

※ ※

Jessa...

AFTER THE WEEK I'd had at work, I would have done anything I could to avoid having to do this. But I couldn't avoid it anymore.

Luckily on a lazy Saturday, the drive out to St. Albans hadn't been too terrible.

The assistant director of Hope House met me on the stairs. "Jessa, it's so good to see you. It's been a long time."

I swallowed the guilt. I knew exactly how long it had been. "Good to see you too, Lulu." Lulu Clement had been there throughout my father's stay. It was residential facility for adults with mental illness.

The psychiatrist on staff hadn't always known what to do with my father, but in conjunction with his old therapist from when I was a kid, they'd worked out a treatment plan. The director of Hope House was an old friend of his from Uni, so there had been some familiarity for him. And I could afford it. Granted, I would have paid anything. I hated not being able to look after him myself, but after a while, he'd become too much to handle on my own.

For him there had been a conspiracy around every corner. And I was always the trigger. Sometimes a visit from me could prompt him into a spiral where he thought people were trying to take me from him. He always called me the lost princess. I'd spent a lifetime being called a princess in a way that was nothing but negative. That's why when Roone said it, it sent me into a rage spiral. I just wanted to be normal Jessa.

When my father was off his meds, he was convinced people with tattoos were coming for the lost princess and he had to save me. Growing up that had made things beyond difficult. He'd insisted I take martial arts, not for fun, but to defend myself against an unseen enemy. He'd insisted I know how to use a gun. I'd learned to shoot but refused to have one in the house given his state.

The last thing I needed was for him to shoot a neighbor.

"I should have come sooner."

"Well it's understandable. You've had a lot on your mind."

Yeah, a complete avoidance of what had happened to my father. It wasn't as dramatic as maybe I made it seem. He simply walked out of the facility one day. He'd made it all the way to London to see me.

But when he'd called, I'd been at work and hadn't gotten his message until an hour too late. By the time I'd gotten it, he'd been hit by a car on the road just four blocks from my office.

It was hard not to blame myself for that. That one hour. That moment that I was probably getting champagne or making sure some starlet wasn't caught without any knickers on, my father had needed me, and I hadn't been there.

The police had tried to convince me that from the time he'd made the call to the time that he'd left, only been about twenty minutes or so had passed. So there was no way I would've made it in time, but still, it didn't matter. I hadn't been there for him.

"His things are here. We held onto them as long as we could. Obviously, he was like family to all of us."

"Yes. Thank you so much. Is uhm, is James here? I'd like to say thank you."

Lulu shook her head. "No, James is in Devon. I know he wanted to see you."

I winced. "Yeah, I'm sorry it's taken me a bit of time. You know, I just couldn't come, I guess."

Lulu took my hand. Her hands had calluses, her knuckles were swollen from rheumatoid arthritis, and she had liver spots on her hands. But her hands were warm and firm, and exactly the reassurance I didn't know I needed. "You did your best love. No amount of you coming more often or being at his beck-and-call was going to change anything. Your father was ill. And off his meds."

"I know. I just—I wish—" I took a deep breath. "I wish a lot of things."

"That's normal sweetheart. But you know what? James is due to be in London in a couple of weeks. Shall I tell him to ring you?"

I would've liked to see James now, while I was here and it was convenient, and I wouldn't be yet again faced with the inadequacy of my duties. But I didn't want to have to face him when I no longer wanted to think about it. "Yeah, we'll see."

Lulu patted my hand as though she understood. "Well come on, I'll call some of the boys to help load his things into your car."

"I mean it's just clothes, right?"

She nodded. "Yeah mostly. He's got some stacks of papers though. You know how your father loved to sketch. I was pretty sure you would want to go through those things, pick out what you might like to keep and what you would like to donate or throw away. I would've done it for you, but you know…"

I nodded. *She didn't know him. You did. Time to stop running away.*

I hadn't exactly run. When I left Toronto to go to Uni in London, I'd done everything I'd needed to. I'd found us a flat and gotten a job with Evans lined up. I'd talked to my university advisor to attend part-time for the first term, until I could get a handle on everything.

Despite his illness, when Dad was lucid, he could work. He'd always been a great videographer, so there'd been some money to move with. Not a lot, but enough to get us started.

Things had gone well for the first six months or so. But then Dad had gone off his meds again. I wasn't sure if it was the environment that had triggered him again, or what it was, but he'd leave the flat every day, determined to prove that there was some conspiracy, that someone was trying to kidnap me. Someone was going to take me away from him.

My whole childhood had been fraught with this. When my mother died, he immediately moved us out of the UK. Out of Europe. To Canada. First Vancouver. And then we'd hopscotched across the country for years. Six months here, a year there. One time I'd spent two years in Quebec. I loved Quebec. But after that stint, once again my father was convinced that someone was on our tail, and he'd moved us to Toronto immediately.

Making friends was difficult, never really knowing if I'd get to stay. But regardless, I tried. Because I learned in the first couple of moves that not trying made things far more difficult. Things would be difficult at home and at school, so I was the tryingest new girl ever. I made friends with anybody who would have me, just to have an outlet.

I opened one of the boxes that were stacked to about my chin level. "God, how many papers did he have?"

Lulu shrugged. "I mean he was always sketching or something you know. You've got some video footage in there as well. If he wasn't sketching, he was filming. Someone had an old donated camera. And on the days he was out, he'd take photos or shoot videos. I think it calmed him."

"Well, Dad was always an artist."

"Yeah he was. Come on love, let's get these to the car."

I left Hope House and St. Albans an hour later, the last of my father's worldly possessions in the back of my car. Several times along the way on the drive home, I was so tempted to just pull over, unload everything, and just leave it. Leave it all behind and never look back. But a little voice kept stopping me. *"You can't do that. He kept you safe, for years. The least you can do is honor his memory."*

But did he really keep me safe? He taught me to be afraid. He taught me to trust no one. He taught me that my life couldn't be my own.

But instead of being afraid of the Boogeyman now that I was grown, I was afraid that my mind would deteriorate like his.

When I reached my flat, I glared up at the stairs outside the main entrance. There was no way. So instead I drove around back to the garages. There were hand trucks in the garage that I'd have to drag to the service lifts. I was in no mood, but it had to get done. The garage lifts only serviced the main hallways, but for grocery runs, they came in quite handy.

Just staring at the boxes made my eyes sting. I blinked the tears away rapidly. I was not going to cry. I was too strong for that. I had this shit totally under control. Swear to God. But still, my eyes threatened to leak.

I had the trolley parked and was loading the first box when

I saw the one person I didn't want to see. *Roone*. For the love of Christ. I was too emotionally raw to fight today.

"Princess, you need a hand?"

There was that word again. The one that made me want to throw things. Accompanied by his swagger.

I sighed. "Maybe right now we don't do the fighting thing? I'm knackered and really in no mood."

He took the box I was unloading from me, then ducked his head to meet my gaze. I wasn't sure exactly what he saw when our eyes met but suddenly, his softened, and he silently loaded the rest of the boxes for me.

"This all of it?" he asked.

I nodded. "Yes. Thank you."

He nodded and led the way to the lift. He still didn't say anything, which was perfect as we stepped into the lift, but also awkward. It was also awkward that I'd been on the verge of tears one second and the next, I was silently admiring his muscles. God. I'd tortured myself enough today, right?

When we reached my flat, he waited patiently for me to open the door then wheeled in the boxes. When he was done, he gave me a smile. "You're all set, princess."

Dammit, just when I was feeling grateful. "Why do you insist on calling me that?"

But he didn't answer, just gave me a crooked smile. "You good?"

I blinked rapidly. Why the hell was I off kilter with him? "Uh, yes."

"Have a good night, princess." Then he closed the door behind him and left me with my memories.

7

Roone…

I still didn't know what had sent Jessa to St. Albans on Saturday. We'd had one of the team watching her. Hope House was a residential facility for the mentally ill, but her father had passed a year ago, so why had she gone now?

More importantly, she'd been on the verge of tears when I'd taken the boxes from her. I wanted to know why. And there was a part of me that had wanted to hold her and keep away the sad things. But a guy like me did not get to comfort the princess.

I dragged my attention back to Evan Millston, who had dragged me into his office first thing Monday morning. "So, you're Rick's pick."

I lifted a brow. "I guess so." I didn't know where this was going, but he was in a bugger of a mood.

Obviously, when I had interviewed with Rick, I was given the job. I had references from Sebastian and the Queen Mother herself that said I'd been invaluable to the royal family in managing their press affairs. He'd eaten that shit right up.

Not to mention I was also an Ainsley. I hadn't advertised that I was one of *those* Ainsleys, but Ariel had told me Rick had done the deep-dive on me, so he'd known.

I had a great résumé, so why was this asshole pulling me into his office?

"I couldn't help but notice the interaction with you and Jessa last week."

Ahh, so we were going to have *that* conversation.

"Yes sir. I'm never one to shy from a little competition. I welcome it. I think it makes both parties stronger."

He leveled flat eyes on me. "You two met at the Chase party, am I right?"

I was still waiting for him to get to the point. "That's right."

He crossed his arms and lifted a brow. "I don't think I have to say this, because obviously you've read the employee handbook, mate."

I could barely keep my lip from curling. "Why don't you lay out for me what I'm supposed to know?"

His gaze narrowed. "Well, if you were paying attention, you would note that there is to be no fraternization between employees. That's a pretty important rule here at Evans PR. We want every employee to feel comfortable in the environment."

Interesting. "Of course. Jessa and I are having a little friendly competition, that's all. Nothing untoward is happening." Whatever the hell that meant. Why did he care so much about fraternization with Jessa?

Unless he wants her, you knob.

Well, that added a new dimension. I'd have Ariel go ahead and run an extensive background check on him. I could handle his posturing, but I was here to remove all danger from the princess. Including over attentive bosses.

"I hear what you're trying to say. Stay away from Jessa. Not a problem." *Over my dead body.* "I'm sure she understands the rules as well."

"You don't have to worry about what rules Jessa under-stands or doesn't understand. I'm talking to *you*. Keep it professional, and there shouldn't be any problems."

Okay, Arsehole. "I hear you. I'm nothing if not profession-al." I inclined my head, giving him a very direct glare. "Am I free to go now?"

When he didn't answer, I stood, and it didn't escape me that I was a good several inches taller than he was. He was forced to look up to meet me directly in the eye. This little friendly chat had put him at the very top of my suspect list for assholes fucking with her. It wasn't a list anyone would want to be on for a very long.

+

Jessa...

"So... are we just not going to discuss just how hot the new guy is? Or are we just going to pretend he doesn't have a shag-me smile? I wish that app would pair me with him. I know he's after your clients, but that does not preclude us objecti-fying him and his very fine ass."

"Chloe!"

"What?" She shrugged. "I mean, come on. He's gorgeous. Even your vajayjay is not so broken you can't see it."

"My vagina is not broken, thank you very much." I sniffed indignantly. "He's pretty... if you like that sort of thing."

"Love, *everyone* likes that sort of thing. But he's persona non grata if he's trying to take your clients. I'll help you bury the very pretty body."

"It's not pretty."

Liar. Okay fine, I was lying. So pretty.

Chloe shook her head. "Still though, I cannot believe you are not all over that."

"Whose side are you on? And have you forgotten that little dealio I told you about with Madison Jeffries? She looked like she wanted to eat him alive, and he looked like he wanted to let her. I have to be smarter. I've got this."

"Okay, well, yes, you told me. And that is pretty gross. I don't blame her though. Have you seen shoulders like that before? He could block a doorway with those shoulders."

"Chloe, focus. He's arrogant, remember?"

My best friend was forgetting the one simple rule; 'Thou shall not lust after thy bestie's enemy.' Though, who could blame her? Because she wasn't wrong about him being hot.

"You don't know him. I can tell he's going to be a pain in the ass."

"Maybe. But if he looked at me like he looks at you, I'd let him be a pain in my arse," she chortled.

"He's not *that* sexy."

She tossed her head back and laughed. "The hell he's not."

Whatever. "I just have to figure out how to deal with him."

"You could just lean into it. Make the man crazy. He already looks at you like he wants to know what you're wearing under your sexy little pencil skirts."

"Oh my God. I do not need to do that. I just want him off my case and on to his *own* clients who didn't first start as mine."

"I'm not saying you should shag him. Though, I volunteer as tribute. I'm just saying use your assets to get him to be less annoying. Everyone knows you're the best. He'll stop fighting you if he's distracted."

"No." I shook my head. "It might be the hard way, but I'll get what I need. I just have to find the best way to drive him insane." I grinned. "This might even be fun."

"I know enough to fear you when you get that gleam in

your eye. Quick question though. Toby... Should we look in on him? I know he no longer works here, but he was on the team."

I frowned. "I've already arranged for a meal service for two weeks. I expensed it. To help until he gets on his feet."

"Evan lost his mind over Toby. He's not going to like it."

"Tough. It's the right thing to do. Toby was a lazy pain in the ass, but he was on the team." I shrugged. You didn't always like your family, but you needed to show up for them.

"I wonder if Evan is going to sack your new nemesis too?"

I frowned. "Evan? Fire Roone? I wish, but the guy hasn't done anything wrong yet. Besides, I want to beat him fair and square. And Evan has no reason to fire him."

"Uh huh. Let's just say, Toby punching a client gave Evan the legitimate reason he's been looking for to sack the git."

I blinked several times. She wasn't right about that, was she?

Chloe rolled her eyes. "How can you not even see it? Evan is super protective of you."

"I'm his protégé." He'd hired me when I was still a newbie. He worked with my schedule and trained me. He was the reason I even had a career right now.

"Sure. I'm just not certain that's the word he'd use."

"That's absurd."

"No, it's not. I'm just saying pay attention. Evan might just get rid of Roone for you."

Roone walked by our office. He and Ariel were deep in conversation. I scowled at him as he walked, and he must have felt my gaze on him because he shifted his eyes, met mine, and winked.

Asshole.

My phone rattled against something in my purse as it rang. I dug around to fish it out. "Hello, this is Jessa."

There was nothing but silence on the line, so I tried again. "Hello, this is Jessa. Who is this?"

There was static, maybe breathing, but mostly silence.

"Hello?"

More breathing, then a hang up. I glared down at the phone. Blocked number. Was it international? Maybe a wrong number?

Something is up.

I shoved down the voice of my father. Just because I'd gotten a random phone call, didn't mean that something was going on or something bad was going to happen. I refused to live my life in fear anymore.

Chloe lifted a brow. "Who was that?"

"No idea. They hung up. There was some heavy breathing though."

"Oh yeah?"

"Yeah. Nice and creepy. I swear to God, if someone is going to be a creeper, they should be a *clear* creeper. You know, with specific instructions."

She laughed. "Right, please leave your panties on the back porch in the back garden specifically at this time, so I can pick them up."

"Exactly. It leaves out any ambivalence."

She frowned. "Seriously, is there something to worry about? Have you had more than one of these?"

I refused to give some weirdo any credence. "Of course not. Just a crank call."

Besides, I had bigger fish to fry.

8

Ariel...

"Mr. Millston, I'm excited you wanted to talk to me. Everything with Jessa has been going great. You were right. She's exactly the right person for what we're trying to do with Meet Cute."

Evan sat back in his seat nodding quietly. "You know, I've been going over it. Everything I see on the app is a rave. Any negative reviews happen to be the result of customers' misuse. And they're things that customer service seems to resolve quickly."

I smiled. Great. At least the deep back story of the app had worked. We anticipated them digging into the background story. It was airtight. No holes. But I was curious as to why he'd called me into a meeting. "Wow, I aim to please. We're a small company, but we're growing. Millions in the bank, zero investors, all my own money. That's the dream. I just want to go to the next level."

He laughed softly. "Ms. Scott, you don't have sell me. I know the pitch. And Jessa is the right person for you. She'll get you the exact kind of clientele needed to take you next level without diluting the brand in any way."

"I'm excited to hear that. She's been fantastic so far. Smart, on her wits. Nothing not to like."

"Right. Of course. She's our best and brightest." He sat forward and steepled his fingers. "Just how does the algorithm go about matching people? If, you know, say someone wanted to make a request of the algorithm, would it be possible?"

"What do you mean *request?*"

The tension in his brow immediately smoothed. "Oh, nothing, not to worry, of course. Just... you know, if say Chloe, Jessa's assistant, wanted to match herself with say Roone? Is there a way for you to directly link them?"

I frowned as if it had never occurred to me that *anyone* would try and manipulate the system. *Not my first rodeo, twat-muncher.* "No. I didn't build any back doors to the system. Unless people are really a match, the system will not put them together. I'm a purist like that. Otherwise, what's the point? Look, Mr.—"

"Evan, call me Evan."

"Evan, okay. I believe in this app. I developed it for a reason. I've had my heart broken before, and I wanted to take some of the guesswork out of it. I wanted something that would truly help people connect, you know?" The irony of it all was that the app actually did work, so if ever I wasn't a Royal Guard anymore, I had a fallback plan.

Like Jessa had said, it was complicated to key in on what would match two people. But if you went on the basics of what they liked to do and their personality types, it wasn't that hard. The irony of it was, Roone and Jessa actually were a match.

"But no one's really *seen* the algorithm."

I shook my head. "Of course not. It's proprietary. If I let

anyone else see it, any idiot could use it for their dating app. And then it wouldn't be special, now would it?"

"No, I don't suppose it would be. But, you know, if *I* wanted to make a request... Could you do it for me?"

No dumbass. But I tried to phrase it nicer than that. I shook my head. "No, I couldn't. Especially if the request is to *not* match two people or to match specific people. Everyone here, as you said, is going to use the app. They'll be matched to anyone in our database who's a good fit. We ask everyone to answer honestly, and the system will match them."

"Yes of course. I just wouldn't want some of my female employees to be matched with people who have unsavory backgrounds. You know, I'm looking out for them."

I forced my lips to tip up into a semblance of a smile. "Wow, how lucky they are to have someone like you to look out for them. But I assure you. The app is airtight. Everyone has been vetted over and over again. There's nothing to worry about."

His hands clasped harder. "No," he sat back. "Of course, there isn't. I just thought it was one of those things I should ask. To get a really full understanding of your application."

"Yeah, any time. Ask me anything you want. But that's just not how it works." We laughed together as he walked me out. As I was leaving, my phone rang, and I made a left to find a quiet corner to take the call.

"Hello, this is Ariel."

"Hey, baby."

I stopped mid-hallway. "Dad?" He never called. And why was his number blocked on my caller ID?

"Yeah. Why do you sound so surprised to hear from me?"

So many reasons. "What's up?" My father rarely called. And I'd made it pretty clear that I was going on assignment. So if he was calling, it meant he wanted something.

He always wants something.

"I can't just call my daughter because I want to talk to her?"

"Dad, I know you. And you knew I was going away. I would've called to check in like normal." Which was about once a month.

"Is it so wrong for me to want to hear my daughter's voice every now and again?"

The guilt slithered in. "Sorry Dad. I'm just in the middle of a case so, you know... I've been busy."

"Sure, sure, I know. My daughter is a big important Royal Guard. You know I tell everyone about you. How important you are, how vital you've been to the King and Queen. I do. I'm so proud of you baby."

Why was it that even though he gave me compliments, I was waiting for the other shoe to drop? I was waiting for the 'ask.'

"Actually, you know, I was calling for a reason."

And here it was. "What's up?"

"I was wondering, since you're not in town, if maybe I could stay at your place for a bit?"

As in my bungalow... on the palace grounds... unsupervised? "What?"

Strictly speaking, the Royal Guard bungalows were meant for the Guard that needed the closest access to the royal family. I had a single bedroom bungalow suite, and I was lucky to get it. I'd been in the Royal Guard since I was eighteen, and seniority-wise, I'd lucked out. "Dad, I don't think that's a good idea."

"Listen, you know I wouldn't ask if I didn't need it. I just need a place for a few days. Your mother wouldn't even let me sleep on her couch. You know how contentious it can get with us. You know that I wouldn't come to you if I didn't need it."

I hated it when he did this. I hated it when I felt like I really had no choice. Like, if it wasn't for me, no one would look out after him. "Dad, I'm not there. And you would need approval on clearance."

"I'm your father."

"Sorry. You still need approval and I'm not physically there to grant it."

"It's just for a couple of days. A week at most. I promise, I'll stay out of the way. It's not like I'll be living down there the whole time. I'll be going to work. I still have the visitor's passes that you sent me so I could come see you. Please Mer, I need your help. You know I wouldn't ask if it wasn't essential."

Using my childhood nickname was low. He and my mom had named me Ariel because of my hair. And they claimed that I watched the Little Mermaid no less than a million times when I was little. "Dad that's low. I could really get in trouble."

"You know, my whole life, I messed up. A lot. But no way, no how would I ever do anything to jeopardize your happiness or your existence. You know this."

I *did* know that. Everything he did was an effort to make our lives better. He just made mistakes.

So many mistakes. But never once had he thrown me under the bus or done anything to deliberately hurt me. "Okay look, you know what my key code is to get in. But honestly, Dad, you better come and go quietly. Peacefully. Do not make a nuisance of yourself. No going to the palace."

"Oh, thank you sweetheart. You don't know how much I appreciate this. I promise. I'll be quite as a mouse. In and out. I just need a place to clear my head."

"Okay Dad. But please, don't make me regret this."

"Never." Even as he hung up, I had to fight the thought that I was making the biggest mistake of my life.

✿ ✿

Jessa …

AFTER ANOTHER WEEK of dealing with Roone, I was surprised I hadn't resorted to drinking yet. For the last two days, everyone had been buzzing about their matches. Chloe was obsessed that she hadn't been matched yet. The texts were constant as she whined.

"Have you seen who you're matched with?"

I sighed as I painted my toe nails. "Hello to you too, Chloe. No, I haven't looked. And I don't care, because it doesn't matter anyway."

"Oh, come on, you have to care about this. *I* care about this. Come on, it will be fun. You actually have to put yourself all-in."

"It's not fun. We're working, remember?"

"But we can work *and* play at the same time. Did you not put in the appropriate details?" She scolded.

She was a first-class whiner. "Sure, I did. I mean, I was always a good student and I like to get things right, but not because I care about what the outcome is actually going to be. The Evans would have it no other way. But you don't see me giddy and staring at my computer or my phone constantly. "

"Oh, come on, Jessa. Have a little fun. Besides, you could use a good shag."

My mouth fell open. "No, I couldn't. I'm fine. I have B.O.B. I need nothing."

"Well, I'm excited. Come on, Jessa, this isn't like you. When you have a client, especially one as cool as this one, you're usually a lot more excited."

She was right. With most clients I'd be all-in, but Roone had me distracted. I'd done the questionnaire and stuck a photo up, but I hadn't paid any attention to anything else. I'd put it out of my head entirely.

I should be far more interested than I was. If I didn't get it together Ariel Scott would think I wasn't invested in her project. I was asking for trouble by not paying attention.

No, you're asking for trouble because for the first time in your adult life, someone makes you itchy and uncomfortable.

I didn't like itchy and uncomfortable. This was going to be a shit show. Besides, I didn't want to be matched. I didn't date. I hadn't dated seriously or even attempted it in over a year.

"Sorry Chloe. I don't mean to be a downer on this for you. True, it's exciting if their app works. You know, from the research I've done, there's not much on them. It's got great reviews by people who seem legit. I've got calls into people's people, to see if they can verify using the app and their happiness level."

I heard a chime. "Was that it? Did you get yours?"

Chloe sighed. "No, that was me, refreshing the screen, still nothing. What if it can't find anyone for me?"

"Chloe! Oh my God, please stop. I'm sure they will find someone who is a perfect match in the system. This is like that other app. The one that like, you know, movie stars use. What's it called again? It starts with an R or something."

"Oh, I think I remember, but I'm still nervous. The last guy I dated? He legitimately ran out of my house with his clothes off. He didn't even bother putting them back on before he left me, so it's been a while since I've dated. I don't know what the latest thing is, or what the kids are doing."

"Don't look at me. It's been so long since I've even been out for a non-work thing, I can't even introduce you to any guys. Hell, I don't even know where I'd meet a man."

"Ugh!" She sighed. "You are so frustrating."

"Sorry I'm not cooler. I'll just stick to my sassy mugs for cool factor. Nerdy cool. It's a thing."

Chloe must have refreshed again, because I heard the chime repeated. "Oh my God! I have a match."

Despite myself, a shot of adrenaline spiked my blood, and I sat up straighter. "You do? Is there a picture?"

"Yes. Oh! He's fit."

"Wait, seriously?" I don't know why I was surprised.

Why was I so damn skeptical? I sighed. "What is his name? What does he do?"

"It says he's some kind of financial analyst."

"Finance? That seems kind of boring."

"No, you should see him though. He is… Wow! Jaw dropping."

"Jaw dropping, you say? Pics or it didn't happen."

The second line on my phone chimed, and I glanced down at my messages. And yeah, wow. The guy could easily be a model. First name, Trevor. They used no last names, gave no social media links, and beyond a general career description, didn't tell you where someone worked. They just showed a photo, a location to meet, a date and time, and a yes or no button.

"Are you going to say yes?"

Chloe laughed. "Are you mad? Hell yes, I'm saying yes."

This made me wonder who the hell *my* match was… not that I was in a hurry. Not that I cared. But still, where the hell was my match?

"Do you have one yet?" Chloe asked.

"Nope, not yet. But you go, click on your match date. Enjoy. I'm going to finish painting my nails and look over the rest of the files. The Tillerman Gala is coming up in a few weeks, and time will go quick. I want to nail down that guest list."

"Okay, you do that. I am going to go count my lucky stars."

I hung up with her, then stared at my phone. I stared and stared trying to ignore the itch that would have me press the refresh button. I wouldn't do it. I didn't care.

I didn't want this. But still, somehow, I refreshed. Still nothing. I glowered at it and finished painting my pinky toenail. When I heard the chime, I jumped, causing me to spread my nail polish across my whole toe, not just the nail.

"Damn it."

I cleaned off the nail polish and snatched up my phone. When I clicked it, I saw I had one new match.

My belly fluttered. This had better be good. Then I clicked the button, waiting for it to load a photo.

When it did, I cursed.

Roone.

I was a 97 percent match with none other than my nemesis.

The universe, it seemed, had a sense of humor.

9

Roone…

NOTHING COULD HAVE MADE ME HAPPIER THAN watching Jessa's reaction when she was paired with me. I'd feast on that one for weeks. It was way too fun to rile her up.

The problem was, now we had to actually go on the date. And Ariel was having a field day.

"Remind me to pay you back," I muttered.

Ariel's laugh rang in my earpiece. "Oh relax, Roone, you'll be fine."

"Getting tossed around in midair is not my idea of fun."

"You're ex-military. I know you SAS guys had to do aerial training. You can't tell me you're afraid of heights."

I shuddered. "My least favorite part of training."

"But come on. With all the parachuting, you can't be afraid to fly."

"I've never liked heights. There, now you know." I'd just given her ammo for future use.

"Well, you should have made it clear on your date form. I selected this activity because it involves trusting each other.

Oh, and the princess has loved this stuff since some circus her mom took her to."

"Wouldn't it be great if trusting each other meant just having a lovely drink somewhere?"

"No, because that is in *your* comfort zone, but it's really not ideal for getting to know someone quickly. We have to make this app believable, remember?"

"So basically, I'm letting you play God?"

She laughed again. "Absolutely, and I love it."

"This is so fucked."

"Relax. It's a safe environment. Neither of you can get hurt. It's something physical. A couple that sweats together is sexy together."

I shook my head even though I had to look nonchalant while I waited. "You're diabolical."

"Oh, that's good. I'm going to make t-shirts."

"You're doing this to torture me, aren't you?"

I shifted on my feet as I glanced over the crowd. I had the height advantage here, but I still didn't see her. I had dressed casually in workout gear as Ariel had suggested. But here I was, one minute to go to the date, and no Jessa.

"I think we have incoming." Ariel said.

I forced my body to relax. No way was I excited for this date. Those nerves coursing through my veins… those were about the acrobatics.

Lies.

The door opened, and all I saw was a baseball hat pulled down low, a woman that looked to be about the right size with a dark ponytail. But a couple of steps in, and I knew it wasn't her. "Nope, not her."

"Are you sure? She was driving Jessa's car."

I frowned again. As the woman approached me, her head was down. But I knew how Jessa walked, and that wasn't it. "Are you sure she came in Jessa's car?"

"Seriously? I'm sitting here on the street looking at it, and you're asking me something so basic? The license plate number matches... and the girl looks like her."

Suddenly my stomach knotted. The woman approached me and then tilted her head up. She was cute. She had Jessa's olive complexion and the same dark chocolate hair, but she was not nearly as compelling. Her eyes didn't twinkle and dance with mischief. She was also an inch shorter and more filled out all around. "Are you Roone?"

I sighed. "Yeah, I'm Roone."

She grinned. "I'm so sorry, but Jessa couldn't make it, so she sent me instead. I'm Haley."

Fuck. I reached my palm out and shook her hand. "Nice to meet you Haley."

On the comms I could hear Ariel howling with laughter. "Oh man, she stood you up and sent a replacement. I like her."

As Haley had her ID checked and stamped, I muttered. "Yeah, while you're laughing, the princess currently unprotected. You better get back to the flat."

That sobered her up. "I'm on it."

As much as I wanted to follow Ariel, I had to see the date through, because no doubt, Haley would be reporting back to Jessa. When I got my hands on her, I was going to tan her ass.

Also, there was a high possibility that I was going to do... other things to her. But, that was neither here nor there. Right then, I had a date to go on.

⚜

Ariel...

WHILE ROONE WAS on his date, I first fired off a text to Jessa about grabbing wine, then I hightailed it to Roone's place. On the way, I called home. I still couldn't believe Jessa's moxie. She'd sent a stand in. Flipping brilliant.

"So how is it working with Roone?" Penny asked.

"Oh, he's fine. Kind of a stick in the mud. I don't think he loves me being in charge."

"He'll come around."

"Are you sure about that? Because right now things aren't going exactly as expected. You'd think a guy who has a slew of women in and out of his place would be more comfortable on a job like this."

Penny laughed. "Roone is different than you think. He's loyal though. He'll make you a good partner."

"I don't know." I wrinkled my nose. "So far, the jury is still out. He's all right. But he has no surveillance skills. And zero skills with women. Jessa's about ready to kill him every day."

"Well, that's because his skills lean more toward security. He has some undercover experience, but not nearly as much as you've had. As for his skills with girls, I'd have thought he was better considering all these women who want to date him."

Finally, I got back to his flat. I opened the hidden compartment in the bookcase and fired up the surveillance. "I know right? He's okay. I think he'll get it together. But I could almost feel him judging me when I started singing my Britney Spears in the surveillance car. I'm telling you, all I had to do was start with the, 'Oh baby, baby,' and he'd start to wrinkle his nose. You should see it… the disdain on his face."

"So then, let me guess, you turned it up and started dancing?"

"You know me to my soul, bestie."

Penny's laugh brought me home again. I was surprised that I missed it. When I was growing up, all I wanted to do was get off the islands. I used to have these dreams of living this fabulous life. I didn't know what I was doing, but I would look bad ass doing it. Wearing leather dresses like Carrie Ann Moss in the Matrix, doing something intriguing, with more money that I could ever need.

Basically, I just wanted to be rich and far the hell away from the Winston Isles. Even after I'd met Penny, it was a constant dream. Mostly, I wanted to be away from my father.

When my parents divorced, I thought my mother would take me. But, as my father had depleted their entire life savings and she didn't have money to look after me, she left me with him.

"Enough about the ginger wonder. How are *you*? You and His Majesty about to give me some nieces and nephews?"

Penny laughed. "I think we have plenty of time for that. I will not become the royal baby factory. At least not yet. I would like children, but I feel like I've just gotten settled into my new role."

"Are you settled?" For the last several months, Penny had been struggling with her new role as queen. With everything going on, the murder of King Cassius, Sebastian finding Lucas, and the discovery of a conspiracy against the royal family that went back for decades, things had been in turmoil on the islands for well over a year. Penny had always dreamed of being an artist, but then she turned into a badass Royal Guard, and that didn't exactly jive with being queen. So she'd had a rough go of it. But she and Sebastian had decided that she wouldn't be in the field anymore, so at least that was a little bit easier on the both of them. She'd settled into a post in Intelligence, but I still didn't feel like I could use my best friend as a resource at any moment. She'd taken way too many risks in the last few months.

"But I think you guys would have the cutest babies, and then I could be Auntie Ariel and spoil them rotten."

"I know, considering you're such a hard ass, I'm surprised you love kids so much."

"Heck yeah. Spoiling them rotten, with their cute little

faces, oh my God, and dimples. *Hand* dimples, they're the best. I would lose interest when they hit about five or six. That's when they start talking back."

"I see you're just dying to be a mom."

Lord no. "I will settle for delightful Auntie." The truth was I wasn't sure I wanted kids of my own. There had been a time when I'd seen all of that in my future. *Yeah, but you were just a dumb kid then.* "Besides, who would have me? Can you imagine? Whatever bloke gets to marry me will be beleaguered and tortured his whole life."

"Well *I'm* not beleaguered and tortured. I think you're delightful."

"Yeah well, you're supposed to." I took a breath. I wanted to ask her if she'd seen my father, but part of me was scared. "And let's face it… you're a little beleaguered."

She's your best friend, she'll look in on him.

"Pen?"

"Yeah?"

"I did a thing. Don't be mad. And I swear, it's only temporary."

"Oh my God, you tried to dye your hair blond again?"

That wasn't fair. "Oh my God, I used the wrong kind of toner, okay? Not my fault." The results had been this horrid, brassy, reddish-gray color.

"That was awful. And you were following me around with that hair color for six months."

"This is actually worse than that."

"Shit. What did you do?"

"Already, this conversation is reversed. I just want to point that out."

She laughed. "Yeah, good point. What's up? What do you need? Anything and it's yours."

"Okay. So, before you say anything, I know this is not good. But my dad needed a place to stay, and I said he could stay at my bungalow." I said it so fast, I doubted she heard me. But there was a bit of silence and then she said, "Let me guess. You want me to go and look in on him? Make sure he hasn't burned your house down?"

I breathed a sigh of relief. Penny understood our complicated relationship. "Yeah, if you don't mind."

"Consider it done."

The relief washed through me. I knew Penny would make sure he was okay, and also that he stayed out of trouble. "Seriously, I owe you. I don't even know what to say."

"First of all, you don't owe me. Remember that time in New York? You saved my ass more than once. Remember all those times when we were kids, and you stuck up for me? Also, remember how you handed Sebastian his ass when he was treating me like a dick?"

I chuckled. "Yeah, vaguely."

"Cool, then you don't have to ask. I'll take care of it. I'll go look in on him tonight."

"Thanks, Pen."

"No problem."

"How is His Royal Majesty, anyway? Is he starting to let you out of his sight yet?"

"It's getting better. He's certainly a lot more relaxed since I'm in Intelligence now, and basically, I'm in the palace all the time. Although, every now and then when I'm headed out for a meeting, I swear he puts a tail on me."

"Well, you did almost die that one time."

"Must I remind the two of you that I did *not* almost die? Robert was stabbed. Not me. No one hurt me. No one was looking for me."

"You were standing right next to him, and I still remember you covered in blood. So if that fills me with the *holy fuck, I've got to keep her alive* feeling, imagine what it does for him."

"Yeah, okay. But I'm only giving him another six months

of this. I've got to live my life, you know?"

I laughed. "Anything else happening? I feel so disconnected."

"He's been a bit distracted. Obviously, everyone here is tense with the whole Jessa situation. Sebastian doesn't want her life uprooted, especially until we know exactly how much danger she's in. He still thinks it's best she remains in the dark, at least for now. But something happened yesterday, and he's been hard to read. From the intelligence briefing today, they said there were some anomalies in the secure files. I don't know what that means yet. We're supposed to be talking to my dad at dinner tonight, so I'll get some more details."

Something fluttered in my heart. Just a little flicker and a skip of a heartbeat. "Anomalies?"

"I don't know what it is. Could be nothing. Could be something. I won't know until I talk to dad, and he's been holed-up with Sebastian. That's not one of my active cases, so right now, all I've got are secondhand tidbits. But when I know something, you'll know something."

"Okay, keep me up to date." I checked the monitors. Jessa was dancing around her flat. "I've got to go anyway. I'm on princess watch tonight."

"You got it. What is she like though? Is she nice?"

"Yeah. She really is, actually. I think you'll like her a lot. She's sweet and funny, and seriously gives Roone a run for his money."

"Hey, you just let her know that your job as bestie is already taken."

"Absolutely. I mean, she's not *that* cool. Besides, she also wavers between giving Roone I-wanna-murder-you eyes, and I-wanna-fuck-you eyes, so her taste is dubious at best."

Penny snorted a laugh. "Come on, you can't be that immune to him. I'm not even into gingers, but that guy is hot enough to melt panties."

"What do you mean you're not into gingers?" I sputtered with mock indignation. "How will we have our polyamorous love affair if you're not into gingers?"

She laughed. "Our love affair shall never end. Besides, you are super-hot. Redheaded guys have just never done it for me."

I considered Roone. "I mean, he's okay. The abs are decent. But he's annoying, so that negates that." The abs were better than decent. He should probably be an ab model if that was a thing.

"Nothing negates abs like that."

"You're not stuck with him twenty-four seven."

Penny snorted. "I swear sometimes it's like your libido crawled into itself and died."

"Yeah, you're actually probably right about that." Except all it took to rev it up was to think about the one person in the world I could not have.

No, not doing that. You just had a chat with your bestie. Why drag yourself into despair and ice cream? So much ice cream.

"Not to worry. I know that love is right around the corner for you. Likely it will be in someplace you'd least expect."

"Yeah well, I'd settle for a really good orgasm. But honestly, I can give myself one of those. I don't need a guy."

"That's right, you don't."

"Okay, love you. See you soon." I hung up and checked the monitor again. Jessa was on her way down the hall. I switched off the monitors, grabbed a bottle of wine, and went down the back stairs then back around to the front of the building to the buzzer.

She let me in immediately and opened her door with a smile. "Hey, I brought booze."

Jessa gave me a wide, tired smile. "Oh my God, you are speaking my language."

I really did like her. I just hoped she could forgive us for what we were doing.

10

Roone...

AFTER A NIGHT OF FLYING THROUGH THE AIR, MY BODY was sore and not in a fun, shagged-my-brains-out kind of way.

Back in my flat, Ariel was still laughing.

"You're not supposed to laugh."

"Oh, come on. It's funny. She gave you the slip and ensured that you still had to go on a date."

"This is about her security protocol."

"And I get that." Ariel closed her laptop and swiveled in her chair to look at me. "But, she doesn't *know* about her security protocol. We're still in phase one. We have to get you close enough and get her to trust you, which she is finding difficult to do for *whatever* reason."

I threw my hands up. "I saved her from herself."

Ariel just shrugged. "Sometimes it takes people getting punched in the face to learn a lesson."

"Whose side are you on?"

"Hers. Just the 'her' she doesn't know about yet. I like her. She's spunky. Obviously, she doesn't know that she's in danger yet, so the two of us just have to work on getting as close to her as possible."

"You think I'm not doing my best? I'm being thwarted by the little princess."

"She's not that little. She's as tall as I am."

I scowled. "Not helpful."

Ariel just grinned. "Admit it. You haven't run across a woman who hasn't immediately dropped her panties for you."

The occasion was rare. "I've run into one or two."

She laughed again. "They just have discerning tastes and can spot bullshit a mile away."

I scowled. "I don't bullshit. You're thinking of Lucas."

"No. You actually don't. But," she shrugged, "you're doing the very alpha thing, which I feel like I've never seen you do before. I have watched you and Lucas tear up the town, and you're usually more charming than this. Right now, you're acting very *clobber her over the head and drag her by the hair.* It's weird. If you just acted more charming, I'm sure she'd find you a lot more attractive."

"That's because she made me want to let out my inner caveman. She's bloody infuriating. How am I supposed to get closer to her if she keeps avoiding dates?"

"That, I can't help you with. But if it helps, *I'm* getting closer to her. I'm her very new bestie."

I sighed. "That's good, Ariel. At least one of us can keep a close watch on her. Maybe she's seeing someone?"

"Oh my goodness, has your poor ego been bruised?"

I scowled. "No. I'm just concerned about the princess's safety." I was wondering why, for once, it was difficult for me to do my job. The one thing I prided myself on doing well. The last two years had been hell between Sebastian's disappearance, the death of his father, Lucas's vanishing act, and now this. I was starting to wonder if I was still any good at my job.

"Relax, I'm just giving you shit. Clearly you're good. Sebastian would not have sent you on this mission if you weren't. So, we just have to find a way to soften up Jessa. I guarantee you, it's not by trying to force her hand. Caveman tactics don't work on her. She doesn't like them."

"I know. And hell, I'm not even a caveman. She just makes me so fucking irritated."

Ariel grinned as I stomped across the wooden floor. "Oh my God. Do you actually like her? As in, not for the role kind of thing?"

I turned to glare at her. "No. This is the job. Remember, I'm a goddamn professional. I'm not Penny, and Lord help me, I'm not Lucas. I can do this job without falling in love with a stubborn princess, okay?"

Ariel held up her hands. "Okay, if you say so. If you want the stubborn princess to play ball, change your tactics. At the very least, you have to get her to like you enough to be your friend so she'll want to spend time in your company and you can protect her. *That* is the job, despite how irritated she makes you. Do you get me?"

I rolled my shoulders. I hated that she was right. I hated that Jessa was just across the hall where I could walk right over there, pound on the door and demand that she go out with me. That was stupid, because I never had to beg anyone. And I certainly wasn't going to start with her.

But Ariel had a point. I had a job to do. And sometimes, it was easier to catch prey with honey instead of vinegar. I was going to be so sweet to her she might even get a cavity. Watch, with my luck, she might not even like candy.

11

Jessa…

LEAVING THE TILLERMAN GALA PLANNING MEETING, MY mind was spinning. There was so much to do. And I was operating on very little sleep.

Last night, the plan had been to have a glass of wine then start going through my father's things. But then Ariel had texted. A glass had turned into three. And those boxes had gone untouched.

But it had been fun. Ariel was funny and irreverent. And it seemed she thought Roone was a pompous asshat too. Okay fine, so she hadn't said asshat. She'd said he was a little arrogant. She'd also said there was something really appealing about him. Apparently, Ariel was a slave to her lady parts too.

So with a slightly foggy brain, I'd had to have several cups of coffee to handle the day. And it was a good thing I had. The director of the opera house had called that morning wanting to discuss logistics. There'd been unforeseen construction needed in part of the building, so we were going to lose some square footage for the gala.

I hadn't had much choice, I'd had to go and meet with him. Which meant, I'd had to let Roone handle the Meet Cute meeting we'd had scheduled for that morning. I prayed to god he hadn't screwed it up.

How badly could he screw up, after all? It was a basic intake meeting to get a feel for the company's marketing ideas. Her likes and dislikes. What had been working for her so far. Chloe had accompanied him, so how badly could it have gone?

You really want to ask that question?

I shot Chloe a test to check in.

Jessa: *The meeting go okay?*

Chloe: *Yeah, fine I guess. But both Mr. Shagable and the client seemed in a real hurry to get out of there.*

I frowned.

Jessa: *Any idea why?*

Chloe: *Both looked surprised that you weren't there.*

Damnit.

Jessa: *Was Ariel angry?*

Chloe: *No. Just confused.*

Fantastic. I'd called and left her a message, but maybe she hadn't gotten it.

Jessa: *Any idea where Roone is?*

It might be a good idea to see how he was feeling after the meeting.

Chloe: *I saw him heading to the gym as I was leaving for my daily hot chocolate.*

I hated that I hadn't been there that morning. While Meet Cute was a priority, I still had other client projects I was dealing with, and the gala required some focus. But I would fix it.

Or maybe you're spread too thin and need to lean on Roone.

Nope. Never going to happen.

He was untested. So for now, I'd just have to find a way to

do everything. I shouldn't have skipped that meeting.

Or maybe he was ticked because I'd blown him off last night. The message I had gotten from Haley was that she'd actually had a lot of fun with Roone, and she asked if she could keep seeing him. Imagine that. He was my date cast-off, and she was trying to keep him.

You don't like him.

I most certainly didn't. But I was still miffed that he'd gone through with the date. Or maybe he thought we looked enough alike that he didn't care.

Haley was a friend of mine from Pilates class. We looked similar enough. Even though she was an Essex girl of Italian heritage and I was a biracial vagabond, we looked an awful lot alike.

How long had it taken him to notice I'd sent a replacement? Not that it mattered, but I was curious.

If you're so curious, you should have gone on the date.

I didn't relish telling the Evans that I'd ditched my date, but hey, I'd been busy. I stopped short when I entered my office. Chloe was likely still on her hot chocolate run, but there was a beautifully wrapped shopping bag on top of my desk. A gorgeous bubblegum pink bag with a black satin ribbon from Ketter's. Linda Ketter owned a fabulous boutique just down the road. She had jewelry, trinkets, and music boxes. Basically, all those pretty kinds of things that your mother or grandmother would frequent to buy gifts for people. I approached the bag warily.

It's not a bomb.

No, it likely wasn't, but the hairs standing up on the nape of my neck told me to be wary. I dropped my notebook on my desk and couldn't quell the rush of glee as I parted the bright pink wrapping. I took the card out first, embroidered, with my name. My fingers played over the decadent lettering. "Since you missed out on our date... "

Roone.

Of course, it was from Roone. Who else would it be from? I told myself I didn't care what was inside the bag, but that was a lie. I cared very much. Reaching in tentatively, I pulled out the black box and then placed it on my desk.

What were the chances that he'd put something awful in there? Tricking me, making me think it would be something pretty.

You don't even know him that well. Why would he even want to fuck with you like that?

This was true, but we'd established a rapport, as it were, and it was my turn to get the shaft. Nevertheless, I flipped open the box with my fingernail, pushed it back, and gasped when I saw what was inside. It was a snow globe, the kind with glittery confetti that fell down. But what was truly fascinating was the display inside the snow globe. Acrobats. Trapeze acrobats to be precise.

When I was nine, my mother and father had taken me to the circus. I'd watched in rapt fascination as women were tossed in midair and then caught. The level of trust, the level of daring, the athleticism. I'd been so fascinated that I'd proclaimed I wanted to be a trapeze artist when I grew up.

Little did I know at the time that the career would actually involve running away to the circus. But my mother had smiled and told me if I really wanted to, I could join Cirque du Soleil. Immediately, I'd joined gymnastics and ballet and all those kinds of things.

Before your life as you knew it ended.

Nevertheless, I loved it. How had he known?

Your dating profile.

Oh yeah, that. I was suddenly wishing I hadn't been so honest. But it had asked for my happiest childhood memory. Without thinking, I'd just put it down.

And that had been my first date. The date I ditched. As if

it were possible to feel even worse. Dammit.

I delicately turned the snow globe over, shaking it up, making the glitter disperse. And then I leaned forward to watch the glittery snow fall. It was beautiful. But I couldn't accept it.

With a sigh, I wrapped the globe back up in its pretty little box and put it back into the Ketter's bag. Chloe walked in just as I was standing.

"There you are. Everything okay with the venue?"

"We'll need to make some changes if we want to use it. I have some notes that I'll need you to type up, and then I need you to start looking at alternative venues. I'll be back in a minute. I need to return something."

She eyed the bag. "Oh, a Ketter's bag. What'd you get?"

"It's not for me."

She frowned. "Well what's in it?"

"Nothing I get to keep, so I'll be back." I left her standing there, eyeing me quizzically. I didn't want to get into it because I knew what she would say. She was all-in for the Meet Cute app.

I didn't even knock before walking right in. The man was doing pull ups, for the love of God. And they were doing amazing things for his biceps… strictly an observation, of course.

He jumped down after his rep. "Jessa, lovely to see you. Would have been lovelier to see you last night."

I placed the bag delicately on the floor next to him. "Thank you, but no thank you. I can't accept this."

He scooped up his water bottle before leaning against the leg press. His smile was slow and lazy. "Sure, you can. It's a gift."

"No. I can't. It's too much. I know how much things in that store cost. And we work together. I can't accept things like this from you."

"Yes, you can. You agreed to use the app, and then you stood me up. Imagine my surprise when the very attractive Haley turned up instead of you. Granted, she was far better company than I think you ever would have been. But I was still expecting *you*."

I tilted my chin up. "I'm surprised you even noticed I didn't show."

⚜

Roone...

WAS SHE INSANE? Of course, I'd noticed. My date had been far too agreeable for one.

Call me insane, but I liked seeing Jessa pissed off. Granted, I wasn't sure why she was so pissed this time, but that was sort of par for the course with us. "You can't be mad about the gift. *You* stood *me* up."

"I just got busy."

"Busy. Right. Why can't you just admit that you felt the overwhelming connection between us, and you couldn't handle it, so you bailed?"

Her mouth fell open, and she sputtered. "Oh, you wish that was the reason."

"Well, if that wasn't the reason go ahead, tell me."

Jessa stood there shifting on her feet, glancing around the gym. "You know no one uses this gym, right?"

Ahh, changing the subject. "Well, the treadmill I ordered hasn't been delivered to my flat yet, so this is what I've got since it's raining outside."

"You ordered a treadmill? That's permanent. I guess you're really moving in."

"Yeah, of course it's permanent. Did you think I'd pack up

and go? No, don't answer that. Besides, even if it's temporary, I still want to make it seem like home."

"That's so strange. Even when I stay somewhere a long time, I never can seem to unpack."

"Oh, what's that? Did you actually just share something about yourself with me?"

She scowled. "No. Not on purpose anyway."

"Well, you could have shared plenty with me last night. But you stood me up."

Jessa rolled her shoulders and turned to leave. "You probably had a lot more fun with Haley anyway. She was positively gushing about you."

My lips curled into a smile. "You jealous, princess?"

She whipped around to face me. "No. I didn't have time for a date, so I chose not to come."

"Well then, why are you miffed that you missed out on a good time? If you'd come, we would have done trapeze. Since I don't particularly love heights, I assume trapeze is something that you would have loved?"

She cleared her throat and shifted on her feet again. "Maybe. And thank you for the gift, but I can't keep it."

I shook my head. "It's yours. I don't want it."

"Fine, then return it or something."

Crossing my arms, I asked, "Just tell me. Why don't you like me again? Because my instincts are always right, and I'm pretty sure when you met me at the party you liked me. Dilated pupils, lots of lip licking, that pretty pink pout."

I leaned closer. I could feel her heat, I could also feel her energy twitching to smack me. Just the thought of if sent an electrical current along my dick. There was something really twisted and wrong with me.

Dick: Who cares. If she slaps you, can we bang her?

Me: No. No banging the princess.

Dick: I hate you.

"So, you liked me then. What changed? Why did you go from liking me and thinking of me as potentially fuckable to hating me?"

"You flatter yourself. I don't hate you. I just find you irritating. I don't like to be bossed around."

"Yeah, I gathered. But does it really warrant this kind of disdain?"

"You really think I have the time, energy, patience, or inclination to loath you? I don't. My whole life has been people like you who think they can tell me what to do, boss me around, and force me into compliance. I hate that. I need my freedom."

"Oh, I get it. No one puts Baby in a corner?"

"Not even the same thing. You were just there, at *my* party, attempting to take over and crisis manage *my* crisis. I don't need a savior."

"Are you sure? Because the way that party was going, it was about to be a mess. You still got hurt in the process."

"Yeah, but the whole point is that it was *my* mess to clean up. Not yours. I don't even know you. But there you were, riding in on your white horse."

I shrugged. "Range Rover actually, but whatever."

She rolled her eyes. "My God you are such an arrogant, annoying—"

All that talk to Ariel about how I didn't want to be a cliché and follow in Penny's and Lucas's footsteps, I'd meant it. Honestly, I had. I had been serious when I said there had to be an easier way to stay close to the princess and still not follow in their tracks. But, I was dicking with myself.

Dick: *Did someone call me?*

Me: *Shut the fuck up.*

Dick: *Oh no. Not now. She's too close. Clearly, you don't know what the fuck you're doing. I'm going to take over now.*

And then I kissed her.

12

Jessa...

THE TRUTH OF IT WAS THE MAN COULD KISS.

Better than kiss. *Seduce.*

His tongue swept over mine, and it had me melting in a pool of hormones right there as need pulled low in my core. Maybe it wasn't him at all. Maybe it had just been too long since I'd had an orgasm I hadn't given myself. I had no idea what to do with myself.

I don't know how it happened, but my arms reached up and slid into his hair as I dragged him closer. This was so bad on so many levels. He worked with me, despite having been matched with me, he *still* worked with me. I didn't like things messy. Not at all. And he was the most stubborn man on the planet. But Jesus, he tasted amazing. Like fresh mint on a cool summer day.

The scent of sandalwood wrapped around me, cocooning me, keeping me locked in the prison I didn't even want to escape. Gently, his hands slid down over my hips and pulled me closer.

I tried to speed up the kiss, to demand more from him, force him to kiss me deeper, but he didn't. He just took his damn sweet time, tasting me, savoring me, as if I was a meal worth waiting for.

Just when I was on the verge of combusting or dying of frustration, he eased back, stumbled, and then swallowed hard. The look he gave me, said it all. *I will tear your clothes off and fuck you on this treadmill.*

What the hell had just happened? I shook my head in an attempt to clear it, but I swayed. To my mortal embarrassment, I swayed toward him.

"Princess…" his voice was throaty, low.

But that stupid nickname… that was the splash of cold water I needed. I blinked rapidly, trying to clear the brain fog, and opened my mouth to give him a string of consciousness that would scald his ears.

But the words were centered in my brain, and it was still offline. It was going to come back at any moment, but until it did, I needed to get the fuck away from him. "Don't kiss me again."

His smile was a slow steady promise. "Of course, princess. Not until you ask me to."

"Never going to happen."

"If you say so. But let's be real clear. You'll be asking me to kiss you again before long."

"Please tell me you'll hold your breath until I do." And then I smoothed down a nonexistent wrinkle on my skirt and strode away from him. As I marched, I told myself that I did not wobble.

And even if there was a wobble, it was the heels. It had nothing to do with Roone Ainsley having a black belt in kissing.

Roone…

THAT WAS SUCH A ROOKIE MISTAKE.

It was official, I was an idiot. I'd made such a fucking strategic mistake.

The *whrr, whrr, whrr* sound of the treadmill filled the gym of Evans PR as I punished my body. I was torturing it with one hell of a run because I couldn't punish it all the other ways I wanted to right now.

I admit, I shouldn't have kissed her. I knew better. That was dumb shit. And it was *never* going to happen again. I wasn't blurring those lines. I had already seen what could happen.

What, two people end up together?

No, not that. Because Penny and Sebastian were different. They'd been friends as children. And Lucas and Bryna were also different because Lucas was already a prince. I was not. Not that it mattered, because I didn't even want to end up with Jessa.

She just made a constant electrical current that pulsed like a loose tooth a child couldn't help but wiggle. There was that good pain, the kind that hurt a little more every time but still sort of felt incredible because it reminded you that you were still alive. That's what Jessa was.

And kissing her was like that. I could still taste the ghost of her on my lips. Cherries. Was that her lip balm? I still remembered the little sighs that she made at the back of her throat when my tongue slid over hers and I shoved my hands into her hair and held her in place. Delving in, taking. Marking her.

She's not yours to mark.

I knew that, I did. She'd made me insane. I'd never intended to kiss her. And I was never going to kiss her again.

You sure about that?

I had to be sure about that. It was a mistake. One the king

wouldn't thank me for. One the prince wouldn't thank me for either. I was pretty sure neither one of them wanted their perfect little sister being mauled by someone like me.

That's right, you're not worthy.

I shoved my father's voice out of my head. He never actually said those words to me, but it had been the underlying message. The way he never acknowledged me or saw me was enough to let me know I was not good enough. And while my mates loved me now, just as I was, the moment I touched their sister in any real way, I was pretty sure that would end.

No. I wasn't going to tell anyone. I was just going to bury it. Take that memory, shove it deep down, put it in a lockbox. That lockbox was getting a lot of use these days when it came to Jessa.

I had to forget it. Otherwise, it was going to eat me alive and I wasn't going to be able to rest until I could taste her again.

13

Jessa...

THREE THINGS WERE TRUE.

One: *I could still taste Roone on my lips.*

Two: *That kiss was a mistake. Also, it was hotter than Satan's balls.*

Three: *I'd started to like his hands on my ass. But that was neither here nor there.*

My problem was while I'd been busy pressing my traitorous body against him, I hadn't exactly been thinking about the team meeting that afternoon… where I'd have to see him again.

It was a full team meeting with Meet Cute. I would rather walk over coals than have a meeting with Roone.

I could still taste him. I could still feel his hands on my hips, tightening just a little as his tongue swept over mine. I could still smell him, like my whole body was cloaked in sandalwood, wrapping around me, hooking into me, infiltrating my every nerve. Oh no, I wasn't looking forward to the meeting at all.

When I charged into the gym earlier, I'd had no thought beyond telling him not to send me anything else. I hadn't really thought it through. But now, seated next to him, still able to smell him, feel him touching me, I realized that going anywhere near Roone was perhaps a mistake.

I also had to sit there and explain to my whole team why I didn't go on my date.

Rick was practically vibrating with energy. "I can't wait to hear about everyone's experience. If it was anything like mine, I think we really have something here with this app. I know we're not supposed to talk about it, but I want to know, who loved it and who didn't?"

Rick's dark eyes were rapt, interested, curious. On the other side of me, Chloe practically wiggled. "I had a great time. Honestly. It was like the perfect date. Like someone had done all the work, knew exactly what I liked and didn't like, and put it all in exactly the right kind of fun first date. None of this, you know, dinner and a movie where you barely talk and don't get to know each other. Really active."

Rick nodded in agreement, practically clapping his hands. "Exactly. That was outstanding. My favorite part of the date."

Ariel grinned. "That is great feedback. That is exactly what we want to hear. What about you, Evan?" It was almost as if she deliberately didn't ask me or Roone how the date went. Did she know I'd stood him up?

Evan, however, was not paying attention to her. His gaze was glued on me. I shifted uncomfortably. Did he know? Was I about to be fired?

Well, if you are, you can leave at a moment's notice.

No. I would not run away from my life, much like my father had done so often. I could take it, whatever my punishment would be.

"I'm actually more curious to hear how Jessa's date went."

Everyone turned to face me. I met Roone's gaze deliberately. "I have to say, I am so sorry, but I did not get to go on my date. I was working on the Tillerman gala, and going on a date didn't exactly seem like the most pressing matter at the time."

"What?" Rick's rebuke was sharp, cutting. "You didn't think it pertinent to actually use the client product that we all said we would?"

"No, of course I did. I just—"

He stood then. "Jessa, I frankly expected more from you. You know better. You know that to give the client the proper experience, you have to be part of it. You need to understand exactly how it all works. You just chose to work on something else?"

"Yes. No. I mean—" This was not how I expected things to go. I took a sip of tea from my mug that said, *Majestic as Fuck*. Not really work appropriate, but I'd been given the mug and several others as secret Santa gifts over the last couple years, so I figured it was ok.

Ariel threw me a bone, even though she really didn't need to. "It's fine. We already have her rescheduled on the app."

Evan, across from us, frowned. "Well, if she doesn't want to go on the date, she doesn't have to. We can't require our employees to date people."

Rick cut him a look. "No, but we can require them to actually use the app. No one's suggesting that Jessa has to sleep with the poor bloke she got matched with, but she does actually have to go and immerse herself in the experience. Wasn't that the agreement?"

The muscle in Evan's jaw ticked. "Yes, it was."

Shit. They were right. It was childish of me not to go. I should have just done it and gotten it over with, and then I could say that I was done with it. But now, it was a thing. "Of course. I will make sure that I do not miss my second opportunity for this date."

Evan's gaze was sharp on mine. "Do we know who your date was with?"

I shook my head slowly, deliberately. "Nope. All I know is that I was supposed to be there, and I couldn't make it. I got the same thing everyone else got. A picture, time, and place. Isn't that how it works?"

Rick nodded his head. "Yep. That's what I got. I will tell you, mine was fantastic, beautiful girl, too. I really want to see her again. And so compatible. Honestly, Ariel, what you have here is something special."

Evan shrugged. "My date was fine. No better or worse than I've done for myself, but Rick is right. Your ability lies in being able to pick appropriate date suggestions for people. It makes a lot of sense. Makes things easy. Takes the guesswork out."

Ariel nodded. "Are there other notes that I should take? Anything you didn't like about the app?"

Evan ignored that question and instead, focused on Roone. "What about you, Mr. Ainsley? Did you go on a date?"

Roone grinned. "Yep, I had a great time. My date was eloquent, funny, beautiful. Not sure I could have done that well on my own."

I ground my teeth. The jackass was goading me. Whatever. I wasn't going to rise, wasn't going to take the bait. Nope. Not I, said the fly. But Roone continued. "She was intelligent, entertaining, game for anything. Perfect date. I couldn't believe my luck."

I was going to kill him. A very slow, torturous death. One he felt for ages.

Don't be mad because he had a good time with Haley.

Rick pinned me with another direct stare. "Jessa, we look forward to hearing about your experience with the app. When's your date scheduled?"

I swallowed hard. "It's rescheduled for tomorrow night."

He grinned. "That's great. Report back to us afterward. And then we can all move forward with the planning for our proper launch. What I'd like for you to do is organize for Ariel to attend the Tillerman Gala. There'll be a lot of great investors there that will make sense for her to meet and engage with. It'll be her first stepping stone to really pitching them without pitching them. Do you understand?"

Even as my jaw clicked, I nodded. Like it or not, with the memory of his taste still on my lips, I was going on a date with Roone. And there would be no backing out of it this time.

14

Jessa…

GETTING A DRESSING DOWN FROM MY BOSS WAS NOT THE way I'd wanted to round out my day.

I'd messed up. And now the impression I'd given my bosses was that I didn't give a shit. *Get your shit together, Jessa.* From now on, despite my feelings for Roone, I was going to have to be the model employee. Which meant playing nice.

Even though I wanted to throw something at his door. With my glass of wine in hand, I settled on the couch, kicked my feet up on the coffee table and tried to forget everything that had happened.

Except there was no forgetting it. Because every time I closed my eyes, there he was again, Roone, his lips on mine, sliding his tongue into my mouth, pressing my body into his, tasting like heaven and hell and everything in between. Worse, the clear memory of my hands winding into that soft russet hair and pulling him closer.

So, that was it, no more closing of my eyes ever.

And then I was handed my ass because I had been in

avoidance mode. I should have just gone on the stupid date. One date. How bad could it have been?

Maybe he'd have kissed you last night.

Oh, God. No more kissing. Not from him. I didn't care how good he was at it.

I dragged my eyes open and lifted my head to stare at the boxes in the corner. I needed to go through those. My flat's living area was tiny, and those boxes were taking up space. Space I didn't have. And I knew myself well enough to know that if I left the boxes there, I'd be in full avoidance mode for as long as I'd be allowed.

Don't be a baby. There's no point in hiding. I needed to just do it. Rip the band aid off.

I placed my glass on the coffee table and went through one of the boxes of papers first.

With the boxes of clothes, there would be nothing inside that I really wanted to keep. It's not like my dad had a favorite shirt or anything. He wasn't sentimental like that. He'd always said to me, "Jessa, don't hold onto things. Only take with you what you can carry." He'd been trying to ready me for whenever we had to move. He knew how hard every move was, but sometimes I didn't have much warning, and there was no time to grab a favorite doll or a favorite toy or something along those lines. There had just been time to run, at least according to him. So I had learned to be just as unsentimental as he was. By force. And it showed.

My flat was tasteful but mostly sparse. The only pictures I had up were one of me and my parents at an amusement park when I was ten and one of me and dad the day I'd gone to uni. Other than that, I didn't have much that meant anything to me. Those were the only two things I'd grab in a fire. Everything else could burn.

I pulled the top box and dragged it back over to the coffee

table. I took another large swig of wine to fortify myself. "Okay, now or never."

Most of the papers were copies of legal documents, and I put them aside for my solicitor to look at. But the rest were an art treasure trove. Lulu had been right. He'd sketched a lot. There were lots of sketches of me, of his surroundings, and of other residents at Hope House.

There were some lovely ones of Lulu. Somehow, he'd managed to capture the kindness in her eyes. Just the way they crinkled, the way she fully smiled. And the way her eyes made it a point to connect with your soul.

At the bottom of the box, there were several sketches of my mother. But she looked older in these images. As if he'd deliberately aged her. Deliberately tried to determine what she might look like today. My heart squeezed when I looked at them. And my eyes were doing that stinging thing again.

Oh hell no. I was not about to get leaky. If I did that, there was no way I'd be able to finish.

And I wanted to get a good night's sleep. Because tomorrow was going to be a long day. And tomorrow night was going to be an even longer night. Because I had to go on my forced date with Roone.

"Now or never."

The next box held much of the same. There was a list of phone numbers of important people to call. Again, I didn't know anything about these phone numbers or the names associated with them, so I set that aside. The solicitor had been a friend of my parents from back in the day. I'd hoped that having some familiar faces around would have helped my father more. But honestly, it seemed as if it just made him more agitated most of the time.

About halfway through the box, there were some other sketches. Several of what looked like maybe a family crest? It looked like a shield of some sort with a Latin inscription and maybe waves of the sea crashing on rocks. There were several of these. Several of a crown. And then there were several of a man I didn't know. A man wearing a crown. I certainly didn't recognize the face.

I wasn't really one of those crazy royal fiends, so any royal who was not Wills or Harry completely escaped my sphere. I had no idea who it was. But I recognized that it was entirely possible that the person wasn't real. Just another figment of my father's delusions. Again, I set them all aside. There were several more of the same crest I'd seen, but this time there was a dagger running through it and what looked like a teardrop or blood or something. And there were more showing several men with matching tattoos on their arms. Different men. I had no idea who they were supposed to be, but he'd put a lot of detail into their faces. I put them aside, as well. I wasn't even sure why.

I knew exactly how ill my father was. I knew that in reality the people in the sketches probably didn't exist. Or that maybe he'd plucked people out of reality and fit them into his delusions. Or maybe these were movie stars that I didn't know. Anything was possible.

It took me another hour to sort through the other stack of paperwork. Of his sketches, I only kept the ones of Lulu, myself, and my mother. Maybe one day if I ever had a kid, I'd want to show them pictures of their grandmother. The way my father saw her. So aside from the stacks of the sketches of my mother and the property documents, I went to throw the others away. But looking down at them, I couldn't.

I had hated his delusions for so long. They'd been as much a part of my life as they had his. I wanted to exorcize them from my brain, from my past. But there was something about them, and I couldn't force myself to throw them away. Because as much as I hated them, they were a part of me and part of him. And maybe one day, I'd also want to explain to my kids what had happened to their grandfather.

When all the boxes had been gone through, I marked the ones that were for donations to charity shops, and then the papers for shredding or the incinerator. And then I made a folder for the sketches. I was going to just put them in a paper binder and shove them on my bookshelf somewhere, but something told me that it wasn't really permanent. Instead I had a better idea. I knew that there were all sorts of places online where I could get them scanned in and made into artwork, so I took out my phone and snapped close-up pictures. Then I used my scanner and added them to my computer, as well. I might never have time to do anything with them, but at least I would have them. A piece of him forever. And they'd be in a more permanent place than something on my bookshelf that would in all likelihood get left behind when I had to leave in a hurry.

You don't have to do that anymore.

No. Maybe not. But the mentality was still there. I didn't want to be sentimental. So maybe I would just keep them in cyberspace, on the cloud where they would forever be with me. And I could still travel as light as I needed to.

Later that night as I climbed into bed, a headache blooming between my eyes, I still couldn't get the images out of my mind. Maybe these were people that he did know. Maybe Lulu would want the sketches of herself.

Or maybe you're just as obsessive as he is.

I padded back into the living room and grabbed my laptop. I emailed copies of the sketches to James and Lulu and quickly typed out a quick few sentences.

I'm not sure if these images depict anyone that was at Hope House. But maybe if he was close to any of these people they'd like to know that he made sketches of them. Lulu I especially love the

one of you in the kitchen making shepherd's pie. As you know, it
was his favorite.

James, Lulu tells me you'll be in the city soon. I would abso-
lutely love to have dinner and chat with you.

Talk soon,
Jessa.

I SENT IT OFF, finally able to let it go. I'd done everything I needed to do. And when I climbed back into bed, I was so emotionally raw and exhausted that when I closed my eyes, for the first time all day, I didn't see Roone.

👑

Roone...

WHILE I MONITORED the princess as she unpacked those boxes she had me drag in for her, the inevitable texts from my cousin came in.

Ben: *Sorry had to travel. Is now an appropriate time to ask you what the fuck?*

Roone: *Sorry about that. I wish I'd had more time to explain it to you. I didn't know that was going to happen.*

Ben: *So, first question, why didn't you phone me?*

Ben: *Second question, are you shagging, the beautiful Miss McLean?*

Roone: *Stay away from her.*

Ben sent a laugh emoji. Hell. I didn't know we were at the emoji stage of our relationship. Lucas had been all over me about my weak emoji game.

Ben: *So, what gives?*

Roone: *Can't go too much into it. It's a job. Undercover.*

Ben: *007 eh, mate?*

Roone: *No, not like that.*

Except it kind of was like that.

Roone: *It's complicated. Let's grab a pint, and I'll tell you all about it.*

Ben: *You're on. Also, you're a twat for not calling before you arrived in London.*

Somehow, I knew that was coming.

Ben: *Well, it's good to have you here. You staying long?*

Roone: *Yeah, it looks like I'll be here for a bit.*

He sent me a thumbs up.

Ben: *Right, I may have to travel at the end of next week. But when I'm back, you and I are grabbing that pint.*

Roone: *Looking forward to it.*

I just had to figure out exactly how much I was going to tell him. There was a time Ben and I had been closer than brothers. But things were different now. Several moments passed before he asked the question I knew he would eventually ask.

Ben: *Have you seen him yet?*

Just the hint of a mention of my half-brother had my gut twisting. It had been years, over a decade. And still, I couldn't let it go. The amount of hatred I felt for Rhys and his family was still strong. It burned inside me.

Roone: *Nope.*

I left it at that. I didn't want to get into it. And when I finally did talk about it, I knew that it was going to hurt, so I'd rather save it for a one-and-done kind of conversation and not do it via text message.

Ben: *Okay. I'll give you a ring when I'm back.*

I didn't relish cutting off the conversation with my cousin, but he knew exactly how I felt about my brother. His family was the reason my mother had died alone. As far as I was concerned, I no longer had a brother. I'd never had one. And if I did, that brother was back in Winston

Isles, not the one by birth who I loathed to the core of my being.

Roone: *Catch up with you soon.*

All I had to do was tell myself I didn't care, and it wouldn't hurt.

Oh, so we plan on lying to ourselves about this one too?

Yep, right now, I was good with all the lies.

15

Jessa...

GIDDY EXCITEMENT ZIPPED OVER MY SKIN. I HAD ALWAYS wanted to try this. Kind of ironic that I was getting to try this with someone I didn't like, but whatever. It was still freaking trapeze.

I've been obsessed with trapeze since I was a kid. I used to beg and beg and beg my father to take me. Then he'd learned that aerial abilities were a good skill to have and aided in martial arts. Granted, he wanted me to have that skill for other reasons, but still, I'd still never really done trapeze.

When I walked into the gym, Roone was easy to spot. I felt, him rather than saw him. My body was already attuned to his location like the traitor that it was.

He was leaning against the wall just inside to the gym. Dressed in low-slung grey sweatpants and a long-sleeved T-shirt, he looked good enough to lick.

No. No licking.

"Let's get this over with."

His lips tipped up in a casual smile. "Nice to see you too, princess."

I wrinkled my nose. "Why do you call insist on calling me that?"

"Because you should always be treated like a princess." He shrugged. "I'm surprised you made it."

A sheepish smile broke out on my lips. "I did. Someone reminded me that sometimes I can stand in my own way, and I'm not going to do that. I really do believe in the app. After hearing Ariel talk about it so much. I decided to give it a shot. A real one this time. No stand in. And I don't want to have the Evans rip me a new one again."

His smile was slow, and I wondered how in the world anyone like him ever needed help from an app. There were moments when he was unwittingly charming and sweet looking. And then he went and ruined it by being overbearing and domineering. But right now, I was getting the sweet and charming side, so I was taking it. "Shall we?"

He nodded. "Yeah, of course." And then he reached over and took my bag off my shoulder before clasping my smaller hand in his huge one. How in the world did I miss that his hands were this big?

The better to touch you in all your secret places, my dear.

This was a date, yes, but not *that* kind of a date.

Who are you kidding?

That was true. I was still thinking about that kiss yesterday.

The way he just owned my lips without much work or effort, it was disconcerting. It was also hot as hell.

His hands were warm. I could feel callouses on them. Under normal circumstances, I would have said he was a paper pushing kind of guy. But, I'd been wrong. His hands had seen hard work. Maybe from the gym? Maybe from using his hands a lot, I didn't know. The truth was, I didn't really know much about him.

His résumé had all the right schools, brief company profiles for past jobs, history and finance, a stint in the Caribbean. Blah, blah, boring blah. To be honest I hadn't paid much attention to it when Chloe had dug it up for me. Maybe I should.

I needed to learn about my enemy.

And if he's not your enemy?

If this were a real date, I'd want to get to know the real Roone. Who was he? Who had he been as a kid? What did he like to do, read, eat? But it wasn't real.

That kiss was real.

Our instructor's name was Gigi. She was a tiny slip of a gymnast-looking kind of a girl, but I could tell she was strong and athletic.

"Welcome to Fly City." She slid Roone a glance. "You look familiar."

He nodded. "Yeah, I was here the other day."

She nodded. "Ok, yeah, I thought I recognized you. You were here with, what was your partner's name? Haley?"

Was it me, or was that a flush creeping up Roone's neck?

"Yeah, that was her."

Then Gigi turned to face me. "I guess you're Roone's *new* partner." I ignored the sardonic bite to her comment.

"Yep, that's me. The new partner."

"Well, you two follow me. It's easy, honestly. The number one thing is trust. You guys will do great."

She sounded like she was from Newcastle, her accent trilling over me. Somehow, when she said she thought we'd do great, I didn't exactly believe her. Trusting men in general wasn't high on my list of things to do. Trusting guys like Roone was next to impossible.

It wasn't until thirty minutes later when I was harnessed

up, staring at the net below with the trapeze bar in my hands, yelling, "Jumper ready," that I really understood that I was going to need to trust the overgrown oaf.

In a second, I was going to jump. I could choose to stay swinging, and then just jump down to the net below, or I could choose to trust Roone to catch me. On the other end of the net, he was ready to catch me on the swing out. He would invert his position so that he was hanging upside down and then catch me. The real problem at the center of this was that I didn't trust *anyone*.

Or for once, you can live your life for yourself. You have a choice. Trust him or don't. Now is the time to decide.

I squeezed my eyes shut and I jumped.

As I swung toward him at a speed fast enough to alarm me, my stomach dropped. What was I going to do? What should I do?

I held my breath, opened my eyes, and let go.

Strong, gently calloused hands caught me easily by the wrists in the hold Gigi had shown us. The rush of adrenaline was pure and fast and sweet, tasting like a frozen lemonade on a hot summer day. We swung gently back and forth, and he grinned at me before finally letting me drop onto the net. I fell with a soft landing and lay there for several moments, laughing.

When was the last time I'd laughed like that?

Before Dad?

It took several minutes to unharness myself and roll off the net. But then Roone met me on the other side. He held his arms wide, and I didn't even have to think about it. I ran straight toward him and jumped up into them. "Oh my God, that was bloody fantastic."

"Uh, that was brilliant. Well done, princess."

He swung me around, and I laughed. When he set me down, his grin was wide and his eyes danced. I couldn't help but grin back at him. And as I held his gaze, his focus dropped to my lips.

Butterflies danced low in my belly, and the synapses in my brain zapped and fired. Roone leaned down, and anticipation lit my nerves, making them jump and dance. I knew what was coming. And it was going to be so easy to—

"Well done, Jessa and Roone. You guys are great. Want to give it another go?"

Damn. Clam jam much?

I shook my head. What the hell was wrong with me? I didn't even like him. But I couldn't even be mad at her because I was going to get to do it again. "Absolutely."

Roone just laughed. "Of course you do."

⁂

Jessa...

AFTER AN HOUR and a half of flying through the air, falling on my ass, nearly hitting my head, several missed connections with Roone, and more fun than I can probably say I'd had in a year, Roone led the way into Sweet Treats, a little café about a mile away from the trapeze place. Once we were settled at a booth and the waitress had taken our order, he turned his attention to me. "So, was it worth actually going on the date this time?"

I couldn't help the smile that tugged at my lips. "You know it was worth it. It was actually really fun."

He grinned. "And you're actually not bad company."

"What? I'm excellent company." I leaned forward. "I don't know how they did that. The app is so intuitive. I mean it's fascinating that they take these experiences that people have always wanted to try and make them accessible. That's the real magic in it, not the algorithm and the matching of the actual

people but figuring out what people actually want. To me that
was outstanding."

"Do you think the people don't matter?"

"Of course they matter. But let's face it. People are basically interchangeable. Women can talk themselves into just
about anything so as long as they find a guy attractive, even if
he's not the right guy for them. Women will bend over backward to make it work. And men well…" I shrugged and eyed
him. "Men are visual creatures. As long as you think a chick is
hot, you'll put up with all kinds of insanity."

His gaze narrowed for a moment, but then he said, "You're
not wrong about that. Men will put up with just about
anything. But you don't think that's chemical? You don't
think that has anything to do with compatibility?"

I shrugged. "Not really. Sure, all that stuff helps, but
studies show that when people work together, or you know,
are in the trenches together, or hell even in close proximity,
those things play more into why people get together than
anything else."

"Aw, it's a shame princess. You don't believe in love."

"I wouldn't say I don't believe, I would just say I am very
skeptical. I believe it's possible. But I've seen too many people
take a dive off the deep end because of love, often for things
that don't make them happy or even fulfill them. So I believe
in the tangible things I can see and taste."

Roone lifted a brow as his moss-green eyes studied me
intently. "Let me ask you a question."

I wasn't sure I was going to like the direction of this question, but I was game. "Okay, fire."

"When was the last time you actually had a relationship?
Not just, you know, somebody you dated because they were
convenient. But someone that you wanted to be with.
Someone who curled your toes and made you giddy and
excited."

I opened my mouth to answer quickly, but then I realized that he had me there. Sure, I dated every now and again, put on a pretty dress. But there had been no one who mattered recently. "Maybe it's been a while."

"Define 'a while.'"

"Okay, so it's been a hot minute since I've felt that kind of snappiness. But honestly, that's not that common."

Roone's voice dropped an octave. "When was the last time someone kissed you like they meant it, Jessa?"

My stomach flipped. *Yesterday afternoon.* "How is that even relevant?"

"Oh, princess, it's relevant."

"Well, maybe it has been longer than normal. But that's not all that matters in life. I could get kissed any time."

He chuckled low. "Yeah, tell me about it."

"I just haven't really connected to anyone to make it mean something, you know?"

His gaze met mine directly then. "Yeah, I know exactly what you mean."

"So as great as I think this app is, I'm not a true believer."

He cocked his head. "How about a bet? I won't kiss you again until you ask me to."

I sputtered. "Which I won't."

"Right. Of course. But we go on three of these dates. If you ask me to kiss you, we call a truce. We'll divvy up the clients based on who's best. If you don't ask me, I'll take what you give me."

I laughed. "But what's to stop me from just never asking?"

He grinned. "Oh, princess, you underestimate me."

16

Roone…

I HADN'T PLANNED TO HAVE FUN. I HADN'T EXPECTED TO really like her.

I was willing to admit it when I was wrong. Maybe I had judged the princess a little too harshly.

She *was* stubborn, obstinate, and always thought she knew what was best. But she was also insightful, smart, and a giant pain in the ass. But she had good instincts. Knew what to fight for. Knew what mattered. And the problem was I liked her. I liked her a lot.

No, you like that zing of electricity every time she's near you.

Yeah, okay fine. The zap between us was annoying. That constant awareness of her. I didn't want that. I *hated* that. She was Sebastian's sister. I was here to protect her. Yes, I was supposed to get close to her, but I was going to do things differently. We weren't going to walk that line. I'm pretty sure the last thing the king wanted was me with my hands all over the lost princess. I didn't care what Ariel or Lucas said. I just had to keep my hands off her. It would be easy. Simple.

Between me posing as her coworker and Ariel posing as a client, she would have a good amount of coverage. And we could be friends.

Those thoughts you're having, they're not very friendly.

We arrived at the flat, and she led the way down the hall. "Well, thank you for tonight. It was actually fun. I'm surprised."

I chuckled. "You're welcome. Thank you for the ringing endorsement. This is where you say I give excellent first date."

"Um, this isn't a real date. You're not getting kissed."

I laughed. "Are you sure about that?"

What was wrong with me? Why was I goading her? Why was I poking at her?

Because you want to kiss her.

No. No I did not. Yesterday was a fluke.

Yes, she was beautiful. Everything a guy like me didn't deserve. But more than that, she was my best mate's little sister. *Both* of my best mates' little sister. She had no idea who she was. Her life was about to get complicated as fuck. The last thing she needed was someone like me making it worse. Even if she didn't know who I was, the real me, the forgotten son, the black sheep, that's not someone a princess will look at as an option, so I shoved aside the flare, and walked her to her door. "Like I said, door to door service. I'm glad you came tonight, Jessa."

She grinned at me widely. "You never use my name. You always call me princess."

I bit the inside of my cheek. "Yeah well, you seem to like it, so I keep using it."

"I don't like it." She wrinkled her nose. "I'm not some prissy debutante."

"I don't think anybody in their right mind would ever call you that."

She laughed softly. "Yeah, you're right. And thanks for keeping your lips to yourself this time."

I lifted a brow. "I just want to be clear, this isn't you asking me for a kiss?"

Just like that the caveman came tapping back at the door. I would love to kiss her again. Love to feel her lips sliding under mine. I wanted to hear those sharp panting breaths she drew in. I wanted to feel her body melt against mine, feel the slickness of her core heat my dick as I pressed up against her. "Just say the word. But I want you to make very sure that you're using the *right* words. Make sure you add please and thank you."

Jessa leaned forward too. The lightness of her perfume, the floral scent, made my heart race. I could hear the *thud, thud, thud* as my pulse clanged. Jesus, what was I doing?

It doesn't matter. Shut up. This is such a bad idea for so many reasons.

Dick: Didn't I tell you to shut up man, if you can't listen, I will take over again.

"I'm glad to see you're still delusional. You keep holding your breath for that kiss. But I will hand it to you. You do give excellent first date."

The flood of heat in my veins had me dizzy. My lips tipped into a smile, and I shrugged. "Oh, I know. Let's get you inside."

"Yeah, right. Okay, goodnight then." She turned the lock and shoved the front door, disengaged the key and stepped inside before stepping right back out.

"What's wrong?"

She swallowed hard. "Someone's broken into my apartment."

Jessa…

SOMETHING WAS WRONG. Something other than Chloe asleep on my couch.

Roone had called her, insisted really. He said it was either her on my couch, or I was staying with him. And there was no telling how many kisses I'd ask for if I did that because I was weak, so Chloe had been the right choice.

I hadn't been able to get back in my flat properly without someone hovering for three hours. But now that I was back in, I could tell something was definitely wrong. For starters, the only thing missing was my rose pendant. But it wasn't worth much, but it was sentimental. Oh, they'd made a huge mess, clearly looking for something. I did a cursory look when the police had asked, but looking again, nothing of value was actually taken.

Whoever had been in here hadn't known to look beyond the surface to get to anything they really wanted. And I really didn't have much to steal. I had a couple of Louis Vuitton's in my closet, and they weren't even touched. One of them was still in the box, unused. I'd left my laptop at work, so that wasn't an option, but mostly, everything else in the flat was disposable. For someone who wanted roots, I never seemed to put down any.

Chloe had been after me for ages. It wasn't like I'd just moved back to London. It had been three years, but I still had some boxes of things that I hadn't unpacked. *That's because you think you're going to have to leave again.* Because my life had been in flux for so long, I stayed ready. Hell, I had a go bag that was packed with basic essentials for any weather.

I heard the door across the hall open and close, and I forced myself to stay put and not run to see if it was him. He'd been so sweet and stayed with me until Chloe had shown up.

Why did he have to occasionally be so sweet? It threw me

off. I didn't even like him, so I didn't know what my problem was.

You do like him.

Just because he'd woken something primal in me did not mean I liked him. Half the time, I just wanted to mess up that perfect wave of his hair. God, there was just something so douchey about it along with his fuck-me smile.

Chloe was right. I needed a good shag. I really wanted to mess him up in more ways than one.

On the couch, Chloe snored.

I really had to stop this obsession. Whatever little childish annoyance we had with each other couldn't go on. For starters, he worked with me. But also, this was my *home*. I had roots. I wasn't leaving.

And I couldn't kiss him ever again. It was dangerous. *He* was dangerous.

Despite everything I told myself, that didn't keep me from staring at the door and willing him to come over. I hated that I was so attuned to him. I hated that he was my match as a date.

I still hadn't figured out how the hell I was getting around that, because there was no way in hell was I going to mess up my career for Roone.

Not today, libido, not today.

17

Jessa...

"UNDERSTANDING BETTER HOW THE APP WORKS AND how it provides these tailored experiences will help us provide the user with a specialized, lux experience. My first date was based on something I've always wanted to do, an experience I've always wanted to have. It felt personalized. It felt tailored to me. So what we're going to do is push the personalization. We're going to push Meet Cute as being the app that caters to your fantasies or dreams, things you've always wanted to do. That's going to be our lead in. It's going to feel special, feel like it's catered to each individual. So, based on that, will the rest of you please share what your experiences were?" I asked.

Chloe was happy to speak up. For her first date, she'd done a tasting room. It was something she'd always wanted to do. It was one of those chef experiences where you end up at a penthouse somewhere in the city, and a chef cooks for you and a group of strangers. "It was fantastic. And Marc, my date, he mostly just wanted to do something exclusive and different.

He'd been trying to get a reservation at that chef's restaurant for months. This killed two birds with one stone."

Rick nodded. "Same thing for me. I've always wanted to drive Formula One since I was a kid. And my date, Amber, her dad was a car enthusiast when she was a kid. He used to talk to her about all these different kinds of cars, took her to car shows, and she's a *Top Gear* fanatic. So we went to a driving course. We had a fantastic time."

Everyone talked about their experiences, including Ariel. But she said, "Well, it's my app, so unfortunately, I sort of know how to beat it. It tends to be inaccurate for me. But I still had a fantastic time. I had to go on an experience that I probably wouldn't have picked for myself."

I nodded. "See, this is exactly what I mean. It should be about the elite experience you can get nowhere else. And that's the publicity we need to focus on. We'll keep it small, just an elite clientele. No Sussex wannabe footballer's wives allowed, and only the biggest and best influencers in social media. I think that's our niche. We keep it exclusive. The more exclusive it is, the more people want it. We're going to have membership cards and things like that, and we'll publicize it amongst the lords and lots of royalty. That's what we do. That's our promotional push."

For once, Roone looked happy when I walked him through our PR plan. "Yeah, that works. You get it. It's not about everyone. It's about only a select few."

After the meeting, Evan pulled me aside. "Have you checked the app lately?"

I swallowed. I really didn't need him asking questions about me using the app to date. I didn't want to lie. "Not yet? Why?"

"I'm so curious what experience you'll get next."

Shit. I needed a better way to ease out of this. "I'll check a little later. I mean what if my date says no to date two. That's more humiliation than I need in the standard work day."

"Oh, right, of course. Keep me posted."

As if. "Sure thing."

I bolted out of the conference room and headed for the stairs. I didn't want to get embroiled in another uncomfortable conversation with Evan that I'd have to lie my way out of.

I shoved open the door to the stairwell.

"So, I noticed you haven't said yes yet?"

"Jesus Christ, Roone. Are you trying to terrify me to death? I'm mulling it over. I'm not sure the terms of the bet apply."

"Oh, come on now, you know you want to," Roone teased. "Unless you're chicken of course."

"No, I don't. And I have never backed down from anything. You have invaded every corner of my life. If I didn't know better, I'd think I'd pissed someone off in a previous lifetime. I mean honestly, in the span of a fortnight, you moved in across the hall, you're working at my company, and you're trying to take my clients."

"Hey now, easy does it. I'm not *trying* to take your clients, I can't help it if your contacts like me better."

"Madison Jeffries does not like you better. And I swear to God on this."

Roone tossed his head back, his laugh low and melodic, and quite frankly making me tingly in all the right places. "You sound nervous. And it sure as hell feels like Madison and I have the perfect working partnership. After all, she requested me for a private meeting. Ariel seems to like me too."

"I'm not going to dignify that situation with Madison with a response. And Ariel *is* fantastic. And she's named me primary."

Roone frowned. "When did this happen?"

"Oh, while you were so busy preening in there with the Evans, she pulled me aside and told me I was primary, so you can feel free to kiss my ass."

"Ooh, you like the kinky shit. I'm down with that. So, date two we can explore that if you'd like."

My hand twitched. I really wanted to hit him across the face. But no, I wasn't going to do that. I was going to stay calm and collected because I liked this job. I liked the stability. I liked being here. I didn't want to have to uproot my entire life again, and if I beat the shit out of him right now, I'd have to. And then I'd have the kind of life I'd had before. Constantly a vagabond. I'd had this job for nearly three years. I liked being a normal person. One who wasn't packed up and ready to run every minute. And he was certainly not going to make me run.

"Oh, you'd like that."

He laughed again. "What guy wouldn't like a kinky girl? I mean you have that crazy-girl vibe to you, so you might be kinky as shit."

"Well luckily for both of us, you'll never know."

"Well, as it turns out, I already know how you taste."

Heat crept up my neck. "*You* kissed *me*."

"Yes. I did. And we both agreed that you'd be asking me for another one, right?"

"Fuck off."

All that got me was a chuckle. "Come on, princess, what are you so scared of? Another date isn't going to kill you. Besides, I thought you said you could resist my charms."

"I can." He knew how to goad me. I didn't want to go on another date with him. *Are you sure?* "I thought you said you could charm my panties off in three dates or less?"

"I did. If you want to be chicken, the bet's null and void."

"I'm not a chicken."

He was so close that every inhale felt like he permeated my synapses in every cell. God, he was so sexy. Problem was the idiot knew it.

"We'll go on this date. I don't care. But you're not getting into my panties. And let's be really, really clear... If I resist you, London Lords is mine, got it?"

He grinned and winked. "Of course. A deal is a deal."

"I don't get it, what do you win? Because all I have to do is tell you no and I get my client back."

His voice went whisper soft then. "Yeah. It's fairly simple. And I know it looks bad for me. Because you just say one word, and that's the end of that. But you and I both know you liked what happened in the gym. Hell, I liked it. And I figure with these dates, it's very unlikely you're going to say no, so you might as well get use to not having Jeffries and London Lords on your client roster."

"Oh God, I'm going to really enjoy it when I get my client back. I'm going to rub your face in it, and it's going to be a sweet day."

The left corner of his lip tipped up. "Just what are you gonna rub my face in? Because I have to tell you, I was really looking forward to—"

I didn't let him finish. I shoved him and yanked open the fire door. "You're a pig."

"Maybe. But you seem to like me." His voice sobered for a moment as his gaze narrowed on me. "You okay though? I didn't want to ask in the meeting."

If nothing else, that threw me. Because the concern in his gaze, that was genuine. I flushed. "Um, yeah. I'm fine. No big deal. The police cleaned up the fingerprint residue, and it's like they were never there."

He studied me. "Of course. No big deal. But you know, if it was a big deal and you don't feel safe or whatever, just give me a shout and I'll distract you with popcorn and cheesy eighties movies."

How the hell did he know about my love of all things John Hughes?

"Thanks for the offer. I'm tougher than I look though."

Roone nodded slowly. "You know what princess? You're tough as nails. Too bad you're going to lose that bet."

"Too bad you're delusional."

Now all I had to do was shore up the lady parts because there was no way I was losing to Roone.

♕

Roone…

I WASN'T PRIMPING and preening. No way no how. Except, maybe I'd fluffed the pillows a couple of times. And changed twice. But to be fair, I'd been in my Evans PR work clothes. I had also made a point to put all the surveillance equipment away behind the bookcase where she wouldn't look, leaving only my laptop out. If push came to shove, I could access her surveillance feed from here, but since she was with me that wasn't necessary. While she was here, I was the only one on duty. Ariel would be on audio based on the bug we had in her purse, if she brought it with her, but other than that it would be just me and Jessa.

At the sound of the knock on the door, I jogged to open it. She stood in the hall, laptop bag and purse on one shoulder, pizza on an actual pizza stone in the opposite hand.

My brows lifted. "Is that fresh?"

She nodded and tucked her hair behind her ear. "Yeah, it is. I get the dough from this bakery down the street. I don't know if you like the weird British toppings like corn and pineapple, so I figured I'd make something that I liked and hopefully you'd like it too."

I laughed and stepped back. "You have this way of making sure you get what you want, don't you?"

She grinned. "Is there any other way?"

I stepped back to let her in, and she glanced around. "Oh, your kitchen is a mirror image of my place? But the rest is loft style."

"I guess so. I love it. It's exactly my style."

Her gaze slid over me. "I never really would have pegged you for a modern, contemporary kind of guy."

"Yeah well, at my last flat I couldn't really change the décor, so this is a nice change of scenery."

"Oh, your place in the Winston Isles?"

I nodded carefully as I took the pizza from her. "Yeah. Let me get some plates."

She dropped her laptop onto my island and took a seat at one of the stools. "I have wine in the bag." She pulled out a bottle of red and a wine opener.

"I see you came prepared."

"Well, I moved around a lot. I know that sometimes the essentials aren't always on hand."

"Were you a military brat or something?"

"No, nothing like that. Just a vagabond father."

"Ah. Well, you are the expert because I have no idea where my corkscrew is."

"No wine opener, no beer opener? What kind of red-blooded British bloke are you?"

"I'm British enough to head straight down to the pub when I need something."

"Right. Good point, solid comeback. Did you miss that just-heading-to-the-pub situation when you were in the Winston Isles?"

I shook my head. "No, not really. There were plenty of pubs in the Winston Isles."

"I've heard it's beautiful. The Caribbean. I've never been."

I set the plates on the counter and tried to find my pizza slicer. Ariel had put that away somewhere. As a matter of fact, she and the staging team that had come in advance had set up the whole kitchen. Which is probably why I had no idea where anything was. She and a few of the rotating team lived in the flats across and down the road from Jessa's unit.

Ariel wasn't exactly domestic. I had already discovered that I cooked more than she did, and she genuinely thought that Maltesers were a food group. More often than not, she popped through around dinner time to see what I'd made. "Where did I put the knives?"

She shook her head. "Already to the rescue." She reached in her bag again and pulled out a pizza cutter.

"Wow. You really do come prepared."

"Yeah, well we have a lot of clients to go over. I set a timer. There's another pizza in the oven at my place just in case this isn't enough."

"Woman, I could marry you."

What? You're insane. Stop talking to the princess.

But she saw it as a joke. Thankfully. "Well, there's a very long queue, so you'll have to form an orderly line to the left."

"I don't see anyone else in line."

"Yeah, there's a good reason for that."

"Oh, come on, despite the slightly prickly personality, you're clearly beautiful. You're smart. There should be a queue."

"Aw, Mr. Ainsley, are you giving me a genuine compliment?"

I shook my head as I laughed. "Don't get used to it." Why was it that she wasn't used to compliments? My heart squeezed at that. While I cut the pizza and plated the slices, she jumped off the stool and started walking around the flat. Ariel and the staging team had put scattered photos around. Some of me and Sebastian. A few with Penny and the whole team. Several of my mother. Where Ariel had even found those, I had no idea.

"Who's this?"

"That's my mum."

Jessa smiled at that. "She's beautiful."

"Yeah. She was. She died when I was 15."

"Shit. I'm so sorry."

"It's okay."

Jessa turned to study me for a long moment. "You look like her a little."

"Yeah, I've heard that before. Although, I mostly look like my dad I know."

She nodded noncommittally. "I uh, I lost my mum when I was ten. And my dad a year ago."

"That sucks. It really sucks. I'm so sorry."

She shrugged. "Honestly, I think I was probably losing my dad long before he was actually gone. He wasn't well at the end."

I knew what she was talking about, but I couldn't allude to it, so I had to ask. Even if I didn't like poking at her wound. "Was he sick for a long time or something?"

She shrugged and then gratefully took the glass of wine I poured. "Yeah, but not like that. Mental stuff. He never quite recovered from when my mom died. And then in the end, he was just more and more delusional, you know? So it was tough. My dad, the guy who raised me, I hadn't really seen *him* in a long time."

"Still sucks." I clinked my glass with hers. "Look at us, getting along and everything."

She shifted on her feet. "Yeah. About that, I figured that

maybe I misjudged you. I thought you were out to steal my clients."

I grinned at her. "I am."

"Yeah, but if you can steal my clients it means I don't deserve them. If they're happy with me, they won't come to you. I have been acting like a brat, and I'm sorry. You're not *completely* evil."

I laughed at that. "Well I'm glad to know I'm not evil through and through."

"No, you're not. So truce?"

"Yeah, sure, I'm down for the truce. Although, I do have to wonder does this null and void our little kiss bet?"

She lifted a brow. "Oh, well see, here's where you lose. I'm not fighting you anymore, but I'm certainly not going to ask you for a kiss."

I clapped a hand over my chest. "You wound me. If I didn't know better, I'd say you didn't enjoy the last one."

Her teeth grazed her bottom lip, and she shifted on her feet, pupils dilating slightly. Oh yeah, she'd liked the kiss.

"My point is that I'm not going to ask you for another. So, I'm keeping my clients, and we might as well divvy up the ones that I don't really have time to work on."

"So, you want me to just give in? Even though we had a deal?"

"The deal is for a kiss. And you and I both know I'm never going to ask you for one."

I cocked my head. "We don't both know that. Because here's the thing. I remember exactly how you taste." I took a step toward her. I watched intently as she swallowed hard. "I remember that little sound you made at the back of your throat when I slid my tongue over yours."

She took another step back, and her legs came in contact with the coffee table.

"You also made this little whimper sound when you could

feel me drawing back. It was so unbelievably sexy. I remember the way your hand tightened just so on my shoulder as I waited for you to push me back, which you didn't do. Instead you clawed your fingernails into my shoulders. So, you can tell me you don't want me to kiss you again. And that's fair. But you can't tell me you didn't like it the last time. If you don't ask me to kiss you again, I won't. I gave you my word. And I'm a man of my word. But don't you go pretending that you didn't feel that."

Her chest rose and fell rapidly as she dragged in short, panting breaths. I was so close now. She was wearing that perfume, the floral one with just a hint of spice as a chaser. I wanted to bathe in that scent. I wanted to kiss every spot where I could smell it on her skin.

You are out of control. Rein it in. Back on the other side of the line.

Problem was I didn't want to go back on the other side of the line. This close to her, I wanted to touch her, taste her, smell her, watch her melt on my tongue.

"What are you doing?"

"Nothing. Just getting my laptop so we can get to work." I reached down and grabbed my laptop from right behind her on the coffee table. I made it a point to brush her body gently with mine. Jesus fucking Christ, I could feel her nipples through her blouse, her heat clawing at me, begging to wind around me. I stood with laptop in hand and showed it to her. "Are you ready to get to work now?"

Her lips were parted, and her eyes were wide as she stared up at me. "Yep, of course."

I smiled down at her. Oh, I had her. I absolutely had her.

I thought we weren't going to get close to her this way.

Shut it. This little exchange wasn't about the mission. It was about what Jessa McLean was doing to me. And frankly, she deserved a bit of her own medicine.

"Let's get to work, princess."

She cleared her throat and nodded. "Yeah. Of course, right, work."

"Yep, after all, that's why you're here isn't it?"

With a sigh she tipped her chin up. "Yep, that's exactly why I'm here, so you just keep holding your breath. Because it's still not going to happen."

I grinned at her. "Whatever you need to tell yourself."

18

Ariel...

I HAD MADE A MISTAKE. I'D KNOWN IT THE MOMENT I said yes, but because he was my father, I'd still done it. And now I couldn't get in touch with him. I scanned the monitors again in Jessa's flat even as I fired off another text to my father, demanding he return my calls.

I had my hands full with this case, and he was pulling this shit? Honestly?

Did you expect anything different?

After I'd asked Penny to look in on him the other day, I'd accessed my security cameras, and I'd seen him coming and going. Unfortunately, when I checked two days ago, I saw him headed in the exact opposite direction of where he should have been.

Toward the palace. We'd had a distinct arrangement. He was to go nowhere near the palace. That had *always* been our arrangement. He could come to visit me, as long as he didn't step foot near the palace. With his background, he couldn't be trusted. And I valued my job there.

I had an important position, and people depended on me. My father could never understand something like that, but if he pulled any of his antics, I'd be out of a job. And then where would I be?

I'd end up just like him. Hustling to make ends meet. For years I'd blamed my mother. I'd been so angry, so convinced that if she'd just loved him more, fought harder, that they could've worked. But over the years, I'd come to realize why she'd left. My only question to her now was why she hadn't taken me with her.

Maybe I was overreacting. Maybe it wasn't that bad, and I just needed to give him a chance. Maybe there was a perfectly good reason he'd been headed to the palace instead of away from it. I sent a couple of quick emails just to check in with everyone at home and to put out some feelers for anyone who may have seen him. This was the last thing I needed right now. This was the biggest mission of my career. He was not going to ruin it for me.

I was still sending emails when Roone approached me from behind. He was a guard, so he knew better. But still, I whipped around, grabbed his wrist, and had his arm twisted in a second.

If he'd been someone untrained, I'd have had good control of his arm, he'd whine like a baby, and cry out in pain. Instead, he countered my maneuver, dropping his body weight and pulling me down with him. Then he had me in a headlock.

I countered with standard headlock escape, one arm over his head and my finger directly on his septum, pulling back and nearly tossing him with a shift of my hips.

"Oh, Shit. Dammit. Uncle."

"Don't surprise me," I grumbled.

"Shit, I'm the only one who knows you're here. Remember, we are a team."

"Yeah, I remember. You just can't sneak up behind me."

Roone glowered at me. "You know for such a little thing, you're awfully feisty."

"You recognize I am a Royal Guard, right?"

He nodded. "Yes, but you look like a little mermaid, so you can see how people would think that you're somewhat of a fairy princess, right?"

I ground my teeth. "No one would call me a fairy princess. I'm a soldier, just like you."

"Relax, no one's saying you're not a soldier. I'm just saying, you do have certain pixie-like qualities to you, so you can see how people might be taken off guard. Which is a good thing, just so you know."

I rolled my shoulders. "Okay, maybe I was being a little touchy."

His brows pulled down. "Everything okay with Jessa?"

"You mean besides her pulling out her boxing gloves and going to town on her body bag?" I indicated the screen where Jessa was practicing her kickboxing. "She told him earlier his new name was Roone."

Like an idiot, the fool grinned. "Aw, she likes me."

I glanced back at the screen. "I don't quite think that's what she's got going on for you, but you can live in your delusional world if you want."

"Look, I know you said charm her and all that good shit, but a girl like Jessa, she wouldn't trust it. Especially if she hasn't earned it. So if I went in there all sweetness and light, she'd know I was up to something, which is not what we need right now. If she has to fight for the friendship, she's more likely to trust me, and we can both do our job. You can be the one she liked right away."

He had a point there. During our first planning meeting, we'd gotten on like gangbusters. I'd used some details from that first lunch to tailor the perfect date for someone like her.

Something whimsical but fun, because she never allowed herself to even relax for a minute. It must be exhausting being the perfect person for everyone.

I rolled my eyes. "Are you making any headway?"

"Well, she's fighting me at every turn, but she seems to *like* fighting me, so we'll take that and run with it. We did have a moment a couple of nights ago when we were working, so she might be thawing a bit."

"Okay, I'm gonna let you run with this angle for now, but don't overdo it. Just remember, the end goal is to stay as close as possible. Which means she has to eventually like you."

"I hear you. I have it under control."

"Why do I feel like those are famous last words?"

"They're not." His voice deepened, and his expression evened out as he met my gaze directly. "Look, I know what it's like to have a partner that I can't trust. You don't have to worry about that with me. I'm doing the job. I'm not going to screw you in the process."

I snorted. "No, but you're going to screw her?"

That got him. His face went pink, and I chuckled to myself. "God, you're so easy."

"You do recognize that I'm trying very hard not to be Penny and/or Lucas in this situation, right?"

"Oh yeah, I know. But, mark my words, the fastest way to protect her is friendship or seduction, which is what you're doing. You're just taking the long way around."

"And you promised to give me leeway. Besides, the fastest way to protect her is honesty. We tell her what's up, and then we can guard her better. Put her under lock and key."

I shook my head. "What, if anything, about Jessa makes you think it'll be any easier to protect her if she knows? It would just make her more reckless. And I did give you some leeway, so don't screw up."

"Got it. Don't worry, we're a team. We'll make this work."

"Yup, team Winston Isles all the way." Even as Roone settled in to help me with this surveillance, I couldn't help but wonder if I was somehow the weakest link.

Had my one stupid decision put team Winston Isles in danger? I certainly hoped not. But the only way I'd know for sure was if I found my father.

❧

Roone…

I'D KNOWN they'd come. Hell, I'd expected Sebastian and Lucas sooner. There must have been something going on if they'd taken this long to turn up.

How they'd turned up though, that had been a surprise. Evan's voice on my intercom was terse and clipped as usual. *Yeah, you're not my favorite person either, you twat.*

But I'd headed on down to the conference room with enthusiasm and a smile. Why the hell couldn't Ariel had done this part of the mission? I was a soldier. I'd gotten my degree in business, so when push came to shove, I could do the job. But I was better when there was fighting involved.

Because she's in charge and you're not.

Right, that.

I knew who I was meeting the moment I saw the guards posted on either side of the door. To their credit, neither of them showed any hint of recognition. "Hey, Evan, what's happening?"

Evan's jaw ticked. "Roone. Obviously, you know His Royal Majesty King Sebastian Winston of the Winston Isles, and His Royal Highness, Prince Lucas Winston. They're interested in Evans doing an RFP for one of their charities, the Artistic

Trust. Since you are piggybacking with Jessa on several accounts, I thought it might not be a bad idea to see what you can do with an account of your own."

My gaze flickered to my mates, who looked tickled to find me in a suit. "Your Majesty, Your Highness, it's a pleasure to see you again. Evan, I'm honored you'd give me the opportunity."

I don't know what he'd expected, but it probably wasn't my enthusiasm, so he blustered for a moment. "Yes, right. I'll leave you to chat about what they have in mind. Roone, find me after you're done, and we'll discuss."

Once he was gone, I breathed a sigh of relief. "Did the both of you need to come?"

Lucas grinned. "Dunno, Seb. He doesn't look that pleased to see us."

Sebastian shrugged as he came forward. "Tough tits. I wanted to make sure everyone was still alive. Besides, I was missing having rational conversations over a pint." Sebastian gave me a one-armed hug, then Lucas did the same.

"Everyone is still kicking. Honestly, you didn't need to come."

Sebastian held up his hands. "Relax. I trust you and Ariel have shit under control. We really do have work for the trust we're dealing with. We're off to Paris for the next two days and then back, so it was nothing to come and see how things were going. Any leads?"

I shook my head. "Other than what was in the report, no. We've already cleared most of the people in her life, but we're taking another pass at her boss."

Sebastian's brows drew down. "The bloke we just met?"

I nodded. "Yeah, that's him. He's a real gem that one. He's been her mentor for years but given his behavior since Ariel and I showed up, there are some clues to suggest he's looking for a different kind of relationship, so we're digging." I rolled my shoulders. "Also, she went out to her adoptive father's facility to pick up his things. Ariel and I weren't able to get into the flat before her place was broken into, so there could have been anything in there. She did scan some of the things, so I just need to clone her phone to access and sift through the data."

Lucas frowned. "Who do you think broke into her place?"

"I don't know. Whoever it was, it was a professional. Looped video, staying in blind spots. No amateur burglar did that on their own."

Sebastian nodded slowly. "What does Ariel say?"

Through clenched teeth I said, "It's in the report, Your Majesty. We're working on it."

He sighed. "I'm not checking up on you, Roone. Honestly, I'm not. I just know how it can be for you when you come back home, so I figured two birds one stone."

Lucas stepped forward. "Look, we didn't mean to throw you off your game or anything. I know I gave you a shit time when you were guarding me, and if Jessa is anything like us, we figured some friendly faces would help."

I forced a deep breath into my lungs. I was still smarting from the assignment I guess. And still smarting from failing last year when I was guarding Lucas. He'd thrown everything out the window when he'd taken off last year. He'd had his reasons, but that had caused a rift between us for a bit there. He and I were on more of an even footing now, but it still irritated me to think about how everything had gone down.

It was important to me to be good at my job. I always felt like I needed to find some way to say thank you to Sebastian for the insane life that I'd led. In the last year or so, it hadn't gone exactly according to plan, but I wouldn't change any of it... except maybe that part about my homicidal partner.

Didn't matter how much time had passed. Marcus's treachery still cut deep.

I slid my gaze over to my best friend. "Have you two seen her yet?"

Both of them shook their heads, but it was Sebastian who spoke. "No, we didn't want to draw attention if someone is watching her."

My gut clenched. "Not to mention taking out the whole royal bloodline in one fell swoop. Ariel must be shitting herself."

"She went from elation at seeing Penny to shouting at me for jeopardizing the op when we saw her this morning." He chuckled before adding. "How is Jessa?"

That was a hard question. "Jessa is a whole other breed of woman. She's nuts, but she's also got this core of steel. I would have thought she'd be hysterical about the break-in, freaking out, and all that stuff. She wasn't. Cool as a cucumber. Pissed off that someone broke in, actually. And then suspicious as fuck."

I shook my head and almost laughed. I had counted the ways she stalked around her apartment, checking very specific items as if she'd always anticipated something like this.

I had the file on her father. Paranoid didn't even begin to cut it with him. Where he could, he went off the grid. Jessa, after age ten, had been moved to several different schools in the states and Canada. From what I could tell, he had a decent knowledge base of general spy craft. A skillset I'm sure he passed on to his daughter.

"She checked it out thoroughly. It passed whatever test she was looking for. If she's smart, she's got all her cash and stuff hidden in the walls. They tore the place up good."

Sebastian swallowed and then ran a hand through his hair. "Look, I know I've had you on long-term job after long-term job, okay? The go-look-after-Lucas thing dragged out longer than it should have. And now this. How are you holding up? You're not even allowed to be yourself on this one."

Lucas at least had the grace to look sheepish. "Sorry again, man."

"Bygones," I muttered.

This was Seb, my best mate. The same scrawny kid I'd looked after at Eton. "I'm ten, mate. No problems."

Sebastian sighed. "Are you sure you're okay with getting close to Jessa? Even that wasn't asked of Penny."

I cleared my throat. "You gave me a job Sebastian. I plan to do it."

He swallowed and rocked back on his heels, shifting his gaze to Lucas, who asked, "So, you two are getting close?"

I was going to kill Lucas. I shook my head. "Nope, I'm not going to give you that kind of mission detail." That was going to be a recipe for disaster, because at some point, it was going to kick in to him that Jessa was his sister. He didn't want that. He didn't need that knowledge. "I'm working on her. Ariel's working on her. We got this. We know what our jobs are. I swear to you, we will keep her safe and bring her home, if it's the last thing we do."

"It won't be. I think you are owed a serious vacation when you get back. Whenever it is, I'll take the time off. You and I are climbing Kilimanjaro."

I grinned. It had been one of those bucket list things that I'd had on my list when I was a kid. I couldn't believe he remembered. "Are you serious, mate?"

"Yeah. We haven't had time for just us in a while. First, I went to New York, then Lucas and his antics, and now, Jessa. We're long overdue."

"Must we always refer to my antics?" Lucas groused.

I nodded and tried not to let the sudden well of emotion choke me. "Yeah, mate, you got it."

Sebastian nodded. "Okay, we'll get out of your hair. Just

know that I'm not checking up on you. I know what you would do for this family. I've never had any doubts."

As he turned to walk out, I finally released the breath I was holding. I hadn't known how badly I needed to hear those words until he said them.

19

Jessa…

WHERE THE HELL HAD ROONE BEEN HALF THE DAY? There'd been a ruckus at the office earlier. Some VIP client, and most of us had been forced to stay in our offices until the client had come and gone. We had work to do on the gala, but he was nowhere to be found. According to him, Rick had needed him.

Yeah but for what? I had been Evan's protégé. Was Rick taking him under his wing? If so, did I really have to worry?

I was too tired to think about it. Being stuck in my office half the day had hampered my movements, and I'd had to get creative about how I worked. I wanted to know who the hell had come in. Chloe was convinced it had been Prince Harry. Never mind that I reminded her that the palace had their own internal publicity engine going.

I needed a hot bath and wine. *Copious* amounts of wine, not necessarily in that order.

I checked with the other senior account managers but

none of them had been called in for the client. So maybe it was just a meeting for the Evans?

But where had Roone been at the time of the meeting? Damn it. Enough Roone. I wasn't going to worry about him right now, because I was going to have my wine and my hot bath. I might even combine the two.

Glass of wine in hand, I sank into the couch. My gaze landed on my bookshelf. Maybe I could use some more photos. If I was serious about staying, then a few sentimental things wouldn't kill me, right?

I frowned staring at the bookshelf. Something was missing. What the fuck was it? I had my books, the one picture frame, a couple of framed prints. *The binder.*

I sat up abruptly, nearly spilling my wine.

When the police had been here, I'd done a cursory look. I didn't have too much that was valuable. Whoever had broken in had made a hell of a mess. I'd assumed that they were looking for something valuable.

Maybe the clean-up crew had moved it? What the hell?

My inner voice screamed. Had someone been looking for my father's sketches? But why? They weren't worth anything. They were personal. But even as I let my imagination run wild, my more rational side slapped it down. *That makes no sense.*

Except someone had broken into my home and taken nothing except the rose pendent. And the only thing I'd been able to notice that was missing was a folder of my father's sketches.

I grabbed my laptop and then opened the file of sketches. What was here that somebody would want?

Just Lulu and my mother. The images of the men with tattoos. But who were they?

I glanced at the tattoos again. I'd had a client, Jillian Brightcomb. She'd launched a lipstick line. She'd also been a tattoo connoisseur.

Pulling out my phone I sent her a text.

Jessa: *Hey Jillian, do you know if tattoo artists keep a database of designs and who has done them? I'm trying to track something down.*

Jillian: *Hey Jessa!! I have a place. They are one of the best in town. Every artist likes to leave a signature, so if it's someone known, they can help you.*

Jessa: *Cheers!! You are a lifesaver.*

Jillian: *No problem. It's Devil's Rim in East London.*

Devil's Rim. I hadn't heard of it. But then I wasn't exactly up on the hot places for ink. I had a couple of tiny tattoos, but nothing major. I was barely a hipster.

Her next text was the address.

I gripped the edge of the countertop. I was exhausted. So tired I could barely stand. But, something was eating at me. I couldn't let it go. Now that I'd started, I'd have to see it through.

It was probably silly. Maybe I'd just misplaced the folder.

You didn't.

Damn it. Why was I so much like him? But I knew I wouldn't be able to sleep until I went down the rabbit hole. So instead of pouring myself another glass of wine, I switched out my shoes for boots. I wanted nothing more than to sleep, but I needed to ask the questions.

I opened my door to find the one person I didn't want to see again today, or any other day for that matter, on the other side my door. "Hi neighbor, how's it going? Can I borrow a cup of sugar?"

He winked at me when he said sugar. And that made me want to both laugh and slap him.

"Sorry, fresh out. All I have is piss and vinegar." I shrugged. He laughed at that.

"Well I figured since we're neighbors, and we work together, and we're trying to get along, we can occasionally share a meal. I've got some takeaway. Vindaloo curry. Since you're full of spice, I figured you might enjoy it."

My stomach grumbled. Oh my God, I would have enjoyed it. But no. I had somewhere to be, and since I was pretty certain he wasn't going to just give me his curry without also insisting on his company, I had to pass. "You know what, it's been a very long day. I'm really in no mood."

"Oh, that's too bad. I guess you don't want to hear about the VIP client I saw today?"

So that's what he'd been doing. *Asshole.* "You know what? I don't even care. I'll see you around."

He called after me as I marched to the elevator. "Where are you off to?"

"I have a hot date."

His brow snapped down. "We haven't even had our second date yet. How are you on a different date for a different app?"

"Hey, all that was said was that I had to use the app to see how it worked. Three dates. No one said that I had to *exclusively* use that app. Besides, our dates aren't real."

His grin was slow, and he leaned against my door forcing my gaze to his shoulders and the way his t-shirt tapered at the waist. God, he was so sexy just standing there being a total pain in my ass. Why was it the one man that I never wanted to see again was the one man I saw everywhere?

"Well you have fun on your date. Just know that you still owe me two more dates. If you want LL Hotels, all you have to do is resist me. You can try dating someone else if you want, but I'll be the one you'll be thinking about."

One of these days I really was going to slap him. Could be any day now. Swear to God.

In my fog of exhaustion, I took a taxi. I couldn't be bothered to deal with the rigmarole of the tube. Within thirty minutes, I was in East London somewhere near the O2 arena.

It was a Wednesday, so the crowds weren't nearly as crazed as usual. I took about two wrong turns before I finally found the place.

It had an old world look to it. Complete with cobblestones out front. But inside, it was a full-on, modern-day ink studio. A girl with a pierced eyebrow, jet black hair, pierced septum, and something poking out of her cheek smiled at me. "Hi, can I do something for you?"

"Yes, actually." I knew what she was seeing when she looked at me; someone too clean cut, someone who wouldn't understand anything about this lifestyle. Yeah, what she didn't know wouldn't hurt her.

She didn't know about the tattoos I had to cover birth-marks. She didn't know about the time I pierced my eyebrow to give myself a different look because dad said I needed to mix it up. She didn't know anything about me. What she saw was a clean cut, perky little publicist. Which was fine, because that's what I needed her to see. "I've got this tattoo I've been trying to locate and identify. Word is you might be able to help."

"I could take a look at it and see if we may have done something like it. But we generally don't like to copy."

"It's not for me. I'm just looking for a person who has it."

She frowned. "We take confidentiality seriously, you know, just like a doctor."

While this was one of the nicer tattoo parlors I'd ever seen in my life, who was she kidding? This was no doctor's office. "Yeah, just like a doctor except not. There's no confidentiality required. Unless someone came in here with an NDA for the design or a copyright form, which is highly unlikely. If you can just tell me if you did the tattoo, and if so, if the person has been in lately, that would be helpful."

She pursed her lips as if she didn't want to help me, but

then she went to the computer, so that was promising. "Yeah sure, show me what you want."

I pulled out my phone and pulled up the picture of the dagger. "I'm just trying to find out who originally designed it, or if you know anyone whose had that tattoo done lately. It's really important." I left out that this was a wild goose chase.

She frowned and stared at it. "I don't see it in our database. You sure it's from here?"

I scrunched my nose. "No. But a friend told me you might recognize the artist's work."

Her brows furrowed even more. "I can't seem to find anything that matches it exactly. Do you know the date?"

I shook my head. "No, I'm sorry. I have no information."

The girl shrugged. "Wish I could help you. If you can give me something to help narrow it down a little further, that'd be great. It might help me figure out whose tattoo it is. In the meantime, what I can do is have Tate make a copy of that photo and have the other people who aren't on duty right now have a look around. Does that work?"

I sighed. "Yeah, it does. Cheers."

I was chasing at windmills. There was nothing here.

It was a hunch. No big deal. You're not him.

But could I let it go?

I left the parlor with a niggling sense of unease. I was missing something.

No. You aren't. Let it go.

I pushed out and made my way back to the main road to catch my Uber. Then I felt it. The eyes on me.

I was losing my mind. I had to be. Is it worse to be paranoid or to be right? There were more pedestrians out now than there were earlier. There were none I recognized, but I couldn't shake the feeling that someone was watching.

Heart thumping, I ducked into the nearest pub and prayed to God there would be a way out the back.

Roone...

"We lost her, you twat."

"What are you talking about? You think it was my fault we lost her? I thought you were the intelligence expert." I searched the Slug and Lettuce pub again, looking for a hint of her, but she wasn't there. Either she'd doubled back, or we'd lost her. How the hell was she able to give us the slip? She was almost as good as Lucas.

No one was that good, but she could give her brother a run for his money.

"Listen double O zero, I wasn't the one who was a little overzealous about tailing my girlfriend. When was the last time you brushed up on your covert surveillance techniques?"

"Well, fuck me. I've got my very own Money Minus."

Ariel smirked. "Oh, I get it a take on Moneypenny with a dig. You've been waiting to use that line for a long time, haven't you?"

I nodded, pretty pleased with myself. "Yeah. I've been hanging on to that one for a while."

"Well stop joking around. We have to find your girlfriend."

I rolled my eyes. "Stop calling her that."

"Well, when you jeopardize a discreet tail, just because some guy checked your girlfriend's ass out, then I've got to give you shit."

"She's not my girlfriend. In case you haven't noticed, I don't even like her."

"Oh, I noticed. *Everybody* notices how much you two dislike each other. I think you forgot that you're supposed to be getting close to her."

"Well," I shrugged, "she likes to fight with me."

"Is that the basis of all your relationships? I thought I was the crazy one. How is it that I'm the straight guy in this partnership?"

I couldn't help it, my gaze flickered over her body. "I promise, you are not the guy in this partnership."

She stuck out her boobs even more, making me laugh. "I know right? Pretty damn fabulous."

I groaned. "Seriously?"

She snort-laughed. "You should see your face right now. And if you're done dicking around, we need to double back and see if we can find little Miss Houdini. If I didn't know better, I'd think she made us and gave us the slip."

"When the Blake Security guys gave us the low down, they were very specific that her father had tried to train her over the years. We don't know how successful he was."

She nodded. "Yeah, I know."

We were just pushing out the doors of the pub, when Ariel's phone rang. She sighed and grinned up at me. "Bingo!"

My brows lifted when I saw it was Jessa. "Hey Jessa, what's up?" Ariel said cheerily.

She was silent for a moment and then nodded. "Yeah, I was just out grabbing a bite to eat. Do you want me to stop by your flat when I get back? Everything okay?"

Jessa said something, and Ariel smiled. "Fantastic. I will bring the wine."

Ariel's lips tipped into another smirk. "Looks like I have a date with your girlfriend."

"She is not my—" Ariel's fit of laughter made me want to throttle her. "Okay, so Jessa wants to hang out?"

She nodded. "Yup. Sounds like she's upset about something, so I'm guessing she definitely saw you."

"Or *you*…"

Ariel shrugged. "She saw one of us, or thinks she saw something. Something that was enough to make her spooked.

So I'll go over there and reassure her that everything is just a coincidence, and then we'll keep a tighter eye on her. I'd hate to have to call in reinforcements. In the meantime, you figure out a way to find that charm you seem to have lost. Because this whole plan relies on you getting extra close to the princess. And right now, you are so far away from that. On a scale from one to never going to get it, you are nowhere near where you need to be."

I didn't tell her just how close I'd already been to the princess. I groaned. "Oh my God, are you always this cheesy?"

She grinned. "Yep. I'm always this *awesome.*"

I rolled my eyes. "You better get home."

"Don't miss me too much."

Nothing to worry about there. "I won't miss you."

She grinned. "Oh right, you'll be thinking about Jessa. Roone and Jessa, sitting in a tree. K-I-S-S-I-N…"

Her voice trailed as I walked away. Sebastian had partnered me with a twelve- year-old. I wasn't entirely sure that this wasn't a punishment of some kind.

20

Roone...

I SHIFTED IN THE PASSENGER SEAT OF THE CAR AS WE watched Jessa. The days when she had client meetings were the worst. We needed to rely on eyes in the building, cameras, and that was it. And given her job, she could pretty much interact with just about anyone. Although, once her work for Meet Cute swung into full action, it would be a little bit easier. There would be more meetings with Ariel.

"You look uncomfortable, Roone."

"Did you have to pick a mini cooper?"

Ariel grinned. "I've always wanted one."

"Why couldn't you drive one on the island? Why did you torture me with this one?"

"It's not my fault you're too tall. I think it's surprisingly roomy."

I groaned and shifted again. "You know, one of these days, I'll pay you back. I'm six foot three."

"Ah, quit your whining."

I rolled my eyes. "For your information, it's called whinging, love."

She mimicked 'whinging' with a high pitch to her voice and tapped away at her laptop. "Keep your eye on the girl, would you?"

That wasn't hard. It was almost impossible to draw my eyes away from her. The seat she picked was right at the window, which was not the safest if someone was trying to kill her, but it allowed me to see what was going on in the apartment. And the bug we had placed in her purse allowed me to hear most of what was happening. Most of it was boring planning stuff. Although, Evan Millston was starting to get on my bloody nerves. He was almost too accommodating to her. He was probing too much into who the app had paired her with. Yeah, well, they'll all find out soon enough.

"Listen, can you do me a favor? Take first shift on Jessa tomorrow. There's something I need to do."

Ariel raised her brow. "You have another girlfriend that you needed to see?"

I swallowed hard and turned my attention back to Jessa. Ariel was too shrewd sometimes. The last thing I wanted was for her to see any emotion in my eyes. "I want to go place some flowers on my mother's grave. Tomorrow is the anniversary of her death."

The ensuing silence in the car was thick and penetrating, and I could feel it winding around me like a boa constrictor threatening to squeeze the life out of me. But then Ariel said something that surprised me.

"Yep, sure thing. Take the whole day. I know her schedule. I can manage it. I'll call in the freelancers if I need to. And I know this great Irish pub. I'll have the freelancers on Jessa tonight, and you and I can get a drink."

I turned to face her, a question on my brow. "Why?"

She shook her head, refusing to look at me. "Because one

good thing my father taught me was that when you're saying I miss you and celebrating someone's life, you pour a good Irish whiskey. These things are important."

I didn't know what to say. But before the thread of emotion choked me, I cleared my throat and muttered a quick thanks. Before we started this assignment, I thought Ariel was a loose cannon. A little too slack with the rules. A little too wild. But, in that moment, I realized she was probably the partner I needed.

⚓

Roone...

THE BLARING ring woke me out of a dead sleep. I smacked the alarm clock several times before I realized it was my stupid phone.

"Someone had better be dying."

"No, not dying. But we got a ping on Evan's background check."

Ariel. Fuck, that girl never slept.

"What did you get?"

"Well, there was a restraining order filed against him. Two actually."

Okay that did it. I sat up, rubbing sleep out of my eyes and scratching my jaw. "What? How did we miss it?"

"Well technically, we didn't. When you told me about your little powwow with him, I ran a deeper check. Just to see. There had been two restraining orders filed against him by the same girl over the course of three years. She would file and then remove it. So I think maybe you and I need to go have a talk with her."

"Yeah, let's go today. After your appointment."

And then it occurred to me that I wasn't going anywhere.

"Wait, change of plan, actually. I'll be with Jessa first shift after all. She emailed me. We've got a meeting for the LL hotels account first thing this morning. I'll need to go see my mum after."

"No problem. I'll rearrange the schedule for coverage on Jessa when she's back at the office. You do what you need to do. I'll run this lead."

"You know we wouldn't have to do all this if she just knew what we were doing."

She sighed. "But it's fun playing Tetris with her guard rotation, and you know we can't tell her, so get used to it."

"Whatever." It had been worth a shot. "Be careful yeah? I don't exactly feel comfortable with you going by yourself. If this girl is terrified of Evan, she could be pretty desperate. Or worse, she might tell him you came to talk to her. Watch your back."

"I'm not an idiot. I'm also not the princess who needs saving. And you can't be in two places at once, so which is it gonna be?"

"Okay, sorry. Forgive me for caring about my partner." I said.

She paused. "Aw, you realize that's the first time you've called me your partner?"

I groaned. "Don't go getting all sappy on me."

"No sap here, I promise. You're starting to grow on me too, like fungus."

I had to laugh at that. "Be careful, yeah?"

"All right. Keep in touch. I'll let you know what I find."

21

Jessa…

I STILL HADN'T SHAKEN THE FEELING FROM LAST NIGHT. I kept trying to tell myself I had imagined it. But my brain refused to let it go.

One minute entertaining my father's delusions, and I was living in fear again. *Nope. Not today.* I rolled my shoulders.

Roone's gaze was screwed on me. "You all right, princess?"

"Yep, fine."

"You're not pissed or something are you?"

I glared at him. "What? Who would be drunk for a morning meeting? I barely even had a glass of wine last night."

He shrugged. "You're just a little green around the gills. That's why I'm asking."

"Well, I'm fine." I didn't know what the hell to do with a sweet Roone.

Madison was unavailable, so our LL planning meeting for the restaurant event was with her assistant, Ryder Jakes.

There was no doubt about it. Ryder was an asshole. He'd *always* been an asshole, would always be an asshole. The last meeting I'd had with him, he'd spent staring at my tits and asked me if they were real. He was a first-class, public-school wanker. But I could handle him.

"Ryder, at present the guest list is three hundred. We'll need to slim down the list if we want to hold it at the restaurant."

Ryder wasn't the sharpest tool in the shed at the best of times. "Can't we just change the venue?"

I blinked at him. Roone came to the rescue. "Well, Madison was clear that she wanted to host it at the restaurant because the chef will have a venue in the New York hotel, so it makes sense."

"Let's put a pin in it until Madison can just—" He checked his phone. "Oh, Madison is on her way, so she can answer your questions."

I checked my watch. "We only have twenty minutes, Ryder."

He shrugged. God, what a waste of time today. We should have rescheduled.

While we waited, Ryder thought a fun game of question and answer was in order. "So come on, you've got to tell me where the hip parties are, Jessa. You would know."

I blinked at him. "I mean, unless it's a planned Evans PR event, I really wouldn't, Ryder. I'm just really not into the scene, you know?" I checked my watch again. We really should be going.

"Yeah, but you're black, aren't you? I feel like that's inherently cool."

Say what now? I ground my teeth. "Yeah, I see how maybe you would think that, but melanin does not mean that I immediately know where the great clubs are. It's not a thing."

Across the table, Roone narrowed his gaze at him. What the hell was his problem anyway? He should be thrilled that Ryder was throwing me off my game. But honestly, he looked like he wanted to grab Ryder's too long hair and slam his face into the polished oak table.

"Oh, it's not just the clubbing, love. You know what I mean. I'm sure you've got contacts. You know, for all the drugs, party drugs. My mate at Eton, Tyson, was a Jamaican bloke. He always had the best supply."

Roone lifted a brow. "Do you hear yourself when you talk?"

Ryder slanted him a glance. "When I'm chattin' to you, you'll know."

Roone just chuckled. "Ryder, you're talking to a lady. Someone who's making your boss and *her* boss very happy. So maybe you shut your mouth and stop saying things that you don't know anything about."

Shit titties. What the hell was happening here? "Okay, everyone take a step back. Ryder, I can assure you that I do not know where the best parties are or where to get the best drugs."

I forced the words through my teeth. "What I do know are the best venues and how to make this event as spectacular as possible for London Lords. How to blend all of this together seamlessly between all of the parties involved. I know how to do that. That's my job. That's what Roone and I are here for. For your party drug situation, you better call Tyson. I can't help you. Do you understand?"

Roone hid his snicker with a cough. Ryder glared at me. "Fuck, what good are you? If you can't get drugs, are you at least a good lay? Is that whole thing true? Once you go black you never go..."

Roone had had enough. "Oi, kid, you had better not finish that sentence. If we file harassment charges against you, I guarantee your boss will sack you when I tell her. Do I make myself clear?"

Everything about Roone, from his tight shoulders to the

muscles ticking in his jaw to his glower, full-on said that he was not playing around. He had zero fucks left to give, and Ryder had basically strolled up to him trying to bum one.

Ryder, for once in his miserable life, sat silently. Something about Roone's stance pretty much said that he wasn't dicking around. Ryder was a trust-fund kid who'd gotten his job through nepotism and his parents' connections, and no one had ever told him no in his lifetime. When Madison Jeffries walked in, Ryder was uncharacteristically silent. The rest of the meeting went off without a hitch, but as soon as it was over, Roone was out the door with me chasing on his heels.

"What's up with you?"

"He shouldn't have talked to you like that."

"I know that. But that's also the job. I deal with shit like that all the time."

His brows furrowed. "You shouldn't have to."

Something was wrong. He was off today. "Are you okay? Because you have been acting very strange. Yes, thank you for coming to my rescue with Ryder. But it was not needed, as you saw. You're not acting like yourself, which makes me think that maybe something's up and you're about to do something horrible or steal another one of my clients, so fess up."

"It's nothing."

"Well it's *something*," I said as I followed him into the lift, where he kept ramming the button for the first floor.

"Nothing, I said."

"You are so hot and cold. What is going on? Look, if you don't want the LL account, great. You get to march into Rick's office and tell him. I'm happy to keep *my* account." I shifted in my heels. There was a tightness around his lips and a sadness in his eyes. Something was off with him. I liked him better when he was trying to get a rise out of me. Also, I didn't want him sad.

That's because you like him.

No. I most certainly did not. But, if he was going to be in a mood, I wanted it to be because I put him there. *Sure you do.* I cleared my throat. "Maybe if you want to talk about it, whatever's bugging you, we could do that too."

He opened his mouth and then shut it. It wasn't until we were outside that he took a deep breath as we waited for the car to come around.

"I'm sorry. I'm just tense today. I have something I need to do, and I'm not looking forward to it."

"Okay, what do you have to do?"

"It's the anniversary of Mum's passing." The car pulled up and he held the door open for me.

Oh, hell. "I'm sorry." I didn't know what to say or do or how to make any of it better, but the shadows in his eyes were too heavy to ignore. "Where is she buried? Did you get to lay flowers?"

"Sheffield Cemetery and no, not yet."

"I know it. Come on." I leaned forward to the driver and gave him instructions. The florist first. And then to drop me at the office. And then to take Roone where he needed to go.

Roone's soft voice nearly broke my heart. "Do you actually mind maybe coming with me?"

"Yeah, okay."

❦

Roone...

HEAVY RAINDROPS HIT the car in fat wet splats. Like little tiny bombs hitting the glass and the metal framing. "You didn't have to do this." Somewhere during the drive, her hand had eased across the seat and taken mine.

"Yes, I did."

"Why are you being so nice?"

"Well, I have been known to be nice before."

"Yes, but not necessarily nice to me."

"I was only not nice to you because you turned up and tried to steal my clients. After you basically spanked my ass in public."

"Yeah, the good old days."

She glowered at me, but it helped lighten the mood.

"Just when I was feeling charitable."

I swallowed hard, not sure where to put the swell of emotions in the center of my chest. "Seriously though, this is a nice thing. I appreciate it."

"Yeah, of course. Just, you know, do you want me to come with you to the grave?"

Her voice was small, soft. The answer was yes. Yes, I wanted her to come with me because this is the last thing on Earth I wanted to do alone. Even though for years I had been doing it alone. Somehow this time just felt like I shouldn't.

"No. Thanks. Besides, it's raining."

"Yeah, I caught that. Come on. We'll both go."

"Jessa."

"What? A little rain never hurt anybody. Besides, there's one thing I've learned since being back in London, always carry an umbrella."

She pushed open the door, and I cursed under my breath as I immediately shoved open mine and ran around the other side to get her. I had texted Ariel what was happening, and hopefully the other guards were on their way. This was potentially dangerous. Out in the open, Jessa was a sitting duck, and this was never my intention for the day at all.

"Seriously, you're gonna get all wet."

She shrugged. "I have a coat. Stop stalling."

She reached into the car and the driver handed her the bouquet of lilies, my mother's favorite, that we'd bought at the Tesco's near the London Lords offices.

"I don't know what to say."

She turned her face up to me, eyes wide and dark with a slight smile on her lips. "How about you say thank you. Tomorrow we can return to our little war, but, today you look like you could use a friend."

She wasn't wrong about that. The umbrella was massive, so at least it covered the both of us. I pulled her to my left side, freeing my right side to be able to reach for my gun if I needed too. Cops in the UK didn't carry guns. But I'd had a special holster made and also had a special dispensation to carry. The surroundings were familiar, massive tombs intermixed with smaller ones, a hodgepodge but somehow still looking neat and pristine, eclectic as my mother would have said. She didn't want a place where everyone had to look the same. Sebastian had found this. It wasn't that she even knew anyone who was buried here. But she'd said it was pretty, so this was where I'd laid her to rest.

As we approached, Jessa leaned in closer to me. Just the press of her warmth was enough to seep into my cold bones and warm me from the inside. The small gesture told me everything I needed to know about who she was. Jessa McLean Winston, like her brothers, was sweet. Kind. A complete pain in my ass, but someone I was lucky to have offering me comfort.

We approached and made a left at the T junction, and then I paused when I saw the man kneeling by my mother's grave. My feet cemented into the ground, and Jessa looked up, a question in her eyes. "Everything okay?"

I shook my head. "Um, no."

"What's wrong?"

"Let's go back. I'll do this another time."

"No. We're here. Is something upsetting you?"

"I just—" I didn't realize how seeing him was going to

affect me. But just seeing him there, as if he belonged, it made my stomach churn.

She glanced up and then finally saw him. "Do you know that man?"

I cleared my throat. "Yeah, that's my brother."

She blinked rapidly, clearly surprised. "Oh, judging by your reaction, I can tell it's complicated."

"Yeah, complicated is the nicest way to describe it."

"Okay, it's your show. What do you want to do?"

"I want to go say hello to my mother."

"Then you go ahead. I'll wait for you here, or I can come if you want." She handed me the flowers and wrapped her hands over mine. The warmth in them chased away the chill in my whole body.

"Thank you. But I can do it. I need to do it."

She nodded. "Okay you take this big umbrella. I have this small one in my pocket. She pulled out a smaller one. When she let go of the big one I had no choice but to hold on tight. She pulled it out and extended the umbrella. It really didn't even cover all of her hair, so I just shook my head and switched umbrellas with her. "I'll take this one."

"But you're huge."

I couldn't help it. "That's what she said."

She rolled her eyes. "Oh my God. Of course,"

"Yeah, of course. You take the bigger one." I knew the larger one would afford her more protection if someone could see her face. "You should stay here."

"Okay. I'll wait right here."

As I approached the grave, I thought of a million things to say to my brother. A million questions, a million rebukes, but when I reached the gravesite, all I managed was "Rhys?"

He glanced up. "I hadn't expected to see you."

"The fuck are you doing here?"

He sighed and stood. "Roone, you look well."

Maybe I stammered. "What. The. Fuck. Are. You. Doing. Here?"

"I didn't know if you were in town. I figured someone should see her."

"You do not get to do this. She was my fucking mother."

Rhys glanced down at her grave. "I know. But she was… kind to me."

"I swear before God, if you say one more word, I'll dig you a grave right here."

"Just listen to me. Please. I know I was a twat. I know my mother was horrible to you. Before dad died, when you'd come over, she was cruel. But I remember when I came over to your house, your mum was always nice. When she died, I wasn't allowed to come and say goodbye."

I glowered at him. "Fuck you."

His shoulders slumped. "Yeah, maybe I deserve that. I'll just leave you to it." He paused. "When you're ready though. We should talk."

I hated him.

No, you don't.

I turned away from him then and planted a hand on the wet gravestone. "Hi, mum. I'm sorry I'm late today." I placed the lilies on the stone and silently said all the things that I'd been wanting to say to her for the last year. I was aware of Jessa waiting, so I didn't want to take too long. I closed out with the usual I love you and I miss you, and I when I turned, I was surprised to find my brother still standing there.

"If you're in London now, I thought maybe—"

I glared at him. "Well, you thought wrong. Besides, I'm not back. It's only temporary."

"You know at some point you're going to have to talk to me."

"No. I don't think I will."

"Then at one point I'm going to find you and we're going

to have this conversation. You can avoid it as much as you want, but we're going to talk eventually."

"If that makes you feel better to say so." I marched past him and found Jessa just where I left her.

She was shivering, but she made no complaint. "Did you say hello?"

I nodded and then stepped under the larger umbrella, taking it from her hand. "I did. I told her all about you too."

"Oh, no. Dare I even imagine what you said?"

"I told her I'd met the biggest pain in my ass ever. Also, the best kiss I've had in a long time."

Jessa stumbled then. "What?"

I grinned down at her. "Come on, let's get you back in the car. You look cold."

"Oh shit, does this mean we're becoming friends now?"

22

Roone…

ALL AROUND US, PEOPLE WRITHED AND SWEATED, THEIR bodies slapping into each other as skin slid over skin, breaths mingled, and groin contact was made.

"Are you ready for this?"

Jessa clapped her gloves together and grinned at me around her mouth guard. "I was born ready."

Date two, per Ariel, was a sparring session at the posh Butterfly boxing gym in Brixton. Supposedly the owner had once fought Mayweather.

I swear to God my partner was trying to torture me. She and Jessa must have come up with a little plan on their own. Jessa was wearing barely there shorts that hugged her ass and showed off every single curve and toned muscle, complete with a midriff-baring sports bra that had her bloody tits shoved on full display.

It was more than an effort not to focus on the gentle bounce of them, but rather on the surprisingly deliberate and accurate punches that were coming from her.

Jessa moved quickly, efficiently. The instructor gave her a few cues here and there, but she wasn't bad. She moved like someone who'd had plenty of self-defense training before.

No killer instinct though. She wasn't really coming after me. Nothing about her said she'd known real terror. Those who had fought before were far less predictable. So far, I'd just had to keep my wits about me, watch my footwork, dance around her.

Jab. Jab. Swing.

The combinations were predictable, but Jessa was also quicker than I'd expected. Light on her feet, like a cat.

A sexy cat, whose tits you can't stop staring at.

The thwack on the side of my head caught me off guard, and I let my façade slip just a little with a narrowed gaze.

Jessa grinned at me. "Pay attention, Roone. If you get distracted, you get hit in that oh-so-pretty face."

"Oh really?" I couldn't help the easy grin. Just letting a little bit of the predator out. Jessa recognized my predatory prowl and then hopped backwards. Shit, I guess she was on alert. It was as if she reassessed me on the fly.

I knew I was supposed to be good, supposed to keep up the façade of the overall nice guy. The problem was with Jessa close, I didn't exactly feel like it. Hell, I didn't exactly feel like myself either. Usually, I was easy going unless I was working. Chilled out, not much bothered me. But around Jessa, every primal instinct fired.

I prowled toward her. She rolled onto the balls of her feet. "Roone, why are you looking at me like that?"

I smirked. "Like what?"

Her footwork was excellent. She'd clearly had dance training too. She never turned her back to me, kept me in her sight at all times. Kept her head on the game constantly checking her sights, checking the exits. She'd had more than a little dance training. More like a lot. But still, I stopped her easily. I was bigger, and no matter how much training she'd had, I'd had more... so much more.

"You're looking at me like you're considering eating me for dinner or killing me."

I chuckled. "Well, one of those is accurate."

She frowned. "Sorry, I didn't mean to pop you in the face. Relax."

I lifted a brow. "I'm not sure why it is you think killing was the option I was going to choose." I flashed my teeth and then pounced. She easily darted out of my way and delivered me a painful jab in the kidney as she bypassed my hold.

"Well, if you're coming after me to eat me, then this is a game of survival, isn't it?"

"Princess, it's *always* a game of survival." Mentally, I ran through all the scenarios where she wouldn't get hurt. Unfortunately, none of those were offensive moves. There were some throws that she wouldn't like that would land her on her ass, but she'd be relatively unscathed. The last thing I wanted to do was hit her. But I could make her life slightly more difficult.

Our coach checked the circle as if he were refereeing an MMA match. Shuffling back and forth, assessing our stances. At some point in our little sparring match, he stopped giving me any instruction. Jessa knew how to move. Her advances were quick as a flash. I deflected them all since I knew she was here to play.

On her final advance, I feinted, then hooked my foot behind hers. She was too busy focusing on the upper blocks, and she didn't see my feet. That mistake landed her on her back.

I leaned over. "Easy now, princess. Are you all right?"

From the ground she groaned, and I reached out a hand to help her up. The next thing I knew, I was catching air. The little witch had scissor kicked me. I groaned as I landed on my fall break then jumped right back up into position.

Jessa hopped up and then pivoted around to face me. "Yeah, I'm great. How are you?"

I laughed, adjusting my stance lower. If she wanted to play, we could play. "So, it's like that?"

She spread her arms and grinned as she danced on the balls of her feet, Muhammad Ali style. "It's always been like that. You just didn't know what game you were playing."

"All right. Let's do it, princess."

The endearment was probably foolish, but I couldn't help it. From the moment I'd seen her, she'd looked the part, but that mouth, that attitude, that nerve. She was so much more than a lost princess.

She wanted to dance, so we'd dance, using the sparring as a way to release the pent-up, clawing need that had been following me around for three weeks. We danced around each other. When the kicks started, I had to pay more attention and restrain her more often.

"Fuck! Jessa. You're going to get hurt."

"Roone, come on. You obviously know how to do this. Let's get the kinks out." She came at me again, this time with jabs, like she was trying to work out her frustration on me.

I deflected easily. I slid my left arm against her punching arm. "Sweetheart, I'll play with you anytime." She tried a back kick, but that just landed her in my arms again. Holding her tight, I leaned in and whispered, "Because you're smaller, you never take your eye off the opponent. Back spin kicks only look cool in a movie."

She grumbled something that sounded an awful lot like "Asshole," which earned her a swat on the bottom. Admittedly not my finest moment, because… instant hard on.

The instructor blew his whistle and we both lay there on the mats, panting. She turned her head and blinked at me. "I guess you really are superman. Mild-mannered consultant by day, badass martial artist at night."

I swallowed and shook my head. "Nah, my mom just made me take self-defense classes a lot when I was a kid."

"That's more than just a few classes. My dad was a pseudo survivalist nut, so I took lots of classes. You could be better than me."

Could? She didn't know the half of it. Was she suspicious? Had I showed my hand?

"Question is did you like it?"

"Well, I took it for a while and I liked it. And now when I feel like I can't let out what I'm feeling, you know, verbally, sometimes it helps to go to the gym and hit stuff and throw myself on the mat."

Her gaze searched mine. So far, we hadn't delved too far into who we'd been, and I wanted to keep the lies to a minimum. But if she probed, I could do it.

"It sounds lonely."

She shifted her gaze from mine and stared at the ceiling. "It was."

I pushed myself up to my feet and reached down and helped her up. "Come on. Let's hit the showers and get some food."

She skipped along. "What does the app say? Where are we going to eat? I hope it's something spicy."

I grinned down at her. "The app says that I'm cooking for you."

She stopped, a slight frown forming between her brows. "You cook?"

"Yeah, I cook. How do you expect me to eat?"

She gestured her hand to somewhere in the vicinity of my chest. "I mean, everything about you says, 'I'm too pretty to cook.' If you can cook, then why are you single? Or are you secretly married? Or are you using the app as a beard for your open relationship status?"

I laughed. "You're crazy. Well, like other people I know,

I've been busy. Work. The only person I see is my annoying work mate. So not a lot of options."

"Seems fair. So, what are you going to make for me?" She bumped me with her shoulder, a flirtatious smile playing on her lips.

The pang that sliced through me made my gut knot. That spark in her eye that had caught my attention when I met her had settled under my skin, making me buzz and hum. I wanted this to be real. I didn't want to be playing at this.

Too bad mate, the soldier never gets the princess.

I cleared my throat. "It's a surprise. Sorry."

"Come on, I'll be your best friend."

I couldn't help but chuckle. "Something tells me that you being my best friend will nearly get me killed one day."

"Possibly. But hey, it's part of the adventure and fun."

"All right, I'll keep that in mind. Come on, let's get a shower and then we can go eat." I just hoped to God that while I was keeping her distracted, Ariel was making some headway into who had broken into her apartment.

⚜

Jessa...

"Where did you learn to cook?"

I watched him as he strained the pasta. "My Mom. She wanted me to be able to look after myself, since she wasn't going to be around to do it all the time." He plated our food then set it out on the candlelit island.

It looked and smelled amazing.

I cocked my head as I took my seat. "Why do you say that?"

Roone lifted a brow. "Say what?" He poured us wine, but still didn't meet my gaze.

"I mean, I know she passed, but I guess I assumed it was sudden. Was she ill?"

He nodded. "Sorry, yeah. Cancer. I was fifteen."

Shit. There I was with my big mouth. "I'm sorry. Fuck cancer."

His lips twitched. "It's okay. And yes, fuck cancer." He raised his glass after he sat and clinked his with mine. "Now eat. You expended a lot of energy."

I was about to argue that he didn't get to tell me what to do, but then I took a bite. The rich tomato flavor burst on my tongue and I moaned. "Jesus, this is good."

"I know," he said with a smirk. Then he added, "I guess we didn't do all the first and second date conversations like normal. Still a lot we don't know."

I sighed. "Yeah, that's right. This app just put us together and so far, it's had you swinging me from trapeze bars and me kicking the shit out of you in a sparring match."

"Oh, just wait a minute now. You did not kick my ass. I took it easy on you. I figured you're still sore from when you got your ass beat a few weeks ago."

I groaned. "Ugh! Why are you bringing up old shit?"

"Because as good as you are, you should have been able to avoid that hit. Those two assholes were so busy screwing around that you got hurt."

"Yeah well, he hit like a girl."

"Yeah, but considering I've been hit by you, that's not really a put down."

I grinned. "Yeah, I do hit pretty hard."

"So, are you going to tell me anything about yourself besides that you have an uncanny knowledge about martial arts and are a genius at public relations, or is that more of a date three kind of thing?" He stood to dish the second course.

He looked so cute, shirt sleeves rolled up, strong hands dishing food, russet hair falling over his brow, I couldn't help myself. That and I didn't really want to talk. We were having such a nice time. Now was not the time to tell him that crazy ran in my family. I stood and walked over to him. "Well, it seems more like a third date kind of thing to me. I'd rather move some other third date things to this date, if you don't mind. Or does the app not allow that?"

Roone's hands paused. "Princess…"

"Well, you could choose to kiss me. Or you could choose to keep playing with your food."

He shifted to make room for me and I stepped into his space. Even standing on tiptoe, I couldn't reach his lips. "Let the record show that you're asking for a kiss."

I frowned. "The hell I am." I still couldn't let him win.

"In that case, allow me to get more creative with where I touch you."

&

Roone…

THERE WAS a rule I was supposed to follow. Except with Jessa so close with the faint scent of rose on her skin, I couldn't think. She was everything I shouldn't want.

Mate, you shall not shag your best friend's sister. Fuck. I'd already crossed so many lines. What was one more?

I didn't mean for it to go so far. But she smelled so good. A little spicy from the pepper I'd used on dinner and a little sweet, like dessert. She smelled fucking incredible.

The little mewling sound she made at the back of her throat while she backed up just drove me further. I couldn't think. I couldn't process information. God help me, I was unable to make any kind of clear coherent decisions right now. My synapses were fried. I'd scorched every single one of them just by looking at her.

With a low growl, I turned her around and backed her up against the counter, bending my knees slightly and angling her just how I wanted. Finally, I just gave up the ghost and picked her up, settling her on the island. My hands were on the back of her thighs and just like that, I hoisted her up.

God, she was the perfect height for this. And just—yeah, right fucking there. My dick pressed against my zipper, throbbing, begging to be let free. To seek out her heat.

Jessa rocked her hips into mine. And I couldn't help but answer every roll of her hips with one of mine. I ran my nose against the column of her throat, inhaling her deep. I planted open mouth kisses along her jawline, the column of her neck, and the hollow of her throat.

Jesus Christ, why was she so—

The moment she scored her nails in my hair and over my scalp, the shiver of need went through the entire length of my body. I couldn't focus. I knew if we kept this up I was going to fuck her right there on the counter.

Just take her right now and give two shits about consequences later.

My dick pressed against her heat, and she whimpered. I needed more. *Wanted* more.

The stretch of skin displayed by her blouse tempted me. Taunted me. I needed to know how soft she was. Just a taste and I could stop. One taste and I'd pull back.

Dick: *The hell you will.*

I slid a hand under the soft jersey. Oh, fuck, yes. My fingers skimmed over her skin, and she trembled in my arms. When my thumb traced over the edge of her bra, she arched her back.

Don't do it. You can't do this.

The angel on my shoulder tried valiantly with one last protest. But the devil that had taken over my soul was having none of it. I traced my thumb over her nipple and her grip tightened in my hair as she rocked her hips.

Yes. All I wanted was her with her clothes off, in bed, with her beneath me, shouting my name. "Go on Jessa, just ask me. I'll make it good. Ask me to kiss you."

"Roone… God. That's so…" Her voice trailed, and there was more whimpering as I teased her nipple. But then she was shaking her head. "So… good. But not on your life."

Fuck.

This was supposed to be a sexy game. Fun. Light. But my dick was apparently playing for keeps. I fucking tore my lips from her neck and deliberately backed away. My dick was screaming for relief and my skin was on fire.

"Okay. Let's finish dinner, then I'll walk you to your flat."

Her eyes blinked open. "Are you fucking serious?"

"What?"

"You're leaving me this turned on?"

I couldn't help the chuckle, despite the steel pole in my jeans. "Princess, to make the orgasm so good you tell your best mate about it, it's going to include kissing. So you don't get one without the other."

She narrowed her gaze at me, and I swore she was going to spit fire. "Nope. Not going to happen."

Sure it won't. "Okay then. Food, then home."

She pouted. "I'm not hungry for food anymore. Besides, I'm across the hall, I can make it on my own."

"I don't know what kinds of wankers you date, but I give door to door service whether you like it or not."

She tilted her chin up. "Fine. I think I've lost my appetite anyway."

I wasn't hungry for food anymore either. My dick screamed at me, but I ignored it. Instead, I cleared my throat. "Okay, off we get."

At her door, she turned to face me, petulant scowl on those pretty lips. "So, you really aren't kissing me?"

Fuck, I wanted to so bad. "Not without you explicitly asking."

She glowered but opened her door and muttered goodnight. Despite my vow not to shag my best friend's sister, I was glad I wasn't the only one suffering.

23

Jessa...

ROONE WAS GETTING UNDER MY SKIN. I TOSSED IN BED. Why was it the one man who was so damn infuriating was the one I also couldn't get out of my head?

I just kept thinking about the way his nose trailed along the column of my neck, his hands on my belly, thumbs gently grazing the skin. His voice. Telling me to just ask for that kiss. How everything would feel so much better if I just asked for the kiss.

Why the hell didn't you ask for the damn kiss?

Because I'm stubborn. Stubborn and mule-headed and stupid. I should've taken the kiss. Would it really kill me to give him a client?

Yes. It will kill you.

Okay. Yeah. It would kill me. I was not giving up without a fight. Just because the man had magic lips, smelled insane and was so sexy he probably came with a combustible-panties warning label, that didn't mean I needed to give in. And true to his word, we'd had two dates now. Two, and he hadn't even kissed me. Easy. One more date and I'd be scot-free.

Except you want him to kiss you.

God. I did. So much. The thing was, it was more than just how he made me feel. He was actually a pretty good guy. I tossed around the bed again and grabbed my pillow, punching it. "I hate you."

My poor pillow was no Roone stand-in.

"Although I don't really hate you. I wish I did though."

I flopped back over hugging the pillow tight to me.

My real problem was that I remembered the look on his face as we drove up to the grave site. Stricken. Sad. Alone. All I wanted to do was reach over and tell him it was okay. The way his fingers had intertwined with mine, that had changed something. As if all of a sudden, we were allies, as if we understood each other. His pain was my pain, and my pain was his pain. Everything had changed. And now, I couldn't get him out of my goddamn head.

He was the kind of guy who would control everything. Cold, calculated control. And no way in hell was I going to let anyone tell me what to do. Too much of my life had been like that. It made me want to rebel just for the sake of rebelling. Even if something was in my favor. And that was essentially Roone. Just looking at him made me want to shake him and scream *just because you said it, I'm not doing it.* Which was childish. Immature. Irrational. I was well aware. But what was worse was the knowing look he'd give me. As if he knew the level of my irrationality and was silently judging me for it.

Well, he hadn't grown up with my father, had he? Being woken from a sound sleep and moving like a thief in the night. Only allowed to take one bag. Leaving behind everything you'd just gotten used to. I'd learned to survive like that. I'd learned to survive with not knowing what came next, with having someone else in complete control of my life. I hadn't even started to become hardened to it until I recognized that my father was just plain ill. There was no boogeyman. No one was coming to hurt me. The old man was just crazy.

But was he really?

Yes. Yes, he was. One break-in at my flat was the one bad thing to happen my whole life. My whole adult life. That did not mean there was a boogeyman. Now, I lived a normal life where I had roots. Real roots. No one was up-ending that serenity.

You sure as hell don't seem serene.

I tossed again. Slapping the pillow over my head and screaming into it. God, I was so keyed up, so tightly wound. All I needed was—

Oh, you know what you need. And you know full well Roone Ainsley is perfectly capable of delivering.

No. I was not going to go and beg for an orgasm from Roone. Hell, I'd been nearly there as it was. That would be just too humiliating.

I reached into the nightstand next to my bed and fumbled around until I found what I was looking for. Old faithful.

It was a little bullet vibrator that would do the trick. Take the edge off. Keep me from doing something stupid like running across the hall and knocking on his door and begging him to just kiss me already.

I dragged my pillow off my face and settled back against it. Sliding the bullet between my fingers over my skin. My belly. Into my panties. I twisted the bullet slightly, activating the vibration. And then I let my imagination wander.

If it was in my imagination, it wasn't wrong. If it was my imagination, he wasn't really controlling me. That was me. My imagination.

Semantics.

I lay still and let myself think about that first kiss with Roone, the way he laid waste to all of my senses. The way he'd gripped my hips, his hands in my hair, anchoring me. Tongue completely owning my mouth. And then I thought about the way he teased. His nose along the column of my neck, inhaling, his lips barely brushing my skin. His hands still gripping. Still asking permission. Begging really. The tip of his tongue, tracing little designs over my skin. The low timbre of his voice as he whispered, "Go on just ask me. I would kiss you so good you would melt. We both want it. Just ask."

That did it. It was the voice. The way he said it. So commanding and authoritative. I was flying. Screaming really. Jesus Christ. Just imagining him talking dirty to me set me off like a rocket.

I panted then dropped back on my pillow. I was in so much trouble. I wanted him so bad I could taste it.

*

Roone...

It was a rare day that Ariel and I both had off, but that's how the schedule had worked out this time. So we were using the time to finish the last reports, to see what we could shake loose regarding the break in. Ariel had even splurged, insisting that we needed to get out. We picked a spot outside of Jessa's main drag, so nowhere near Central London. We went all the way out to West London, Chiswick, for breakfast. It was a place along the Thames River called Annie's. It was perfect. Quiet. Quaint, with checkered table cloths and well-worn wooden chairs. And we could still manage surveillance from here. Today, Jessa had a team of four on her, but from the looks of it, she wasn't leaving her flat anytime soon.

"Okay, so do I need to ask how you're feeling?"

I frowned. "You're asking me about my feelings? Remember, you and I, team Elsa, conceal don't feel."

She chuckled as she sipped her coffee. "Yes. But I mean, I do know it was the anniversary of your mum's passing. How are you holding up?"

I sighed. "Fine, I guess. It was rougher than I thought it would be."

"If you need some time off, we could have you call in sick to Evans. I can get some temporary help."

I shook my head. "No. I prefer to work. Besides, you don't get sick days on a mission."

Ariel grinned at me. "There's no crying in baseball."

I lifted a brow. "What does that even mean?"

Her jaw dropped. "A League of Their Own. It's a classic."

I shrugged. "Don't know it."

"Oh my God. We're going to have to resolve this immediately. Matter of fact I'm making a note."

I shrugged. "If you say so."

"I know Jessa went with you. From the looks of it, you guys bonded?"

How did I put this? "Yeah. She was — helpful."

She studied me for a long moment and then sighed. "Roone, look. I gave you shit for the way you were handling the Jessa thing. But I get it. You are who you are. You have a certain code about you. I know it's tricky because she's Sebastian and Lucas's sister. I know it's awkward because clearly you guys have some serious chemistry."

I shook my head. "I know how to do my job."

"Of course you know how to do your job. We wouldn't be on the same team if you didn't. You recognize Sebastian gave you the highest position of trust on his team. To look after his family, literally to take care of them. He sent you to New York for Lucas. And he sent you here to London for his sister. A sister who knows nothing. Lucas at least understood what was at stake. That's a great deal of trust. So, you being all in your feelings about, whatever... not being in charge, about not being good enough, or whatever the hell is going on with you. You need to can it. If anything, he trusts you more than he trusts me. I'm just the bestie who comes with his wife. Package deal."

I frowned at her. "He trusts you."

She shrugged. "I know he does. I'm damn good at my job. I demand it. And you know full well how the king feels about you. I'm watching you tear yourself up, pretending you don't like this girl. But you *do* like her. And you're also worried about her. And you want to do the right thing. So you know what's it like to hold the weight of the world on your shoulders, just your shoulders, because obviously you would be the only one strong enough to handle it."

I frowned. "I never said that."

"You think you have to say that? You're a soldier. You don't say much. You deflect anything that's real feelings. But I see how you look at her. I saw it the first day. I get it. It's the lying that's getting to you. She doesn't know the whole truth. But she knows most of the truth about you. All I'm saying is if you're into it because you're into it great, you don't have to try to pretend. If you want her, you want her. It'll be a little bit tricky, but I think we can all manage that."

My jaw clicked. "It's all well and good for now. But first, it's going to hurt her when she finds out the truth, and second, Sebastian's not going to be as cool as you think he is."

"Well, why don't you give him a chance?"

"Because when you give people a chance they disappoint you."

"Has Sebastian ever disappointed you?"

I frowned. "No but — "

She shook her head. "You have known him since you were eleven years old. In all that time, has he ever disappointed you?"

I gnashed my teeth together. "No. But, there was never a

scenario like this where he'd have to look at my shortcomings."

Ariel laughed. Tossed her head back. "What shortcomings? You have been his protector, his friend. If anything, I'd want you for my sister if I had one. I'd be like, 'Date that guy, he can protect you, he would do anything to keep you safe. He will literally go to the ends of the earth. He will keep you from drowning.' We all know how you saved Lucas. He was toast because he wasn't thinking."

"Yeah, that's another thing. When you fall in love you make stupid decisions."

Ariel shrugged. "Yeah, I can't argue that one. I've watched people do some dumbass shit. Hell, I've done some dumbass shit myself. But you know what? You like her. And from the looks of it, she actually likes you too. So if you can like her and keep her safe, then why don't you? It's silly, watching you try to keep yourself so rigid. Your moral code is excellent. It's kept you alive. It keeps other people alive. There's no ambiguity with you, which is great. But, it also keeps you alone. I'm just saying, if you actually like the girl, and if she actually likes you back, then make that line nice and gray. Because life's too short. The both of you know that. So go ahead pretend you don't like her. Pretend you don't want her. That's fine, no skin off my back. But if you're going to insist on honesty and transparency from everyone around you, the least you could do is provide the same."

She had a point. Hell, what was I really supposed to say? I don't like her? I did. She was smart and funny, and half my day revolved around getting to see her and getting her to say something outrageous to me. Hell, I goaded her just to see if she'd do it.

And sure enough, she always rose to the occasion with a retort or a flip off. But there were still rules.

Well sometimes, rules were made by dumbass rule makers.

As we finished our breakfast, I tucked our conversation aside. I might not think it was a good idea, but Ariel had a point. I wasn't fooling anyone. And maybe I could keep her safer if I allowed myself, even just for a moment, to get a little bit closer.

24

Roone...

THE TILLERMAN GALA BROUGHT OUT ALL OF LONDON'S bold and beautiful. I'd helped a little with the preparation, but it had been mostly Jessa and Chloe since they had the contacts from the previous years.

Champagne was flowing, the food was sublime, and Jessa made it all appear seamless and effortless.

"Mate, you need to stop staring at her. Evan is gonna blow a gasket."

I dragged my gaze off of Jessa. "I'm not staring."

"Yes, you are. The two of you are doing that eye-fucking thing across the room. Keep it in your pants, would you? I don't think boss man is going to like it."

I scoffed. "You think he's a problem for me?"

Ariel chuckled under her breath as she tapped away on her phone. "Potentially. We are still under cover, remember? That little thing where you pretend to work for him so that you can stay close to her and keep her protected? If he fires you, it makes your job that much more difficult."

I nodded and ground my teeth. "Yeah, I remember."

"It's the whole reason why we're here. If her boss is behind the break-in at her flat, he's more dangerous than a basic run-of-the-mill stalker, which we could handle, but we need more information. So, I'd rather we remove him the legal way and not because you kicked his ass so badly he has to be put into traction."

"All of that does have a certain appeal."

"Super funny. Little Roone standing down now?"

I rolled my eyes. "Everything is under control."

The hell it is. Mostly because my pants would not contain the erection I'd had for half the day. I had to get my shit under control. It turned out I *was* just as bad as Lucas. I'd been sent in to protect the princess. I was an idiot.

I was falling for a girl I couldn't have.

"If it helps, I think she's into you too. But seriously, you need to stop because if dipshit number one is actually a stalker, you have a problem. It means he's unstable, which means he could do anything, which means he could spook her, which means you and I will be S.O.L., so get it together."

She was right. I did need to get my shit together.

Remember what's at stake. Remember what your job is.

And I did remember. But she was in the room, so the humming buzz under my skin was all about her. I followed her into the hall. "Where are you going?"

A smile teased her lips.

Dick: Hello beautiful.

Me: Shut it.

"Emily Winthrop came this way. I wanted to grab her before things got real crazy."

"You're not trying to ditch me to go and get a proper burger, are you? The food is abysmal. Take me with you."

Her gaze shifted around to the stairwell. "Follow me. I

know where the good stuff is in the kitchens, three floors down."

"Now you are speaking my language."

In the stairwell, she paused and turned around. "Or were you just looking for an excuse to get me alone?"

A growl escaped before I could stop it. I was an idiot. "This is such a bad idea for so many reasons."

She swallowed hard. "Who are you telling? All the reasons. So bad. All the bad ones."

"You've been watching me today." I closed the distance between us.

"Someone has to keep an eye on you before you steal all my clients."

This is stupid. You're going to get yourself caught.

The problem was I didn't give a shit. I wanted her so bad I ached with it. Every cell, every muscle. I almost didn't care about the consequences. "You lured me in here with the promise of palatable food."

She blinked up at me. "Would I lure you in here? I'm not a villain. I'm sweet. I swear."

I grinned down at her. "The hell you are."

She shrugged. "Okay, a little sour too."

That humming vibration I always felt with her intensified. The closer I got, the more euphoric I became. The buzz was skipping over my skin, licking at my synapses. I couldn't stay away. It didn't matter what it was going to cost me, I had to have her, even if it was just a taste. Even if it was just for now.

Damn straight, it would just be for now. You're not good enough for her and you know it.

Sebastian will definitely know it. And soon she will too. I felt like an impostor.

You are *an impostor.*

I shoved those thoughts away and focused on the woman

in front of me. If I was going to hell, I might as well go in a blaze of glory.

I took her hand and dragged her down another two flights of stairs, so we'd be less likely to be discovered.

"So are you going to ask me or not?"

Her gaze went to my lips and then she whispered, "Kiss me."

Relief coursed through me. "About time." And then I slid my lips over hers and pressed her to me as she moaned. For now, she was mine. She just didn't know it yet.

The kiss went from a meeting of the mouths to a desperate attempt to fuse our bodies. In that moment I would have killed to lift up her dress and sink into her bare. I backed her up into the corner of the stairwell, bracketing her in with my big body. Then, bracing my hands on either side of her face and angling her head so I could deepen the kiss, I teased her lips with the tip of my tongue until she parted them. I slid my tongue in on her sigh.

Even as her body melted to mine, my brain tried to register a warning. *Do not get too close. You can't keep her.* But as I licked into her mouth, I refused to heed the warning.

My hand scooped down her back and made contact with her ass, drawing her closer to me. The hard ridge of my erection throbbed against her belly, and she moaned into my mouth.

I levered myself lower and wound my arm round her waist. Understanding what I wanted, she wrapped her legs around me. I growled as her tongue slid over mine, gliding against it as she worked her heated core against my erection.

This was so stupid and dangerous and out of order. But fuck if I could stop it.

Quickly, I pressed her more firmly into the shadows, and she realized she had to extend no effort to hold on. All she had to do was keep her legs around me, and I did all the work of holding her up. Slowly, as if I had all the time in the world, I devoured her lips. My tongue dipped playfully into her mouth.

Jessa dug her hands into my hair I slid my tongue in and out of the warm depths of her mouth in time to my hips rocking into hers. Or maybe that was her rocking her hips into me? All I knew was that I wanted to be closer to her heat. Feel the delicious way our bodies fit.

With every stroke of my tongue, she moaned, and I took what I wanted from her. Everything she was willing to give.

I cupped her face as I sucked on her bottom lip, teasing her, my thumb gently stroking her cheek. My other hand skimmed up her torso, then stopped as it reached the start of her deep 'v' of cleavage. Jessa drew in a shuddering breath and arched her back into me, waiting for me to touch her. Gently, my thumb traced where the material met flesh. She tried to pull me closer, but she had no leverage and was at my mercy as I drove her slowly insane. When my thumb finally nudged aside the flimsy material, her double-sided tape put up no fight. When the fabric gaped, exposing her pebbled nipple to the air, she shivered, and I groaned.

"Fucking gorgeous," I whispered against her lips. I sucked her tongue into my mouth before slowly drawing back again. With her eyes still closed, Jessa tried to follow my lips, but I held the back of her neck firmly. Eyes heavy with lust and longing, she dragged them open, the question ready on her lips.

I watched her with clear need and fire in my eyes, but my gaze held hers. I needed to see the connection to convince myself it was real. Still holding her gaze, I rolled her nipple with my thumb and forefinger, gently plucking. Fuck me, she felt like satin. "Damn. You are so fucking soft."

"Oh, my God. I, I—"

I drew a slow circle around her exposed nipple. When I

spoke, my voice was ragged. "I want to taste you here." I rocked my erection against her center and added in a whisper, "I'm going to taste you here too. In fact, I'm going to spend the majority of my time here, exploring every inch of you with my tongue."

Jessa drew in a shuddering breath. *Yes.* She wanted it all. "I, I—"

But I interrupted her by kissing her nipple softly. She tasted faintly sweet like the nectar of the rose scent she wore. It was like a hit of the most potent drug. "Shit, I don't think I can stop." I groaned against her skin.

She arched her back. "Then don't."

I drew her nipple into my mouth again, taking deep pulls. Heat snaked down my spine, making my skin tight and itchy. Jessa slid her hands into my hair and moaned as I sucked harder.

I released her and let out a low growl as I panted. "Jesus, princess. I need to stop before I can't." As if to punctuate my words, my body pressed into her. I was so close to coming, and all I'd done was suck on her.

She moved her head up and down. "More…"

Dick: *Yes, what she said.*

Fuck, if I listened to him there was no telling where I'd be.

Dick: *Inside the princess feeling her come around —*

Nope. Shit. We were in fucking public. However long we'd been there, I'd completely forgotten that I was on fucking duty. *Fuck.*

Instead of my thumb teasing her nipple some more, I brushed the fabric of her dress back into place. My fingers kneaded the back of her neck. Why couldn't I stop touching her? Gently, I slid my hands to her waist and picked her up again before setting her gently onto the ground.

"What—I—"

I cleared my throat loudly. "You pack a hell of a punch, Jessa." I then took a very deliberate step backward.

She was silent for a long moment as she stared at me. Then, as if her brain finally clicked online, she shoved at my shoulders. "Oh my God, we need to get back before anyone misses us."

"You okay?"

She swallowed. "Yeah, I—you. That was…" her voice trailed.

The smirk played on my lips. "Yeah, what you said. Let's get you back."

"You know it would help if you didn't look so damn smug."

I laughed. "Oh, princess, you haven't seen smug yet. Wait until I give you at least three orgasms."

"You're impossible."

"So you keep telling me."

Jessa…

"Where are you off to, sweetie?"

I wiggled in my dress, trying to adjust the stupid control thingamajiggy undergarments that had ridden up when I'd been busy snagging Roone. In public…like a god damn teenager. "Honestly, if you must know, my Spanx are killing me. I need to take them off."

Ariel laughed. "Right there with you sister. I'll come with."

"Okay, no big deal."

My gaze scanned the crowd for Roone. He was embroiled in some conversation with the media mogul, Frederick Brice. The two of them were chatting away as if they'd known each other their whole lives, so I was sure he'd be fine for a few moments. We might have reached an impasse, but it's not like I trusted him with my clients now.

Ariel followed me down the hall. Several other women were trickling the same way that we did. I tugged her down another hallway. "I think there's one down here too."

She slid her gaze back toward the main lobby and then shrugged. "Okay, if you say so."

Sure enough, there was a bathroom. Unfortunately, it was only one stall. I went in while Ariel fixed her makeup, and I had never been happier to rip off a pair of control wear in my life. All this just to not have panty lines? It wasn't worth it. I needed to breathe. My thighs, they needed air.

I leaned onto the toilet for a moment. Just breathing deep. Finally, I staggered out in my heels and tossed the damn thing in the trash. "Oh my God, if I ever wear another one of these things again, shoot me."

"Weren't you the one telling me I needed some of these?"

"Yes, but I declare it too high a price to pay to not have panty lines. So freaking what?"

Ariel laughed as she shuffled into the stall. "Amen, sister."

My phone rang, but I only had one bar. "Hey," I said just as she started to moan and, I assumed, wiggle out of her undergarments as well. "I'm just going to take this right outside the door. I'll wait for you."

She hesitated for a moment. "Oh, do you have to take that right now?"

"Yeah, silly. I'll be right out here." I stepped out and answered. "Hello. Jessa McLean." But there was silence on the line. "Hello? Hello?" I glared at my phone. I still only had one damn bar. But we were right next to one of the exterior doors, so I shoved it open and stepped outside into the darkness. "Hello?"

"Jessa?"

The voice was familiar enough to have me frowning. "Yeah, who is this?"

"It's Toby."

Toby? "Adamson?"

"Yeah, listen. I need to talk to you about what happened, you know, at the bar. I'm really sorry—" As I was doing my walk and shiver dance, someone grabbed my elbow. I dropped my phone, cutting Toby off. "Hey, what the fff—" A hand slapped over my mouth, squelching my scream.

Another arm wrapped around my waist and then picked me up.

Oh fuck! But with one calming breath, I remembered what my father used to tell me about staying calm in the face of certain madness. He always used to say, 'You can't think if you're not calm.' Except, he never seemed calm himself. He was always frantically muttering about something, keeping me safe, keeping people away from me. But maybe, just maybe once, he was right. I forced my body to still and my brain to go quiet for just a moment. And then I remembered all the things he taught me. The things I didn't want to learn at the time. All the things I thought were way too intense and a little bit crazy. Things I'd practiced with Roone the other day.

As if in slow motion, my body knew what to do, and I quickly executed the moves. Backward headbutt, reach behind for the balls, grab, twist, yank. As soon as I was released, my elbow went back into his gut, creating space, and then my foot pounded on his instep. Hard. With heels on. My assailant howled and buckled to his knees.

I turned to face him and delivered an elbow, right on top of his skull. With my mouth free and my body now loose, I screamed bloody murder. "Help! Somebody, help me!"

It only took a couple of seconds. He stood and wavered, and I bolted for the door, yanking it open, screaming bloody murder. "Help me. Somebody, help!"

Ariel came running out of the bathroom. A security guard and a couple of men in tuxes ran down the hall toward me. Ariel quickly ran for the door. "What happened?"

"I don't—" I sucked in a couple of deep breaths and planted my hands on my knees as I dry heaved. "I don't know. There was a guy… I was on the phone. I couldn't hear… no service and, and… he just grabbed me. And, and… I don't know what happened."

Ariel quickly wrapped an arm around me, gently soothing and rubbing my arm. "It's okay. You're okay. You're fine. Listen to me, nice and calm. Do you remember how tall he was?"

I frowned. "How am I supposed to know that?" But somehow my brain knew, even if I didn't. He'd been taller than me in my heels. Which meant, at least 5'11. Actually, more like six feet. "I think he was about six feet."

"That's great. What else? Do you remember anything? I know it's dark outside, but what color was his hair? Dark? Blond hair?"

I shook my head. *Think. Think. Think.* And then as if sliding into a view finder, I remembered. "His hair was lighter. Light brown. Sandy blond."

She nodded. "Any tattoos you could see? Any identifying marks?"

"Well, he has a cut over his eye, where I landed my head-butt, but there was nothing else I could see. Nothing like face tattoos or anything."

"Good girl. Nice and easy." She handed me to someone and then turned to say something to the security guard. I didn't know who it was, but strong arms wrapped around me and cocooned me in warmth and sandalwood.

Roone.

I glanced up, and his green eyes were focused and intent on mine. "Are you okay?" His voice was more vibration than sound to me.

"I don't think so."

He nodded. "Okay, I'll get you home."

That was easier said than done though. All the hullabaloo had drawn lots of guests of the gala. My bosses being among them.

Evan shot through the crowd. "What the hell is going on here?"

Roone kept his arms around me. "Some asshole nut job outside just tried to grab her."

Evan frowned. "What, like a mugging? Who the hell would have done something like that? This is a charity function."

Roone shook his head. "If you don't mind, I'll take her home as soon as she's done with the police."

Evan opened his mouth as if to object, and then Rick stepped forward. "No, of course, we don't mind. Take her home."

Ariel came forward and gave me a squeeze. "Jessa, you're having the worst luck."

"Tell me about it. I'm starting to think I made a mistake waking up this morning and putting on those Spanx."

Both Evans furrowed their brows. Ariel, on the other hand, chuckled. "I don't know about that, but let's have you give your statement then we can get you out of here."

It was funny, between her and Roone, I felt completely safe, secure, considering what had just happened. Ariel handled me and the police expertly. She kept the crowd at bay, kept me talking to only people that mattered. And then Roone squired me away from everyone.

Evan looked like he wanted to say something, or insist on escorting me home, but Rick said he was needed to run interference. They had guests in at gala they needed to attend to. After something like this, they needed to run their own PR, so I was left in the capable hands of Roone. Someone whose hands I wanted to be in. The car dropped us off and Roone escorted me to the lift, gently keeping his arm wrapped around me as he walked me to the door.

When we reached it, he merely stuck out his hand in silent request for the key. And just like he'd done the night of the break-in, he searched everywhere before letting me come in, and then he sat me down on the couch. "I'm going to make you a cup of tea."

"Yeah, this is one of those times that I think tea might actually help."

"I'm sorry this happened. It shouldn't have, and we're going to find out who did it, who's responsible, okay?"

He leaned down in front of me, his eyes level and solemn, making sure to impart the seriousness of what he was saying. He wasn't going to let something hurt me. I didn't know why, but I absolutely believed him.

A few minutes later, my hands shook as they wrapped around a mug of tea. When was the last time that had happened? I didn't even realize I was rocking into Roone, who was scooted right next to me. He took the mug out of my hand and set it on the coffee table. "Easy does it. You're okay. I'm right here."

"All my life, I thought my father was in-in-insane." I couldn't even get the words out.

He shushed me some more. "Your dad? What does he have to do with this?"

How could I even explain without looking crazy myself. "I know I sound crazy, but that guy, the way he grabbed me… it seemed like he was trying to take me somewhere. Not hurt me right there, ya know? My whole life, Dad insisted I needed to be vigilant. At first, I thought he was just extremely overprotective. He never let me go anywhere. Forced me into martial arts. Told me one day people were going to come for me and I needed to be ready. In the end, he made no sense. I had to have him hospitalized for a time because I thought he was a danger to others. But what if he wasn't crazy at all?"

"Okay, easy does it." He pulled me tighter, and I couldn't help it. Stupid sandalwood was like a relaxation potion. The moment he held me firmly against him, I relaxed, even though I didn't want to. "Look, maybe your Dad was right. Maybe there is some bad boogeyman out there. Let's not discount that. But let's stop for a moment and think it through. The most likely assumption is that the events are unrelated. But this is for the police to figure out. Not you. I don't want you doing anything that's going to put you in danger."

I ran a hand through my hair. Goddamn it. I was losing my shit if I was going to start to think of my father's ramblings and secret texts.

"No you're right. I just – I don't know what the hell is going on. I've worked hard for this gig. I have worked my whole life to get here. I'm finally stable, and now all this shit keeps happening?"

Roone kissed my forehead. "Just let me hold you, okay?"

I wanted to fight him. I wanted to insist that I could take care of myself. But in all honesty, his arms arounds me, cocooning me against his broad chest, made me feel safe, though I knew that safety was relative and an illusion.

And maybe he was right, maybe the break-in and the incident at the gala were unrelated. But if they were, that was one hell of a coincidence, and I didn't believe in coincidence.

"Come on, let's get you to bed."

I didn't want him to go. I felt helpless saying it, but I held on to his hand. "You stay."

Roone pulled back, his gaze searching mine. "Yeah, of course."

"Somehow, I figured when you finally said those words to me, it would be far hotter. This feels like a disappointment."

He chuckled low as he pulled me to my feet. "Don't worry. I'll make up for it. First, you need to get some rest."

"Leave it to me to get stuck with a gentleman."

"There will come a time when I stop being a gentleman. When that time comes, we're going to make sure this place is sound proof. Because there will be screaming, and it won't be because you're in pain."

Oh, well then. "Careful now. I might hold you to it."

"I'm counting on it."

25

Roone…

I HEARD JESSA'S BEDROOM DOOR OPEN AND I SAT UP, shifting my gun from under my pillow to under the couch. Guns weren't a thing in the UK. Police didn't carry them, let alone private citizens. I'd have a hell of a time answering questions about it if it came to it. But I needed it. I had to be on high alert because I'd disabled the cameras.

I still wasn't sure why I'd done it. Nothing was happening. *Liar.* But I just knew that Jessa had her pride. She wouldn't want anyone to see her breaking down.

I'd been lying on her couch running through every moment of the night before, trying to find the holes. Because there was no way I was sleeping tonight.

First someone had tried to take her. Tried to hurt her. Second, she'd rubbed her body all over mine. No way in hell I'd ever sleep again. And having another wank wasn't going to help.

I'd already had two in the shower and my cock was still ready to rumble.

Dick: Go on. Let's do this. She wants you.

No. I wasn't playing. Tonight of all nights, he didn't get an opinion. She needed me, so I was going to be the bloke that was there for her. Not the bloke she hate-shagged because she was having a shit night… okay, a shit couple of weeks. Besides, she didn't know the truth about who I was.

"Jessa? What's wrong?" After I rubbed my eyes to adjust them, I immediately wished I hadn't. The sight of Jessa in tiny, black undies and a cotton camisole that stretched thin over her breasts and barely covered her belly was not what I needed. Fuckin' hell, I could see the dark areolas of her nipples. I wanted her so badly I could taste the essence of her on my tongue.

Dick: I concur.

Brain: Maybe what she really needs is your dick to feel better.

Fuck me. My brain had gone over to the dark side.

I ran my hands through my hair. I was tense. I couldn't do this. I'd resisted for weeks. Even after tasting her, I hadn't gone there and for that I deserved a fucking medal.

But now, my stupid brain was conjuring up all the reasons why this was a good idea. A couple of hours with her pinned beneath me, then on top of me, then in front of me would help take the edge off.

But it wouldn't lessen my desire for her. I'd been living with it since I got here. And my need level was raging.

Her voice was soft. Husky. "Roone," she whimpered, "Are you awake? I… uh… couldn't sleep."

"Bad dreams?" Why the fuck did it sound like I'd swallowed a frog whole? I simultaneously wished for and hoped she wouldn't ask me to hold her.

She shrugged. "I'd have to be asleep first."

I cleared my throat. As she strode closer, I picked up the

scent of flowers, and my dick twitched. "What do you need, Jessa?"

"I—could you maybe sit with me for a bit?"

I scooted back to make room for her. When she sat, my arm went around her automatically, as if she belonged there.

I had no right touching her. She would feel betrayed when she found out. So would Sebastian. That didn't stop me though. I could make all the excuses in the world about how I wanted to comfort her. Or about how being around her chased away that hollow feeling inside. I had more fun fighting with her than doing just about anything else.

But none of it mattered. Because at the base truth of it, I wanted her. I wanted her so bad my blood thickened and ran hot. Every word from her lips made me want to antagonize her so she'd say something else crazy.

"You weren't asleep were you Jessa?"

Against my shoulder, she shook her head. "I need a little help getting to sleep."

Dick: I volunteer as tribute. I'm a very good helper.

I struggled to hold on to control. "Princess…" My voice trailed because all the reasons why this was a very bad idea escaped me. My fucking brain had shut down.

She slipped under my arm and stood directly in front of me. "I don't know why I came out here. I thought I could…" With a deep breath she continued. "I was lying in bed freaking out, but also wanting you. I thought if I just came out then I'd be able to seduce you or something. But I have no idea what I'm doing."

My mind blurred as she stood before me. With her sweet pussy directly at eye level, I couldn't traverse the length of her torso to meet her eyes. Tearing my gaze away from my prize wasn't an option.

I swallowed around the sawdust in my mouth. "Princess, is

this what you want? There are things we should talk about. But if you're saying you want me, I'm not saying no again."

I forced myself to shift my gaze up. She nodded, and I smiled up at her. "I need the words, love." God if she gave me the words, there would be no going back. I wanted her too much. The last part of me that was able to think wanted her to say no, to walk away. It would be safer. The larger part of me could give a fuck about consequences.

"This is what I want."

Fuck. Also, hell yes.

She hesitated. *No need to be shy, princess. I know exactly what to do.* I reached up to her neck and pulled her down for a kiss. I wasn't slow. I wasn't gentle. I took her smart mouth like it belonged to me. I did what I'd been dying to do since I saw her at the party at the bar. I kissed her like she belonged to me.

Yeah, I'd kissed her before, but I'd been holding back, convinced I could stop myself from wanting her too much. I was a fool, clearly.

I slid my tongue over hers, trying to absorb every single flavor. Trying to sear myself on her memory.

When I pulled back she panted, and her eyes were glazed. I slid my hands to her ass, gently testing with a light squeeze before dragging her down to straddle my hips.

With soft hazel eyes, she searched my face then shifted her hips ever so slightly, bringing her heat right up against my straining cock.

I fucking throbbed. The only things that separated us was the flimsy scrap of material she called underwear and my boxer-briefs. *Fuck. Fuck. Fuck.* I wanted to slide into her so deep I couldn't find my way out ever again.

I wasn't supposed to have her. But she was mine now. I needed to take care of her. Which meant getting my shit under control. I needed to go slow.

When she placed a soft kiss on my lips, my whole body

tensed. The scent of her lotion intoxicated me. The way her soft fingers brushed against my bare chest made me tingle.

Jessa bit her bottom lip, then slanted her lips over mine again and kissed me. Hard. As if I could hear the steel snaps of my control break, I slid my hands up her back and into the nape of her neck. Taking control of the kiss, I angled her head so that we fit better. I used the tip of my tongue to tease the seam of her lips until she opened for me again. Once she did, I took.

Frustration and need boiled out in that kiss. I demanded that her tongue meet mine. I teased and sucked on her tongue in a sensual rhythm that spoke of how I was going to ride her. Soft hands caressed my back and clung to my shoulders as her hips rose and descended over me.

Shit. And I'd thought dry humping as a teenager was frustrating. Clamping both hands on her hips, I held her still and continued to devour her. When she came, I would be inside her. When her orgasm hit, it would be with the slick walls of her sex around my cock.

I broke the kiss and traced a path of open-mouthed kisses along the column of her neck. My hands controlling the movements of her hips now, I eased her moist heat against my throbbing erection in a pace that I could manage. I tucked her close, then tilted her away, tucked her close again, and away. Over and over I set the new pace, letting her know that I was in charge.

She tasted sweet and spicy. And her hair smelled like heaven—summer strawberries. With a growl, I shifted our positioning, flipping us over and tossing her beneath me on the couch. With too rough hands, I tugged at the fabric of her panties, and a small tearing sound echoed in the quiet of the flat.

Jessa moaned at the sound, and if possible, I felt more heat pouring off her already wet center. Her fingernails dug into my back, scoring the skin, and she called out my name. Fire burned where her nails tore flesh.

Taking the cue from her, I reached for the hem of her camisole and shredded it from belly to neckline, baring her breasts to my view. Her nipples were dark chocolate tips and fuck me, did I ever have a sweet tooth.

I sucked one pebble into my mouth and grazed with my teeth. I tugged gently and used my fingers to pinch and pluck the other puckered nipple. When I'd had my fill of one, I moved to her other breast and laved at her like she was ice cream on a hot summer day.

"Roone, please." Her hips rolled up, and my dick insistently twitched against her. Her eyes flared. "God, of course you're big."

I grinned against her nipple. "I was telling the truth about that."

She reached between us and with one stroke of her delicate hand, she had me on the brink of orgasm. *Fuck.* Lust raged in my veins, and I couldn't for the life of me remember why I was supposed to go slow. I was on fire, and only she could put me out.

Impatient, I divested her of the remainder of the barely-there panties, the same way I'd taken care of that worthless cami. Merely hearing the tearing of the rest of the fabric brought me closer to the brink.

Impatiently, I kissed down her body. I nipped at her hip bone and her hips jerked up off the couch. "Roone, oh my God. You don't have to. I—"

What? Was she mad? No way was I making love to her without tasting her first. I cut her off with a stroke over her clit.

"Oh God."

I repeated until she started to shake, then I wrapped my lips over her clit and sucked. Jessa dug her hands into my hair and pulled it tight. Yeah it hurt, but the fuck I cared about battle scars.

Although I did start to worry when I slid two fingers inside her pussy and her legs clamped around my neck. "Shhh. Relax. Just let it feel good."

Jessa's panting and pleading that it was too much, made me smile. "Just tell me to stop." I waited. "Go on."

Her laugh was throaty. "You're such a tease."

"Oh, I'm not tease, princess. I plan to deliver. I just want you to have some fun on the way."

I stroked over that spot inside and she screamed. While I stroked, I sucked. It only took seconds, but she drenched my hand, and her thighs quivered around my fingers.

"Oh my God. Oh my God. Oh my God."

Her body arched up and back as she shook. "Roone, oh God." I couldn't tell if that was one long orgasm, or if one had rolled into two. Either way, she held onto my fingers like they held the answer to world peace.

I brushed my stubble against her inner thigh. With wide eyes, she stared up at me like she was holding her breath.

I stroked her wet slit with the backs of my knuckles, and she rolled her hips into the caress, moaning for me. Her wetness coated my knuckles with her juices. "God, you're so wet." I stroked again.

Jessa tossed her head back. "Jesus, Roone, please don't tease."

I chuckled as I slid a finger inside her, reaching into her slick depths. Slowly, I retreated then added another finger. With my thumb, I teased her clitoris by making light circles. She was still coming down.

Her hips rocketed off the couch, and still I slid my fingers into her.

When she widened her thighs, I inhaled. I loved her scent, spicy and decadent. I wanted to go back for another taste, but I'd make love to her first. I needed to feel her around me.

She attempted to tug me up by yanking on my hair, drawing me closer to her. "Roone please, I need you. I can't—"

I kissed a path up her body again, pausing momentarily at her breasts. With a muffled curse, I reached for my wallet on the coffee table. I snatched a condom out, ripped the foil with my teeth and had myself sheathed in seconds. Then I positioned my cock at her entrance. With one stroke, I slid into her to the hilt. She cried out as I groaned through gritted teeth.

"You are so tight." I withdrew an inch and re-seated myself inside her. "Fuck... feels good."

Ecstasy and white-hot bliss exploded in my body. I buried my face in Jessa's neck as I struggled to conquer the blistering need to claim her hard and quick. She felt like heaven. Soft, silken heaven wrapped around my cock. A hundred armed men could have come charging through her front door, and I would have been powerless to leave her.

"Roone, please." She dug her nails into my back again.

Through clenched teeth, I muttered, "Shit, Jessa. Stop that. Otherwise, we won't be here for long."

She placed an open-mouthed kiss on my shoulder. "I don't want to stop. I want you." Her hands slid to my ass, massaged the bunched muscles, then drew my hips forward and tucked me further inside her.

That was the moment my body snatched control from my brain. I drove into her with enough power to make her gasp.

Her legs locked around me and she met me thrust for thrust, rocking into me. Pleading. I grazed her neck with my teeth as I fucked her. I wanted to leave a mark. I wanted the world to know that in this moment she was mine.

My hand in her hair gripped tight. I forced her to arch to give me more access. All the while I kept up the pace. I could tell before I think she knew, that she was about to blow again. It was that first telltale quiver.

"That's it, princess. I love to watch you come."

And come she did, squeezing my dick tight. Trying to hold on to it for an eternity. If I could have, I would have let her. And then the heat came, the white-hot fire on the tail of lust, threatening to blind us both.

It curled up my spine like a lover's caress and exploded as I came. No matter what happened, I would die to keep Jessa McLean.

Fire burned in my chest. Because all I had to do to keep her was not tell her the whole truth.

26

Jessa...

I KNEW EXACTLY WHERE I WAS OR RATHER WHO I WAS with. As the streaks of sunlight threatened to blind me in the morning, I knew what I'd done last night on the couch. Then again in my bed. Okay fine. What I'd also done against the wall on the way to the bedroom. And I was terrified.

I'd been awake for forty minutes. Trying to find the courage to get up and shower to face it all or to snuggle in and just sleep for another hour, so I was stuck in limbo. Also, I kind of wanted to see if he'd do what he'd done to me last night again, because 'one more for the road' was something I'd always wanted to say.

No. You know how this is going to end up. And it's not going to be fun for you.

Are we sure it won't be fun? Because, orgasms.

Nope get up. Get in the shower, freak out in private. Maybe escape to go get breakfast then conveniently forget to come back until he's gone. And then put the wall back up.

I tried to expertly slide out of the bed. I had not had many opportunities for one-night stands. Okay no real opportunities. I'd had maybe one one-night stand, and it was really more like a two-day fling when I was on vacation in Vegas with a friend. There had been no need to sneak away because we were getting on separate planes, never to be seen or heard from again. But this, this was different. I would see him across the hall and at work. And there was no pretending that this hadn't just happened and that I hadn't just lost my ever-loving mind.

I shuffled slightly. I was trying to take one of the sheets with me, but he had that duvet wrapped firmly around him.

As I stood, his hand reached out and wrapped oh so gently around my wrist. "Where are you going?"

I swallowed hard. "Um, shower. Then you know… food?"

"That sounds like a question not a statement."

"Can you let me go? It's cold out here."

"I have a solution for that." He tugged me down into bed and quickly covered my body with his.

I squealed. "Oh my God."

He kissed me softly, expertly melting away the temporary wall of ice I'd started to construct. "Now, where are you going?"

"I am going to shower. You know, I have things to do."

He shook his head and lifted a brow. "It's okay. I can wait."

I glowered at him. "Fine. I'm having a hard time stiff-upper-lipping this, so I was going to run away, shower, sneak out of my flat, pretend to go have a coffee and breakfast, then maybe return when I thought I wouldn't run into you. Only then will I maybe call Chloe. Have a girl chat, you know? Where she'd tell me, 'You go girl! You got some.' And I'd tell her, 'Oh God, I'm not actually sure what this means.' You know that sort of thing."

His smile was lazy before he dipped to nuzzle my neck. "I have a better proposal."

Yeah, that was his super power. The nose thing against my neck. I was weak. Weak for the neck. "Roone. I really don't know what this means."

He pulled back, and his eyes were serious. "I don't know what this means either. But I do like you. And let's face it, you like me too. You might not want to, but you do. And we make an excellent shagging team."

I snorted a laugh. "I mean, you're okay. But I'm the real champion in this duo."

He chuckled then. "Oh, so that time you were screaming, 'Oh my God, yes right there, yes. Oh my God.' That doesn't mean you like me?"

"Oh my God." I smacked his arm.

He quickly and efficiently captured my wrists above my head. "Oh, you were the one saying it. I didn't force you."

"You were busy giving me lots of orgasms. That the standard response."

He shook his head. "Nothing about you is standard. Like I was saying, I like you too. And this complicates a lot of things. But considering I've been living with a perpetual hard on since I first laid eyes on you, I'm not really going let you go now that I've tasted you."

My inner diva preened. "Really? A perpetual hard on, huh? It's a wonder you're getting anything done."

"I know. Especially when you walk by and say something sassy. God, you're so sweet, but that little bite of attitude? Guaranteed turn on."

I scoffed. "You just like difficult women."

He frowned. "Who said you were difficult?"

I frowned and tried to shove down the feelings of inadequacy. "Nobody." *My father.*

"Well, whoever that idiot was, you're not difficult. And you're not trouble. You're just perfect, and you just need someone who can actually handle you."

"I do not need to be handled." I wiggled in his grasp.

"And by handle, I don't mean control you." His grip tightened ever so slightly, warning me that physically, he was superior. "What I mean by handle is someone who can support you and thinks you're fantastic and can sometimes partake in your craziness. That's what *I* mean by handle you."

Well then... "Oh." How the hell was I supposed to fight and struggle if he was being sweet?

You're weak.

I was weak. But, the hard length of him was pressing against my center. His hips rolled ever so slightly, and the promise of orgasm tripped my synapses, so I couldn't really think properly. *Later.* I'd think about all the ramifications of this later.

"You ready to stay in bed with me now? And we'll figure out all the complicated things after, like *way* after, you've had so many orgasms you don't even think of leaving my bed anymore."

"So, you plan to control me with orgasms?"

There was that classic grin again, slightly off center, lopsided. Totally panty-melting sexy. "Princess, I'm pretty sure you're the one controlling me."

⚜

Roone...

I WAS PRETTY SURE the princess was trying to kill me. With every smile, every flip of her hair. Every trace of her fingertips over my muscles. She was killing me one step at a time. Because I knew I wouldn't be able to let her go so easily.

You shouldn't have crossed the line with her. You should have told her the truth. It didn't matter that I was under orders not to. None of that would matter in the end. The problem was I still couldn't let her go.

Yeah. I crossed a line. But even knowing how it would end up, I would cross it again because I'd never wanted anyone so much in my life. So, she could slowly kill me, and I would accept it. Because to me it was worth it. I deserved it.

"What are you thinking about?" Jessa asked softly. She kissed my nipple and gently used her teeth to graze it. A shiver of lust ran through my body. *Jesus Christ.* How was it possible that I could go again already? I should be out for the count. Three times last night. Twice this morning... I should be dead.

Dick: I'm a rock star.

Me: Pretty sure this is all Jessa.

Dick: Yeah. It is.

She giggled as my cock brushed her thigh. "My God, you're a machine."

"Well, you're the one kissing my nipple, so really, this is your fault."

"Sure, blame the poor innocent woman who had no idea that endless orgasms were in store. I think my vagina hurts."

I frowned. "Shit, was I too rough?" Was it the doggy style? I'd lost control a little with that last night. Gripped her hair too tight. Just thinking about the curve of her back and I was throbbing again.

She bit my nipple again. "Just rough enough. I meant you might have to kiss it and make it all better though."

I couldn't help the smile that crept over my face. "Oh hell, yes."

She giggled and tried to duck out of the way. "But first I need sustenance."

"What do you have in the fridge?"

"I have the makings of breakfast."

"I'm good with that. Just know that I have zero intention of letting you get dressed."

"I can't just walk around naked to cook."

I bit her shoulder. "Spoilsport. Besides, I get the impression you've walked around naked plenty. Not to mention I'll be doing the cooking. No princess of mine has to make her own breakfast after she tried to kill me with sex."

"Death by cock. Why did I never know that was an option before?" She giggled. "What time is it?"

I glanced over at the bedside table. "It's half ten."

"Shit. I was supposed to have a lunch meeting with someone."

I frowned at her. "Who? I feel like we already established that all bets are off for the whole work situation, so who are you meeting with?"

She ran her hands through her hair. She was busy lifting up the sheet, trying to find the pair of underwear she'd snuck on before I ripped them off. I wouldn't tell her that I'd actually ruined them until later.

Maybe she didn't have to know.

"This isn't a work thing. It's another thing."

I lifted a brow. "Woman, if you think I'm going to let you out of bed to see another man, you've got another think coming."

"I just told you my vagina hurts. Do you really think I could see another guy?"

I shrugged. "Hey, you're an overachiever. I'm just letting you know now, I'm not letting it happen."

"It has nothing to do with that. You know I'm not seeing anyone."

I grinned at her. "Yeah, I know. If you were, there's no way would you respond to me like that."

She smacked my shoulder.

"Ow."

"Quit your whinging. You know full well I can hit you harder than that."

"That I do. So, what is it? What's your appointment?"

I willed her to tell me the truth. I knew she had a meeting with James Morgan who ran Hope House. But it was really important to me to have her tell me. We needed to cross the threshold together. Especially after last night. I wanted the truth from her.

Oh sure, she has to tell you *the truth, but you don't have to tell her?* Bile rose in my throat.

"You're going to think I'm crazy."

I sat up. Letting the sheet drop fully to my waist. Her gaze drifted over my shoulders. And then down my chest to my abs. I flexed on purpose just to see her pupils dilate because yeah, I'm a bloke.

She shook her head and then dragged her gaze back up to my eyes. "You're doing that on purpose."

I nodded. "Guilty. Now, your meeting?"

She ran a hand through her hair. "There's this bloke who ran the residential facility my father was at before he died."

I frowned. "Okay?"

"As I told you. He wasn't well. He was diagnosed with a delusional disorder when I was eleven. For the most part, with therapy and medication, he lived relatively a normal life. But one little change, something would be up with his medication or I'd start a new activity at school, and he'd stop taking his meds and just..." Her voice trailed.

I toyed with a strand of her hair. "Go on?"

"Since I was a kid, dad was really obsessive with thinking someone was going to kidnap me or take me away. So much so that in our time in Canada, he had me learning martial arts and marksmanship. At first he made it fun, like it was a game. And we'd learn together so it was more father-daughter bonding. But then he started getting extra weird with security. He'd decide that someone was following us, and we'd have to move."

I frowned. "Wait, just like that?"

"Oh yes. Sometimes, he'd pick me up from school with a small backpack for me and that would be that. No warning. No time. A few times it was in the middle of the night where he'd wake me up and off we'd go. I learned to not really care about lots of possessions after that."

It was one thing to read about her life in a report. Another to see how it really was for her. "I'm sorry. That sounds horrible."

She shrugged. "It was what it was. But even as his illness got worse and worse and the delusions grew, and I dragged him from shrink to shrink, he was steadfast. Even when he *was* on his meds, he insisted that someone was out to get me. He didn't spin as much and overly obsess, but he was unwavering. My safety was his number one concern."

"What are you saying?"

She sighed. "I guess, my whole life I thought he was ill. I never gave his delusions any credence. When he was on meds and still held fast that I was in danger, I doubled down on therapy. The fact is I never took him seriously. And lately, I'm starting to think I should have." She sat up on her knees as she shifted the sheet. "I went to Hope House to collect his things. I sorted through them and sent some sketches he made to a couple of people who worked there. A few days later, someone broke into my flat and stole the originals of those sketches."

What the fuck? This wasn't information we'd had before. The building had been dark when she'd been broken into. She'd told the police nothing was taken. "Did you tell the police?"

She shook her head. "No. I didn't notice until a few days after, and I don't know, it seemed like I was making a mountain out of a molehill. But then, I sent the scanned sketches to a friend to try to see if she could identify the tattoo in them, and then I was followed."

Shit. That one had been us, the night we lost her. But what fucking tattoos? "You scanned the sketches?"

"Yeah. He was an artist. More videos and photos, but he also loved to sketch. He did it all the time. So I thought I'd send the sketches to James and Lulu at Hope House so if any of the residents were in them, they could keep them if they wanted."

"Smart. Now what do you mean you were followed?"

She chewed her bottom lip. "I know. I sound like I'm suffering the same delusions that he was. I know there is a risk of a hereditary link. But I get myself checked once a year. And I think I'm ok."

My gut curled in on itself. I had to fucking tell her. *You can't. You are under orders.* I hated that she thought she was ill for following her hunch.

"First I was followed, and then someone tried to grab me at the gala. What if all this time, my father wasn't ill and no one believed him? What if *I* should have believed him?" A tear escaped and rolled down her cheek.

I tugged her close and held her to me. "Hey, it's okay. You had a rough go. We don't know anything for sure yet. And look, even if he had a reason to believe you were in danger," *which he did you twat,* "from the sounds of it, that might have fed into his disorder. And you can't know that for sure. If you want to chase this theory to see if it leads down the rabbit hole, then let's back it up to before anything happened. Let's look at the tattoos."

She swiped at her tears again. "You keep saying we."

I sure as hell wasn't letting her do anything alone. But also, I wanted to help her. It was about more than just keeping her safe. I wanted her to have a little peace. "Yeah, we. Look, I don't have all the answers about last night. But I like you, despite you giving me a hard time."

"What?" He eyes went wide. "You turned up and started to try to steal my clients."

I rolled my eyes. "I was *assigned*."

"You also hoisted me over your shoulder like some kind of tart."

I shouldn't have laughed, but I did. "You were the one wearing no knickers."

"I swear to God I will kill—"

I kissed her to stop her. "I know, you'll kill me. I look forward to all the ways you'll try. But the point is you're smart. A little brazen, fun. Funny. And you keep me on my toes. You also have this soft center that you're terrified to let anyone see. You're kind. And I like you, genuinely, as a person. Also, I'm addicted to shagging you. That sound you make when you're about to come... the breathy one... I could die hearing that sound and I'd be happy."

She stared at me. It looked like she was contemplating whether to hit me or not. Instead, true to form, she said something cheeky. "You've gone ahead and fallen in love with me, haven't you? I've got the magic snatch."

It took me three beats to process the words before a laugh cracked me open. "Lord, woman."

She grinned, then shrugged. "I like you too. But I'm going to warn you, I have zero idea how to do this. I've never had a relationship before. I'm probably not good at it."

I pulled her to me and kissed her softly. "We can take a day at a time. Why don't we start with looking at the sketches since they are important to you? Then I'll make you something to eat. And then maybe we can shag in the shower?"

"Seriously, how can you even go again?"

"It's your fault. I just look at your lips and then envision all that you could do with them and boom... instant hard on."

Jessa shook her head. "How do you feel about shagging a

woman with a shower cap on? I have so much hair it'll take hours to dry and straighten if I get it wet."

"You'll soon learn I'll take you any way I can get you."

She pulled her hair back into a bun, then wrapped the sheet around her as she padded into the living room for her laptop. When she returned with it, she pulled up the sketches.

As I flipped through each one, I masked my expression. The arm tattoos were all too familiar. My former partner had had one just like it. As had Robert Sandstorm, the traitor who had conspired to kill the king.

I cleared my throat. "So that looks like a crest? With a dagger or a knife?"

She nodded. "Yeah. I don't think I've ever seen a tattoo like that. I took it to a tattoo parlor recommended by a friend, and they're looking to see if they can track it down."

Fuck me, I'd been sent to protect her, and she'd still unwittingly stumbled into a royal conspiracy. Shit job of protection I was doing. "Okay, so you want to ask James if he's seen the tattoos?"

"Yes. And if he recognizes anyone in the images. And well... I've been avoiding him since Dad died. I feel guilty for not looking after him better."

"Jessa, you can't do that to yourself. Your father was ill. And you took care of him the best you could. You shouldn't blame yourself for anything."

She nodded against my hand. "It's just hard. And hey, you called me Jessa."

I frowned. "Did I?"

"Is it weird that I think I prefer princess?"

I leaned forward and kissed her softly. "Then princess you shall be." She kissed me back. More insistently. "You keep doing that, and I won't feed you for another few minutes."

"I'm not *that* hungry."

"In that case, let me get one more scream for the road. And then we're going to eat."

I slid my hands into her hair. I couldn't help it. Is this what it had been like for Sebastian? Knowing full well he couldn't tell her the truth but needing her just the same? With another kiss, I lost myself again.

Roone...

AS IT TURNED OUT, THE COUNTERTOPS IN JESSA'S apartment were the perfect height for shagging. We finally managed to cobble together breakfast with some eggs and bacon and toast. But she begged off in the shower to try and get ready. While she did that, I reengaged the cameras. I knew she was safe in her flat, but better safe than sorry. I also knew that I had to check in with Ariel.

When she was out of the shower, I kissed her briefly. "I'm going to grab a quick shower at mine and change clothes, okay? And then we'll go together?"

Her smile was so sweet I almost opted to stay. "Yeah, that's perfect." She stood on her tiptoes and brushed her lips against mine once more. God, every time she did that all I wanted to do was club over the head and drag her somewhere safe and bury myself deep inside her.

What was wrong with me?

I let myself into my apartment. I wasn't the least bit surprised to find Ariel. "The conquering hero returns."

"You realize I could have come in here with Jessa, right?"

She rolled her eyes. "You realize that I can hear everything that goes on in the other apartment through the bug in her purse, right?"

A flush crept up my neck.

"Yeah, I turned off the sound once the two of you started with the, 'Tell me you want this.'" She shrugged. "Unfortunately, the louder screaming could be heard without the mics. I mean hey, if you're a stud, you're a stud."

Shite. I rolled my eyes. And started yanking off my t-shirt.

"I don't need the show."

"Well you're going to get it. Make it fast. We're off to meet the director of Hope House." Quickly I filled her in as I brushed my teeth and grabbed clothes.

"Jesus. This princess just stumbles into clues we need without even looking. While you meet with him, I'm going to place a bug in his car just to see if he has any information."

I popped in the shower and was out in five. Shoving my feet into shoes, I asked. "About last night. Just how much *did* you hear?"

"I mean, I turned off the purse mic once I realized you weren't killing her. With all those 'Oh my Gods,' I wasn't so sure there for a minute."

"Shut it."

Ariel just laughed. "I see you got over whatever was mentally blocking you?"

"Stop being a dick."

"I'm a girl. I can't be a dick. Generally, people call me a bitch."

"I'm not calling you a bitch."

"Good. Because then I'd have to run after you going, 'Oh my God. Oh my God. Oh my God. Roone, Roone, Roone.'"

I tossed my jumper at her. "My God, you might as well be a bloke."

She laughed. "Hey, you're the stud. I see once you decide to do something, you *really* decide to do it. I mean, hey."

"Glad I can impress. Anything else I need to know?"

She shook her head. "But you're good, though? You're tight?"

"Oh yeah, I'm right as rain. Keeping the truth from her feels completely normal. I assume I'm still not allowed to tell her?"

She shook her head. "Nope."

"Bullshit. But whatever. I just don't want her hurt."

"Let's just see what leads we get out of the director."

"Yeah. I'm hoping he's got more information than we do, because right now we've got nothing, or not much of anything."

She nodded. "And just so you know, that smile on your face looks good on you. I hope I see it more often."

I watched her walk out the back door as she dragged the beanie cap over her head.

⚜

Jessa…

"JAMES, it's good to see you."

He shook my hand and nodded. "Who's this?"

I swallowed. Why was I so flushed? "This is my, um, friend? Roone?"

James's brows rose. "You sound like that's a question."

Roone laughed. "I'm working on being her boyfriend. But she's a bit cagey, so we're just going to stay with friend right now."

James laughed. "Good to see you branching out, Jessa."

What was that supposed to mean? "I— He's a friend

who's a boy. That's about it." Roone winked at me and took my hand. James seemed happy about that.

"Why don't you guys have a seat."

We were at a little café near the South Bank which was surprisingly difficult to find. It looked like part industrial neighborhood and part gentrified Hipsterville. There were all these little alcoves of men with babies strapped to them and moms with super expensive jogging strollers. But then there were warehouses still scattered among the newer businesses.

Roone glanced around. "The whole place is changing. Every time I come back, it's different than I left it."

James eyed him up and down. "Where'd you grow up?"

"East London, actually. Near Walthamstow."

"Your accent though, that's..."

"Yeah, that's courtesy of Eton."

James's brows furrowed then. "Okay then. That's fascinating."

I could tell that James was going to do an extensive lookup on Roone later, but whatever. I sat forward.

"We haven't seen much of you since your father passed, so I was hoping you were well."

"I—I'm good. Work you know."

"I see you're getting a more balanced life. Your father would be happy for you."

I slid my gaze to Roone, who was giving a rather complex breakfast order. How was the man still hungry? *Maybe you wore him out.*

Something with egg whites and something called chorizo? I suppose I had branched out a little. Did this count as a date? Hell, this was further than I got with 99 percent of the men I went out with. Not that the pool was large. "I guess I'm starting to."

James sipped his tea. "We got the sketches. Thank you. Your father was extremely talented."

I sat up. I hadn't known how to broach the subject, but this was the perfect opening. "Actually, I wanted to ask if you recognized any of the people in the sketches besides Lulu. I know that he sometimes drew things randomly, but I didn't know if they maybe were real people at Hope House."

"Unfortunately, I don't recognize any of them, no."

I tried not to let my heart sink any further. It wasn't likely that he would know them. But I couldn't let it go. "Oh, well. Thank you."

James's eyes went soft. "But you know what? You might ask this bloke, Phillip Winchester. He and your dad were close in Uni. I was closer with your mum."

Roone's hand tightened on my knee. "Did the tattoos look familiar at all?"

"I'm sorry. I wish I could tell you something. Jessa, you know how ill your father was."

I, of all people, knew. But after everything that had been happening, I couldn't ignore what he'd been telling me for years. All I had to do was decipher the clues.

28

Roone…

WHILE ARIEL WAS ON JESSA DUTY TONIGHT, THERE WAS someone else I needed to see. I followed the directions Ben had given me to find the bar in Brixton. I still couldn't believe it. Brixton was so gentrified now. There were gastro pubs and microbreweries littered all over the place. What had happened to all the Jamaican rude boys? That could be the title of a song. When I was a kid, Brixton was a rite of passage where you'd find some underground club. The neighborhood had been rougher, but somehow it had felt more like home.

When I walked in, the place was full of hipster types with their beards and ironic T-shirts under suit jackets. It looked like an Instagram stylist had had their way with the whole place. I found Ben in the corner next to the pool table with a pint. He waved me over, and I wandered my way through the crowd until I reached him. "Hey, mate."

"Cousin." He came around and clapped me on the back. "Jesus, let me look at you. You look great. Island life agreed with you then, yeah?"

"Yeah, it did. Not sure when I'm going back though." Especially not with this new lead on the tattoos.

"So, tell your favorite cousin everything. Like how you got hooked up with the most delectable publicist in London. Seriously mate, I have tried for a year to get her to show interest. East and Bridge too. But nothing. You turn up and she's looking like she wants to shag you against the wall...then kill you praying mantis style."

I coughed out a laugh. "Not sure that's exactly how she was looking at me."

"Oh, come on. I could feel the tension." He studied me closer. "But you, you don't have it anymore." His mouth fell open. "Aw, mate. You've shagged her, haven't you? Lucky sod. Tell me she was fantastic. Please don't ruin my imagery and tell me she just lay there. Tell me it was at least a wild ride."

"Piss off, mate."

He lifted a brow. "Woah. *Not* just a shag then. All right cousin. So now that you're in love with your 007 mark, how are you going to pull off your mission?"

I rolled my eyes even as I chuckled. "Who said she's a mark?"

Ben pointed at me. "It's what you *didn't* say. You're acting as a publicist now?"

"Excuse me, I'm a consultant."

"Whatever the fuck that means." He lowered his voice. "You're fucking Royal Guard to a *king*. Not to mention former SAS. Don't expect me to believe you had a sudden career change."

"I hate that you pay attention."

"I'm not daft."

"You know I can't tell you what I'm doing, right?"

He nodded. "Yep, I know. Just don't treat me like an eejit, yeah?" He added, "She's not in some kind of trouble, is she?"

He actually cared about her? "No. She's fine."

"As long as you're not yanking her about. She's a nice girl."

"I'm not. You have my word." I was just lying to her about what I was doing here. But I was being completely honest about falling for her, so there was that.

"You're really not going to tell me?"

I shook my head. "Nope."

"God, you're so boring. I was hoping to get some juicy gossip."

"Mate, you love gossip more than a teenage girl."

Ben just grinned at me. "You know it. Besides, gossip is good for us. It keeps us connected to our community."

I shook my head. "You're a nutter."

"Maybe. But you look happy, though. Just how is the king?"

"You know Sebastian. He's taken on the weight of the world now."

"Didn't I hear something about him having a brother?"

Ben was remarkably well-informed. "Yeah, it's a thing. Long story."

"We've got time. Let's get you a pint."

A brunette walked by. She was gorgeous with dark hair and a little edge of crazy about her, and she eyed us up and down. But especially my cousin. Ben grinned right back at her. "Oh, love, did you know they call me Big Ben?"

She laughed at that. Of course she did. Ben had always had a way with women. He loved all kinds of women. If he had one failing, it would be that. He loved women too much. As if that was a thing, but still.

The woman, however, did not even blink. She just tittered as he flirted. And that was the way with Ben. When she made her way over to her friends, he winked at me. "Always gotta keep the options open, mate."

"It's good to see some things never change."

"So tell me, is my cousin in love?"

It's a distinct possibility.

It wasn't anywhere near a possibility.

You should've thought about that before you touched her.

I shifted uncomfortably and picked up one of the pool cues. "It's complicated."

Ben grinned. "It's never complicated. Women are women. They are designed to bring us to our knees."

"I'd have to agree with that."

He studied me for a long moment. That was the thing about Ben. He seemed like a playboy, always joking. Always there with a laugh. But there was something shrewd about him. He was hyper aware of other people. Honestly, that's why people loved him so much. He was a natural born leader. People wanted to listen to him. Because around him, they felt seen. "Look, I don't know Jessa that well. But I do know you. And I know how you looked at her. If you're into her, I wouldn't let that one go. That would be stupid."

"This from the bloke who changes women as often as he changes kleenex?"

"Ah, you wound me, cousin. Let's just say this is coming from a bloke who knows that when someone twists you up like that, when you're borderline obsessed with them, you probably shouldn't let them go."

"Okay, I'll take that under advisement."

He shrugged. "Well, it's good to have you home however long. Make sure I actually get to see you again."

"Yeah, I'll make sure I arrange that."

Ben nodded solemnly. "You know, for what it's worth, I have someone go out to your mom's gravesite periodically and clean it up and leave fresh flowers."

I blinked at him. "Why?"

"Because you're my cousin. And I never felt right about not being allowed to go to her funeral. So, if I could do something to make your life a little bit easier, then why not?"

"Thanks, mate. I don't know what to say."

He shrugged. "No need to say anything. I will tell you though, my guy who goes to clean out there says he's seen your brother there more than once."

The bottom fell out of my stomach. " Yeah?"

Ben nodded. "Yeah. Are you planning on seeing him while you're here?"

No way I was getting into this conversation with Ben right now. I sank my shot and leaned back onto the cue. "The plan was not to see him. And so far, that's my only plan."

"As plans go, that seems pretty solid to me. But maybe you'll want answers and change your mind. But then again, that could just be me."

Jessa…

"To GIRLS' night."

I had no choice. Ariel was looking far too happy and enthusiastic, followed closely by Chloe as they clinked their glasses. "Fine. To girls' night."

Chloe grinned at me. "You'd think you'd be happier about girls' night. Or are you disappointed that we're not Roone?"

I rolled my eyes. "I am not disappointed. I don't need a man to make me happy. I am perfectly happy already. Look at me being happy."

Chloe laughed, and Ariel glanced up as the waiter brought us our first round of appetizers. "What you're seeing is that she's desperate to get back to work right now."

"I am *not*. I am enjoying an evening out. With friends. This is me relaxing."

Chloe mouthed, *No it's not.*

"I saw that."

My friend laughed. "Well, it's true. Although, since Roone showed up, you've certainly looked less stressed. Inquiring minds want to know... Any reason you're less stressed out?" She grinned at me and waggled her eyebrows.

"No. I have nothing to offer."

Ariel laughed. "Come on, some of us are in a drought here. Your potential hookups are giving me life right now."

"There's no reason you're in a drought. If that's the case, it's by choice."

She shrugged. "Maybe. What about you, Chloe? How is the app date guy?"

Chloe beamed. "Oh my God, he's great. Very cute. And our chemistry's scorch-the-sheets off the charts, so I'm not going to complain."

I raised my glass to Chloe. "Good for you. Enjoy. Have some fun."

Chloe rolled her eyes. "What about you, though? You deserve fun."

I couldn't help the flush that crept up my neck. "I have fun." I'd had all kinds of fun over the last couple of days. Roone was... God, how did I end up here? He was all the things I thought I wouldn't want in someone. But for some reason, when he talked to me, all I heard was him, all I *saw* was him. He had the potential to be dangerous for me. "What about you, Ariel? You must have had some great love affairs at some point?"

She hesitated and chewed her lip. "Well, there was someone once, but that ended a long time ago."

Smelling blood in the water, I leaned forward with my drink. "Oh my gosh, do tell. I promise you, it's far more interesting than what's happening with me and Roone right now."

Ariel raised her brow, telling me full well she didn't believe me. But we would fight that battle another time. "No, not necessarily, but, it's ancient history now."

Chloe whined. "Oh, come on, tell us."

Ariel flushed a deep shade of red. "Okay, okay. There was a guy once. Someone I thought would be great. You know, like when you're young, that kind of all-encompassing, all-consuming kind of love. But I wasn't good enough. His family didn't approve. And in the end, he chose them."

Chloe moaned. "But that's so tragic."

Ariel shrugged. "Yeah, I guess it was."

I narrowed my gaze. "There's something you're not telling us. Is there something about this guy we should know? Like is he someone famous?" Sensing blood in the water, I leaned forward some more. "Come on. Tell us."

Her face went beet red this time, matching her hair.

"Oh my God. No, he wasn't famous-famous. He just was recognizable. You know, I just... God, I don't even talk about this to my best friend."

I grinned. "But you know what? We're safe. Because there's no way we would even know who he was."

Ariel chewed her bottom lip. "Yeah, I guess so. I mean, it seems too ridiculous to even think about it now. But I was in love, you know? Like head over heels, *we are going to be together* kind of love. Only to discover, that he didn't feel the same way about me."

"What happened?"

"We were secretly seeing each other for a while. On what was supposed to be our first public date, he ghosted."

I lifted my brow. "Was he married? You seem so down to earth. Like you would never do that. I can't see you putting up with some kind of secret relationship."

She nodded, her red hair swinging around her shoulders. "Yeah. I know, right? But when we were supposed to meet, he was a no-show. We'd made this whole fabulous plan for the future about how we were going to move abroad and do all this stuff, but instead I ended up going on my own for six months. When I came back, I—" She shifted her gaze around. "Um, I got to work. That's when I got started on the design for Meet Cute. The rest is history."

"Do you ever see him? Have you seen him? Have you talked to him?"

"No. At the time, I thought maybe he would try and reach out, but it never happened. And I don't know, I just sort of tucked that one away."

Chloe shook her head. "But I don't understand. How does your best friend not even know?"

"Well at the time, she had left for university. And honestly, it was just this summer thing. And now, when I say it out loud, I recognize it sounds insane to plan my whole life based on three fantastic months, right? I was just so embarrassed when it ended that I just never told anyone. I was just mortified that I'd thought someone like that would want someone like me. But I'd really believed it."

"Just for the record, you're fantastic. I'm sure he's regretting that decision now."

She shrugged. "I don't know. It would be easy enough to look him up, but I won't be ever doing that. I have no desire to punish myself."

Chloe took another sip of her wine. "God, I swear, men can be such twats."

I nodded. "Yeah, they can be." But really, what did I know about it? I don't know what prompted the honesty, but I said, "It's a bit embarrassing to even say this, but I don't even know what it's like to be in love."

Chloe laughed. "You're not serious."

"Yes, I am."

Ariel shook her head. "But you're beautiful. You're smart. You're driven."

"I've just never had a chance. My dad had us bouncing us

around all over the place when I was a kid, and I went to several different high schools. And then during Uni, I was mostly looking after my dad. I dated some, but like that fall in love kind of thing, get swept away in it all, I've never had that."

Chloe smiled. "Well, maybe you have it now?"

I blushed. "I don't know what I have now. What I have now is something dangerous because he is verboten. Evan would fire both of us, and Chloe, he'd fire you for knowing and not saying anything."

Chloe snorted. "Nah, boss man would only fire Roone because *he* has a thing for you."

Ariel laughed. "What? What is this madness?"

Chloe giggled. "Oh yeah, Evan has had a thing for Jessa since she started at the firm."

Ariel's eyes went wide. "Oh really? An office thing?"

God no. "That's not true. That's Chloe's *theory,* and not the best theory she's ever had."

"It's true." Chloe insisted. "I can tell by the way he watches you. If he looked like Roone, it'd be hotter. But he's not Roone. So sometimes it's a little creepy."

I sniffed. I'd never once been interested in Evan. He'd always *just* been my mentor. "He's perfectly fine-looking, handsome even with his dark hair. He works out. But that's not the point. The point is he's my boss, and I also feel absolutely zero there."

Chloe took another sip of her wine. "I'm telling you. I still remember when you were hired. We were all in the assistants' pool together, but he honed right in on you. He'd just lost, what, two assistants in a row? Both quit with no notice. I thought he was coming to make you an assistant. But he took you under his wing and gave you some great shots. You, ever the kind bestie, dragged me with you."

"I didn't drag you anywhere. You earned your spot."

Ariel chimed in. "You know, I mean, I could see it. He did seem awfully concerned for you at the gala."

"Oh my God, you're both delusional. The whole point is, I can't even get caught up in this whole Roone thing. It's fun, and he is so unbelievably sexy. But honestly, it's not going anywhere because he makes me crazy, and it's also way against the rules. I like this job. I *need* this job. I don't know if it's worth the risk."

Ariel met my gaze levelly. "Yeah, but isn't all love really just a giant risk? If Roone's not worth the risk, then who would be?"

She did have a point there.

29

Jessa...

"Do you plan on telling me where we're going?"

"Do you always ask so many questions?"

I fiddled with the blindfold over my eyes then groaned. "If you plan on chopping me up in little bits and pieces, I will have you know that Chloe knows where I am."

He chuckled softly. "I should certainly hope so. I had a little help planning this."

"Ugh. There's a traitor in my midst."

"Okay, okay. Calm down. We're here." He stopped just behind me and planted a kiss behind my ear.

When Roone had told me to dress comfortably and dress for fun, I hadn't known what that meant. I'd donned my petticoat skirt, flat boots, a long-sleeved tee, a hoodie and a jean jacket over that. I had no idea what we were doing, so I'd dressed for London in the fall. All I knew was that we were outside because I could feel the gravel beneath my boots.

Behind me, Roone fumbled with the blindfold and then separated it. When I blinked my eyes open, I immediately shut them again because the lights were so bright. When I blinked then more cautiously opened them, I gasped. "Oh my God, this is Play Town."

He grinned. "Yeah, it is."

I whirled around. "Oh my God! This is Play Town!" I shouted again.

He laughed. "I know. I saw that picture in your flat the day of the break-in. I made some calls. It turned out I know the guy who bought the place and refurbished it. He is planning to eventually turn this into some kind of an adult playground thing. But, in the meantime, welcome to Play Town, your childhood revisited."

I squealed with giddy excitement and wrapped my arms around him, giving him a tight bear hug. "Thank you. Thank you. Thank you. I loved this place when I was a kid." Play Town sat on the outskirts of Slough. My mother had brought me every year. Almost like a rite of passage.

With a quick glance around, he took my hand. "Come on, let's go have some fun."

"Oh my God, we're totally doing the roller coaster first. Oh no, ferris wheel. No, funnel cake."

Roone chuckled. "Maybe we'll save the funnel cake until after we've been on rides?"

"No, funnel cake *before* the ride is part of the adventure. Can you stomach it? Get it?" I asked with glee.

"I think we don't need to risk it."

"Okay, maybe not. Especially if you're chicken."

"Oh, you did not just call me chicken."

"Hey, just calling it how I see it," I giggled. I'm giggling. Who am I? Had I been kidnapped by pod people? "Seriously though. Thank you. This is incredible. I can't believe you thought of this."

"Yeah well, it's a date, and judging from those pictures,

this place meant something to you, something important. I wanted you to enjoy it."

"Roone Ainsley, you are something else. This wasn't even a Meet Cute date."

He shrugged and tucked his head. "Yeah, the app is great, but I figured I could do pretty well on my own." I could see this red hue creeping up his neck. "Come on, let's go get you a funnel cake if you insist."

"I didn't know you had this sweet side to you. Hell, I don't know if anyone has ever been this sweet to me."

"Well, it seems that maybe you've been dating assholes. But we're fixing that now, right?"

"It would seem that way. This is perfect I love it."

We did get funnel cake first. One funnel cake, two forks, and more powdered sugar than could possibly be good for either one of us. As we ate with our fingers and laughed, Roone made me systematically walk the park, picking out which roller coaster I wanted to do first, then second, and third, and which games I wanted to play. By the time we were done with our assessment and our priority order, the funnel cake was long gone and partially digested in our stomachs. So clearly, he did it on purpose. But I hadn't even realized it because I was so happy.

At the first roller coaster, he hesitated even as I skipped into the first row of seating. I waited anxiously. "What's wrong?"

"Is now a good time to tell you that I don't really *love* roller coasters?"

My heart sank. "What? Everyone loves roller coasters. Is it the height?"

"No, not the height. It's just the whole pitching about trying to make your stomach fall out of your mouth thing."

"Oh, come on, it will be fun. I'll hold your hand." I

lowered my voice so that the ride tech couldn't hear me. "I'll hold something else if you want."

Roone skipped in quickly. "Well, why didn't you just say so?"

The safety bars settled over our laps and then the gate was closed. As we lurched forward and started the climb to the first drop, Roone clutched my leg. "I'm not sure this is the best idea I've ever had."

I put my hand over his and grinned. "It's going to be fun."

He leaned over and kissed me, lingering softly over my lips before we fell.

An hour later, we'd ridden all of the roller coasters twice, and then played a couple of the games. Apparently, when it came to the drag racing, Roone was not taking it easy on me. He was in it to win it, and he did win... *twice.*

"You were cheating," I grumbled.

"Don't be salty."

"I'm not being salty. I'm just saying that this is my special date and you're the one who won the giant giraffe."

"If you're nice, I'll let you cuddle with it tonight if it'll make you feel better."

I glowered at him. "No, it does not make me feel better. That giraffe should be *mine.*"

He shrugged. "Next time, win it."

I shook my head and laughed. "You're such a dead man."

"Oi! Love, don't hate the player, hate the game. If you want something bad enough, suck it up and work for it."

I narrowed my eyes. "Oh, I'll show you working for it." I reached for him to give him a pinch, and he quickly evaded my grasp, instead turning me around and kissing into my neck.

"You smell fucking incredible do you know that? I could live right fucking here."

"That can probably be arranged."

"In that case, my job is done. One last ride then we'll call it a night. And if you're nice, I'll even let you name the giraffe."

"Well that's easy. His name is Stretch."

"Stretch?"

"Yeah. I had a toy giraffe when I was a kid. That was his name. It seems like a good name as any."

"But don't you want some other name?"

"Okay, in that case, his name is Stretch Two."

He chuckled low. "Completely rational."

"Always."

He reached for me, kissing me as he swung me around. For one moment I closed my eyes and pretended that I could fall and Roone would catch me. That nothing bad would ever happen to me in my life because *this* man held me tight.

You know better than to put that kind of trust in anyone.

I did know better. But that didn't mean it wasn't fun to pretend. When my eyes fluttered open and I glanced up, I froze in his arms.

"Jessa? What's wrong?"

For what must have only been a second but felt like an eon, I couldn't breathe, I couldn't talk. Instead, I shoved against his shoulder, grabbed the giraffe, then vaulted over the duck shooting booth.

The kid manning the booth's eyes went wide, but I placed a finger over my lips and implored him with my eyes to stay quiet. All the while, I looked for a way out. If I was caught, my life was over.

On the other side of the booth I could just barely see Roone's face. "Jessa what the—"

He was interrupted. "Roone, is that you?"

I knew that voice well. It was the whole reason I was hiding behind the duck shoot. Evan Millston.

"Hey Evan, how's it going, mate?" Roone's voice was perfectly relaxed as if I hadn't just pulled a Houdini.

"Uh, it's fine. What are you doing here?" Suspicion dripped from every word.

Roone stayed calm though. Even though we'd both likely be fired, he stayed cool. "I had a Meet Cute date. I was supposed to meet her here. But so far she hasn't shown."

"That's too bad." Except the way Evan said it, he sounded like he didn't think it was that bad at all.

"And you?"

"Looks like Meet Cute had the same idea. This is Chantal, my date."

A feminine voice said, "Nice to meet you."

Had Evan seen me? How long would I have to hide here? Pleasantries were exchanged, and then Evan excused himself and his date. I stayed hidden for another few minutes before Roone poked his head over. "You're clear to come out now."

I stood slowly, dragging Stretch with me. "Shit. That was so close."

Roone's jaw was set tight, and his gaze was always on the move. "I know. I'm sorry, but it's time to go."

"Yeah. There'd be no way to explain me being here too. Your explanation was shaky enough."

"Yeah well, let's just say I'm not exactly buying his explanation either."

"Why not? What other reason could he have for being here?"

"Don't know, but something's off."

Roone was still the perfect gentleman, but on the walk back to the car, I could see it. The subtle shift in him. The walls had been re-erected. It was probably for the best. If I wanted to keep my job, to keep my roots, I couldn't keep him.

I just had no idea how to break the news to myself.

Roone...

I TRIED FOR LEVITY, but I could tell exactly where her mind was. "Stretch, you're gonna stay with Jessa now. She's gonna let you come see me on weekends."

She didn't even crack a smile as I handed her the giraffe. I'd been shaken seeing Millston too. And since Ariel was behind the dates, I knew he wasn't there because of the app. The real question was how he'd *known* to be there.

"He doesn't know anything, princess."

She swallowed hard. "I'm telling you, he does. I could hear it in his voice. He knows."

I reached for her again. "It'll be all right. I promise. We've been careful."

"Careful. Are you kidding? We were almost caught tonight. I just – I don't know why, but I've been risking every-thing with you, and I shouldn't be."

My stomach fell. "Jessa. Come on. Don't say that, okay? We'll figure this out. If push comes to shove, I'll leave before I let this impact you."

She shook her head. "What? That's nutters. I couldn't let you do that. You're actually good at this. I couldn't let you be fired and me stay. It's not right."

I held on to her tighter and pulled her to me as my heart raced. I wasn't letting her go. I'd just gotten started. Just started to — I wasn't going to let this happen. "Let me figure it out before we do anything drastic. Before anything happens." I wanted to tell her the truth. I wanted to just spill the beans and let the truth hang between us. We could figure it out after that.

She shook her head. "Roone, this was never supposed to

work. I'm pretty sure we knew that. If somehow we haven't both lost our jobs already, we need to stop."

"Princess, we're just getting started. Whatever happens, don't let him do this. I liked you from the moment I saw you. I liked you more when you fought me throwing you over my shoulder. But do you know the real moment I knew I was fighting a losing battle?"

Her lips quirked. "When I stole your keys?"

I shook my head. "Not even close. Although, that was when I vowed to make you weak with orgasms so you couldn't run away."

She rolled her eyes. "Of course."

"No, the moment was when I helped you carry in those boxes. You looked at me, and you were so vulnerable. I could see you. The real you. The one who tries to be strong and is afraid of failing. The moment I saw her, I knew I couldn't stay away. Even when I most certainly should have."

"You can't tell me things like that."

"Why not? It's the truth." Shit, I wasn't above begging. It didn't even bother me that Ariel could likely hear us. I didn't want to let her go.

She shook her head. "I don't know what I was thinking. I let my guard down, just for a second."

"I liked that your guard was down. And this will be okay, I promise. He doesn't know anything. He's just trying to make you spin out and panic. I will take care of this, I swear."

"How do you plan on doing that? I need this job. This job is everything right now. It's all I've ever wanted. For the first time I have roots. I can't just walk away."

"You are better than this job. They honestly wouldn't thrive without you. You know it, and I know it."

"It doesn't matter. What matters is I need the job. I can't throw it away just to break the rules."

Shit. How had our roles become reversed? I was the rule

follower. I liked my rules. Liked that they made sense. Liked everything neat and tidy. Now I was on the verge of begging for complicated. "Look, just give me a couple of days, okay? We'll figure it out. If you still feel the same way, I won't stop you."

She looked like she wanted to argue, but she let me pull her into my arms and hold her tight. It looked like Ariel and I were going to have to deal with Evan after all.

30

Ariel...

"EXCUSE ME? ARE YOU WILLOW JAMES?"

The woman turned in front of me with a smile and a question in her eye.

"I'm Ariel. I wanted to ask you, if it's not too much trouble, about Evan Millston?"

Her eyes shuttered all of a sudden. And then she gathered her things from the tabletop at the café. "I'm not gonna talk about him. If you'll excuse me."

"Willow, I'm sorry. That name probably brings up memories you don't want to talk about. But I think a friend of mine might be in trouble with him, and I'm trying to get the facts so I can help her."

"If your friend is somehow caught up with Evan, tell her to end it publicly and painfully. The one thing he'll hate is a scandal."

"That's good to know. But they're not together. She works for him. He's just... maybe it'd be helpful just understanding what happened to you?"

Willow slung her backpack over her shoulder. "I can't talk to you."

I really hated to do this. The poor girl already looked terrified. "Can't or won't? Did they make you sign some kind of NDA?"

"You don't understand."

I put up my hands. "Look, it's completely off the record. I just need to understand what we're dealing with."

She slowed her walk, stopped, and turned to face me. "Look, I worked for him too. I was his assistant four years ago. I was still in college. I was more an intern really, it's not like they paid me a lot. He was helpful. Real helpful. At first, I was a little creeped out because I thought, 'Oh, that's weird. Why is he so helpful to an intern?' But then I realized that was just how he liked to do things. But before I knew it, he sort of... it felt like he was... he felt proprietary toward me. When I got a boyfriend, things got really bad. He just miraculously turned up where we'd be for dates. I would swear that he was around my flat. I finally quit, got a restraining order, the whole deal. That was four years ago, and now I still sometimes think that I see him."

"Did he ever hurt you?"

Willow shook her head. "No. But working with him was difficult. The moment I got a boyfriend, every question became about 'oh did your boyfriend allow you to do that?' Or 'does your boyfriend want you to eat that?' Or 'does your boyfriend know that you wore that to work today?' The constant digs, the picking, the needing to know who my boyfriend was. All of it was just so stressful. He never hurt me, but..."

"If you know anything, anywhere you can point me in the right direction."

"There were rumors that there had been this other girl,

someone he'd gone to college with. I don't know her name. She left Evan to work with Rick. She left him to *date* Rick."

My brows snapped down. "His partner?"

Willow nodded. "Yeah. It was a huge scandal. I guess in college Evan had dated her, and after school when they started their own company, Rick dated her. I don't know how that worked out with all of them, but I know that the girl was so freaked, she left the country. Got some fancy job in Toronto or something. But she would tell Rick all the time that Evan was just around. He didn't believe her. She filed an order of restraint too."

"Has anyone heard from her since she moved? A postcard, letter, email, or something?"

Willow frowned. "I don't know. Maybe an email or something. If you want I can look around for you."

I breathed a sigh of relief. "Yes." I pulled out my card and handed it to her. "I appreciate you talking to me. I know I shouldn't have ambushed you, and I'm sorry. But I'm very worried about my friend."

"Yeah, I understand. I'd be worried too. Hopefully she's got someone looking out for her?"

I smiled to myself. "Yup. That's basically the plan."

❦

Jessa…

I'D MADE A MISTAKE. A horrible, awful mistake.

I'd completely miscalculated what it would be like to see Roone around the office. Not that I'd been avoiding him. There was nothing to avoid. After all we were just colleagues, work mates, friends, sort of. Whatever. *Also, you shagged him so good, your vagina needs a break.*

Also true.

But locked in an office with him at Ben Covington's office, discussing the restaurant announcement, I could feel the tension between us. I'd had another meeting just prior to Ben's, so I opted to meet him there.

Liar. Okay fine. I hadn't wanted to ride over with him because his stupid soap would make me weak and melty. I was not a weak and melty person. I was strong. I was not going to lose everything I need and want because of some guy.

"The feedback from the team has been positive so far. They're all excited to work with Evans. And just so you know, Ryder has been dealt with. Permanently reassigned."

I blinked at him. I hadn't said a word. Had Roone? Fuck. Another example of him dealing with something I knew how to handle.

"Well we're looking forward to all the milestones. Marketing has been working on packaging and imagery already, so we'll have designs for you to look at in time for the next meeting."

Ben was watching me, but I was off my game today. Distant, distracted. I felt like I was walking through a fog. Ben stood and shook our hands. The guy was huge. No wonder they called him Big Ben. And he was stupidly good looking in that almost-too-pretty kind of way. But I barely notice because all I could focus on was Roone. It was as if he were sucking all the air out of the room and I couldn't breathe.

As soon as hands were shaken and we were released from the meeting, I bolted. I just needed air. I needed to get to a bathroom, splash cold water on my face, and just take a moment to myself.

Blindly, I searched for a bathroom until I finally stumbled upon a receptionist who pointed me to one down at the end of the hall. I was vaguely aware that Roone was somewhere behind me, calling out my name, but I couldn't stop. I shoved open the door intending to close it behind me, but Roone was right there. "Princess, what's wrong?"

"You. You are what's wrong. Before I met you, shit, I was on my game. Game face. Nothing rattled me. I was so good. I could do the work of three on my own. You turned up, and I can't even make it through a client meeting. All I can do is think about you and never touching you again, and it is fucking with me, and it is not fair. And I realized just how stupid it was for me to think I could handle this, that I could handle *you*."

I knew I wasn't making a lot of sense. I was blubbering. Honestly, it was embarrassing. But once I started talking, there was no stopping it.

"I just wasn't supposed to like you. And then I liked you. And then I more than liked you. And it isn't fair because Evan knows, and I need this job. I know you don't think that it's important, but this is *mine*. I fought for this little piece of real estate in the world, and I want to keep it. I promised myself I wouldn't move or run, and now I just can't stay. Every day locked in rooms and offices with you, knowing I can't touch you because it's against the rules. And I broke the rules, so now I might get fired."

Roone's hands were on my shoulders. "Jessa, breathe."

His command shut me up. Which consequently, I also hated. "Don't tell me what to do."

His lips tipped up at the corner. "That's how this works. I tell you what to do, you fight me. I like the fight."

"You realize that's not exactly healthy?"

He shrugged. "No. But pretending that we don't want each other, that's impossible."

"Yeah well, it can't happen."

"Let me be really clear, you and I, Jessa McLean, *are*

happening. It's just a matter of how long you want it to take. I can wait as long as you need me to."

I stared up at him. And my jaw unhinged. "This is crazy."

"Yeah. It is. And there's a whole slew of things I probably need to talk to you about and tell you. But that's all you need to know right now. I'm not going anywhere. So if it takes you a million years to make up your mind, fine. I'll wait. I'll be right here."

"You are the most obstinate, stubborn—"

Roone, of course, impatient as ever, didn't let me finish. His lips brushed over mine, but gently. Then he pulled back. "You were saying? I plan to kiss away any protest you have unless it's the words 'I don't want this.' You tell me you don't want me, and I'll leave you alone, I swear."

"You're a lot of things, but you're not stupid. You know I want you, but this isn't what I planned on. This is really unfair. I'm not ready. I just—"

He kissed me again.

Electric currents ran over my skin.

I gasped and parted my lips as a shudder ran through me. Roone groaned low and dragged me closer. His tongue slid over mine, and I couldn't think. He tasted like something sweet and sinful and dangerous, and I couldn't get enough of him.

When he sucked on my bottom lip, I moaned, meeting his tongue with my own and lazily looping my hands around his neck. I threaded my fingers into his hair, and Roone growled low, his possessive nature coming through.

His thumbs traced over my hipbones, and I shivered. He angled his head and deepened our kiss. Roone kept up the teasing until I panted and breathed out a soft whimper.

With his hands in my curls, he angled my head so he could kiss me deeper and then pressed up against me.

Shit. Could I give this up? This high? This feeling of flying?

It was all I'd ever wanted. To love. To have someone take care of me for once.

But the roots I'd planted, the plan I'd wanted for myself was in jeopardy. But Roone… For once I had a risk I wanted to take. One I wasn't necessarily ready to give up yet.

31

Jessa...

THE COVINGTON MEETING HAD ENDED AT SIX. THEN Evan had called me in to run a favor for him. He had some papers he needed delivered, and Roone had insisted on accompanying me.

I was still keyed up from the kiss he'd given me after the meeting. Like I was walking this lust tightrope and Roone was the net below.

He hadn't so much as held my hand as we walked up the stairs into the block of housing units. But once we turned down our hallway, his fingers gently brushed mine. The hit of electric current was nearly enough to make me moan. Who was I kidding? I wasn't going to be able to stay away.

One more brush of our fingers and Roone dragged me over to his door and fumbled with his key.

Once we were in, he kicked the door shut and we began tearing at each other, my bag forgotten somewhere near the door.

His hands dug in my hair as he angled me for deeper kisses. With each step, pieces of clothing dropped.

We were naked on his couch with me levered over him. He'd tossed his wallet onto the coffee table once he'd slid on a condom. Slowly, he dragged me down over him, his teeth biting into my lip, and I sank down, my eyes going wide as he nudged me open.

Oh, that delicious stretch as I accommodated to fit him. God, he felt so good, his cock sliding in and out of me slowly, which was just what I needed, just what I'd been craving.

With a growl and his hands on my ass, he shifted our position and stared up at me from under his hooded eyes. "Ride me, baby, it's your show."

And I did. Rising over him again and again, I took what I needed. I let go of the fear. Let go of the worry and just felt.

Roone clamped his hands on my hips and held on, digging his fingers into my flesh.

As he drove into me with thrust after thrust, he stared up at my eyes, adoring, full of lust and… something else I couldn't quite place. Unable to take the intimacy, I closed my eyes, wanting to only focus on the feelings, how he touched me, how the desire and need unfurled within me. But Roone had other plans.

With his thumb and forefinger, he took hold of my chin. "Look at me, Jessa."

I stubbornly refused to open my eyes. And he immediately stopped thrusting. I snapped my eyes open. "Roone!"

"I asked you to look at me."

Heat flushed my face. "I can't… it's too much."

He shook his head and started moving inside me again. "No. It's perfect." Pulling me close and levering himself up so we were in a more seated position, he kissed me slow and deep, brooking no argument from me. When he pulled back from the kiss, he resumed the deep thrusts, gently this time, as if we had all the time in the world. "I want you to be well aware of who's inside you. Who's making you feel this. How much you need it. How good it feels."

Pleasure rode my spine, urging me to go faster, and I rocked against him. "Oh my God."

Roone pumped inside me again. "I'm glad you know." Capturing my nipple, he pinched gently, and my inner walls quickened.

He repeated the motion. Harder this time. I groaned as bliss chased the initial sting of pain.

"You like that?" His piercing green gaze settled on me.

I nodded. "Y-yes."

He repeated it, and I tossed my head back. "Roone, please. I need—"

With his other hand, he reached between us and stroked my clit.

"Roone!" To allow him better access, I braced my arms behind me on his knees as I enjoyed his deft thumb and his hard strokes.

My orgasm crashed into me so fast I lost my balance on his knees and fell back. Shocks rippled through my body, and I groaned.

With a muffled curse, Roone grabbed my hips and held tight as he increased his pace. With three more thrusts, he jerked and threw his body back. Inside me, his dick twitched, and I knew he was coming.

Unable to move on my own, I allowed him to pull me close. He kissed my temple and my forehead and my cheeks before settling the throw blanket around us. I made to get up, and he stilled me.

"No. Not yet. I want to hold you for a minute."

As sleep snuck in like a thief on my consciousness, I prayed I would never have to leave his arms.

✤✤

Jessa...

I WAS FALLING FOR HIM.

There was no point in hiding it, at least not from myself. But that meant I had some decisions to make. From the time we moved back to London, my whole life had been focused on my father and keeping him as well as I could. I'd taken care of him, making sure I could afford to pay for his care. When he was gone, I focused on my job. My life. What I had built for myself. But I hadn't really focused on me properly. I'd gone through the motions, but I hadn't actually lived. I hadn't actually moved forward. I was in a holding pattern.

The same kind of holding pattern I'd been in my whole life. Not really here, nor there. My whole life was just blank slate of not really living. And despite his best intentions about my safety, I'm sure this was not what my father would have wanted for me. I know it certainly wasn't what my mother had wanted.

So, I was doing this thing. This thing that was going to cost me everything. The roots I had worked so hard to plant would all go up in smoke if anyone found out.

But Roone, the way he held me, the way he made me feel, had convinced me it was worth the risk. That skin-tingling, bone-melting, irritating fire was under my skin. Whether I wanted to fight with him or kiss him, at least I was feeling.

Real feelings.

I'd spent the weekend making love to him. It had been insane. For the last week, at work, we were perfectly professional. Even the sniping had died down. Although, I told him we had to pick that back up so that neither Evan or Rick would notice. Chloe though... Every time we pretended to snipe at each other, she just gave me a sly wink.

After the gala, the Evans had hired security. Just someone who would walk me out to my car and make sure I didn't go anywhere alone. I didn't go to the parking garage on my own. Since Roone was with me most of the time because we have the same clients, being alone wasn't really a concern the rest of the time, but it was awkward.

I didn't honestly know how long I could go on pretending. Because as time went on, it was about the little things. I wanted to hold his hand. I wanted to walk around with him in public just being us. I wanted to do tourist things like eat at cafés and stroll around the Victoria and Albert Museum. I just wanted to be free. *With him.*

It was after work hours when Roone came into my office. "Want to try to get out of here?"

"Yeah, but I'm waiting on a call from James. He said he had an address and phone number for that Phillip Winchester guy."

His brows lifted. "Well that's good. I'll stay with you. We can talk about the proposal for London Lords. I have some ideas for budget cutting that could still be beneficial just by using a different vendor. There was this bloke—"

My phone buzzed, and I held up a finger. "Sorry. It's from James."

"What's it say?"

I stared at my phone. "I have a phone number and an address."

"Why don't you look happy about it?"

"I don't know. It was one thing to ask James about the sketches, you know? It's another thing entirely to call up an old friend of my dad's and say, 'Oh hey, do you think anyone would have seen these tattoos before.' I don't know, somehow drawing another person into the conspiracy theory makes it feel like this is real. That all of a sudden, it's not tidy or neat. Honestly, I've never been a tidy, neat person. I'm a little bit messy. I'm kind of a hot head, but I get things done. But now, I'm..." My voice trailed.

Roone's voice was soft. "Scared?"

"Yeah, terrified."

"Well, I'm here. So you call him. What's the worst he could say? 'I don't know anything about these tattoos. Great sketches though?'"

"Yeah, I guess you have a point."

He waited patiently. Anyone walking by would think that we were just having a meeting. He was relaxed, sort of reclined in his seat. I was hunched over my desk, grabbing on to my cell phone.

"Come on, it's 5:30. Make the call, and we'll get something to eat. We'll order in. Feel like a curry?"

My stomach grumbled. "Oh my God, I would love a curry."

"Great. You make the call, and I will order online. By the time we make it back to our flats, we'll have dinner. Actually, know what? We'll pick it up on the way."

I couldn't help but smile. I lowered my voice in case anyone could hear us. The door was still open, so I had to be careful. "I don't know why but I get the warm squishes thinking about us ordering take out."

He winked at me. "Wait until I tell you that there's going to be dessert too."

I giggled. "Be still my heart." His smile was lazy. And the way he looked at me made my stomach flip and dance. "What?"

He shook his head. "Nothing. You do that. I'll do this."

I picked up the phone and dialed the number.

Someone picked up on the first ring. "Hello?"

"Hello, I'm looking for Phillip Winchester."

"Yeah, this is him."

I said, "Hi, my name is Jessa McLean I believe you knew my father, Andrew McLean, and his wife, Elisa."

"Oh my God, Jessa! It's been years."

"Yeah. I suppose maybe when you saw me last I was quite small."

"Yes, indeed you were. Maybe eight, nine?"

"Listen, I'm not sure if you knew, but dad, he passed away last year."

"Yeah, I heard. But by the time I found out, the funeral had already passed."

"Oh no, that's not why I'm calling. I picked up some of his things from Hope House, and there were some sketches he'd done. I thought maybe you could take a look at them and tell me if you recognize anything or anyone in them."

"Oh, sketches you say?"

"Yeah. You know dad, forever drawing. It won't take long. I can meet you somewhere. Perhaps a coffee shop? It should only take ten minutes of your time."

"Yes, of course, I would absolutely love to meet."

"You would?"

"Of course. How about tomorrow evening, happy hour. I teach at the university at King's Cross. There's a café close by. When you pass the train station, make a left. Tea and Vine, I think it's called."

"Yes." I scribbled it down so I wouldn't forget. "I can absolutely do that. That's fantastic. Thank you so much."

"Sure thing. I look forward to seeing you again, Jessa. I wonder if you turned out looking like your mother."

I smiled softly. "I hope so. People used to tell me that all the time. But not a lot of people who knew her are around now."

"Well, I'm sure you do. I look forward to seeing you." Then he hung up.

Roone lifted his eyebrows expectantly. "Well?"

"I'm meeting Phillip Winchester tomorrow. Hopefully, he can tell me something useful."

Roone nodded. "Yup. See? We'll get to the bottom of this."

I grinned. "You're still saying we."

"Yeah," he looked around and made sure no one could overhear us. "Because like we discussed, you're stuck with me."

I laughed and stood. "Wait. We have a meeting with vendors tomorrow. You and Chloe will have to take it."

He frowned but nodded. "Okay. Consider it done. But I want all the news when you finish."

"Deal." For the first time, maybe in my whole life, I was looking forward to going home. Because I knew that home would involve conversation with someone about our days and what we loved, and things that made us happy. There was nothing to regret, or fear, or miss at home. I could happily be there because of him. "Okay, I will head out first. I'll meet you at the tube station, and we'll walk together."

He shook his head. "You know what? We can walk out together."

"Are you insane? I'm pretty sure the Evans are still here somewhere."

"Yeah, no shit. But you know what? Doesn't matter. Still safer for you to have someone with you, so we can just be two mates heading off for a curry."

I chewed my lip. "Yeah, okay." I hated to say it, but I was so afraid, though there was no way I was admitting that out loud. Tonight would be for fun things. The things I'd always longed for in my life and finally had. Everything was going exactly how I'd always dreamed and for once, I was going to enjoy it.

Jessa...

LATER THAT NIGHT, a knock at the door aroused me from my sleep haze. I'd fallen asleep during the superhero movie. Roone had fed me well, then he'd licked me until I'd been too exhausted to scream. And then he'd held me as we watched some telly.

I was getting way too attached to him. *No such thing. Now shut up and enjoy.* Roone just tightened an arm around me and tried to keep me tucked against him on the couch.

"Roone, let me go. That might be Chloe with work."

"No, just stay here," he muttered. He lifted his arm and helped me up off the couch. Sometime after making love, we'd thrown on shorts and T-shirts to start our bad-TV binge.

I knew there were a slew of conversations coming. Things we had to iron out. I was enjoying the hell out of myself for the moment, but soon, there would be much talking.

When I looked through the peephole, I was surprised to find someone I recognized. Detective Inspector Spencer. He'd been the one to speak to me after my father died.

"DI Spencer?" I said as I dragged the door open. "What can I do for you?"

His eyes were grave. "May I come in?"

The color leached from my body. Something was wrong. The way he was looking around told me something was *very* wrong.

"What's wrong?"

He frowned and pulled out a small notebook. "I wish I could say this was a social call or even that it was about your father's death. But Jessa, I have to ask, has anything unusual happened the last few days?"

My gaze darted straight to Roone. He came over at that point and nodded at DI Spencer. "You don't have to answer that," Roone said.

"I have nothing to hide."

DI Spencer's brows furrowed. "Why would you have something to hide?"

Roone shook his head. "Jessa."

DI Spencer glared at Roone. "Well, strictly speaking, I would suggest you wait until your solicitor gets here."

What the hell was going on? "Solicitor? What do I need a solicitor for?"

His gaze met mine directly. "I hate to break it to you, but Toby Adamson is dead."

Gray flecks of snow flipped over my consciousness. That was all that registered. "What?"

DI Spencer nodded. "The reason I'm here is that there's some evidence at his house that suggested maybe you'd been there, or that he'd been here and removed it from your flat."

Did I hear that correctly? "What? I've never been to Toby's flat."

DI Spencer reached into his pocket and pulled out a small plastic baggy. Inside was a delicate chain with a rose pendant on it.

"I've been looking for that. It was my mother's. It was stolen when my flat was broken into weeks ago."

Roone gripped my shoulder. "Jessa. Stop talking."

DI Spencer slid him a glance. "He's right. You *should* stop talking. This is just a friendly conversation. I saw reports at the station of a couple of incidents you were involved in during the past few weeks, and I'm inclined to think that the break-in here and the mugging at the gala was him. Sometimes people become fixated."

I thought about the hang-up calls I'd been receiving of late, but that made no sense. Why call me and get my guard up if he was planning just to mug me later? "What? Toby? No. Also I was on the phone with him when someone tried to mug me."

"I know it's hard to imagine, and sometimes it's impossible to see because there's whole parts of the story that don't line up. and we need to piece them together. It's also not unheard of for people to use recordings in those type of kidnap situations."

"But—he was a kid." No way was he the one scaring me.

Roone wrapped an arm around my shoulder. "Can we ask, when did he die?"

"Last night around eleven p.m. Stabbed."

Who in the world would want that kid dead? Suddenly my hairbrained theory that my father wasn't as sick as I thought was on the rocks. But still, I couldn't figure out the why of it. It made no sense.

I couldn't find the words, so Roone spoke for me. "Thank you for notifying us, DI Spencer."

"Of course. Miss McLean, if you can think of why anyone might want him dead, you call me, yeah?"

I nodded, too numb to speak.

When DI Spencer was gone, Roone pulled me close. "This is going to be okay. You're okay."

I nuzzled in. "I know what he said. I don't believe him. There's no way Toby came after me."

"I know. It seems unlikely, but we'll investigate *tomorrow*. For now, let's get to bed so I can hold you."

I knew I should be strong and start making calls to see if Evans PR could help Toby's family in some way, but I couldn't bring myself to do it. Just for the night, I was going to accept comfort.

I could fix this in the morning.

32

Jessa…

As I rode the tube, I smiled down at my phone. Roone was sending me inappropriate messages. I knew what he was doing. He was trying to keep my mind off of Toby. And all things considered, he was doing a pretty good job of it. The first thing I'd done when I woke up was find out where the services would be and arrange for flowers.

Before I'd left for this meeting, Roone had fed me and done everything he could to keep my mind off of it. And bless him, he was still trying.

Roone: *Show me your tits.*

Jessa: *No. I'm on the train.*

Roone: *Go on… just stick the phone under your blouse and take a picture.*

Jessa: *You're impossible.*

Roone: *I'm pretty sure that's why you love me.*

Oh shit. Did he know? *No, you daft cow, he's just being facetious. It's like 'love ya, not serious.' He doesn't know you're falling for him.*

Should I address it? *NO!*

Jessa: *No, pretty sure it's your big cock.*

I was a chicken shit. But I wasn't ready to examine any of the feelings I'd been having. I was going to enjoy him and pray that no one from work found out. Oh, and I should also try and figure out how to get around the little no-fraternization rule.

God this should be easier.

Why couldn't I ever do anything simple like fall in love with a nice normal bloke? Why, oh why, did everything have to be so complicated?

Roone: *Okay that's good. I can work with that. I'll just keep you so high on orgasms you have no choice but to fall in love with me.*

Like an idiot, I grinned. Like every stupid girl before me smiling because some man wants me to fall in love with him by way of giving lots of orgasms.

Jessa: *Ah, I'm onto your nefarious plan.*

Roone: *You will have no choice.*

Jessa: *I probably never did.*

I turned off my phone then. I didn't want to be distracted. If Phillip was taking the time out to meet with me, I couldn't be cheesing off because Roone was asking me to show him my tits. I also couldn't be urgently looking around because I was considering it.

I walked up the stairs into the station and followed the directions he'd given me. When I found the café, I popped my head in, looked around, and found an empty table by the corner. An older gentleman, probably mid-50s, came up to me. "Jessa? My goodness, you do look just like your mother."

I blushed and touched my cheek. "I'm not sure why, but that makes me really happy."

He smiled. "Well, it's a compliment." He opened his arms wide. I felt a little odd about stepping into them, but when I did, I felt safe. Like I'd done this before. I might not remember him, but there was something extremely familiar about him, like he was someone I could trust.

"God, it's been a long time. Have a seat."

I took my seat again, and he joined me.

"Again, I'm so sorry about your father."

"Thank you. It was difficult, but maybe he's at peace now or something. I don't know."

"He loved you very much. I may not have seen him much in the last decade or so, but that much I know. He did come to see me, about two years ago. But I didn't see him again after that."

I frowned. "He came to see you? James didn't mention that he'd come to the city."

"I think maybe he'd been here to visit you. I don't know. He was lucid, so that was good."

"I have absolutely no recollection of that visit. I mean obviously, he was my dad, so he'd come to see me plenty. But I was always closely monitoring him. You know, just waiting…"

Phillip nodded. "For the other shoe to drop. For the delusions to reappear out of nowhere. And it wasn't really even out of nowhere, because you know it's always there. It was a constant. But just when you get comfortable and complacent, you're reminded?"

"Yeah, I guess you knew him well."

Phillip nodded. "Yeah. But despite his illness, I loved him. And it hurt to see him like that."

"Yeah, I know." I didn't want to go down the road of how sad we all were because then I would start crying in the middle of a public place, and I really wasn't down for that. "Oh, so let me get out my phone and show you the sketches."

"Yeah, I'm curious as to what you think I can help with."

"Well, I don't know. I don't even know if I'm chasing a ghost or people who aren't real. In some ways, I feel as crazy as he was. Like why am I even bothering? But I have to know, you understand?"

"Sure. And I honestly wouldn't worry."

"Is it that apparent on my face?"

He nodded. "Yeah, you're not him Jessa, and I'm—"

I shook my head rapidly. I pulled up the file and showed him the phone. "It's not really that much of a worry."

He frowned. "I feel like there's something I need to tell you."

I shook my head. "No, if you could just look at these." I knew I was being irrational, but I didn't want to talk about it, and I didn't want to hear his platitudes.

He leaned forward and took my phone. He frowned as he saw the tattoos in the sketches. "These men don't look familiar to you?"

I shook my head. "I've never seen them before. But you know how it was with dad. These three people worked at the grocery store. This is the mailman, but the tattoo stays constant. Apparently, he sketched it for years. There were so many of it. Different faces, obviously, but this group are the only ones that had it tattooed on their arms. Like they were real people with these tattoos, you know?"

He nodded.

"I'm sorry, their faces are unfamiliar. But there is something I do need to tell you."

He opened up his jacket and pulled out a folder.

"What's that?"

"I really wish I wasn't the person who has to do this. When I saw your father two years ago, he asked me to keep these things for you. Obviously, I was well aware of his illness. But I've also known your father a long time. I knew your mother. There was a time when they had trouble."

I frowned. "What? What are you talking about?" My

stomach started to curl in on itself, making a tight knot. One I was afraid I wouldn't be able to unfurl any time soon.

"I don't know exactly what happened. But I know they had a rough patch, even before Elisa got pregnant with you. A few of us thought they might split, but they didn't. And you, you were the light of your father's eyes. He adored you to no end."

I smiled blissfully. My eyes were stinging a little as I thought of him, and then I rapidly blinked to stop the water from filling them. "I loved him, and there were times that I hated him. And now, obviously, I feel guilty for hating him."

"All that is natural. After your mother died, any balance and influence she'd had in his life was gone. And his illness probably would've been far less severe if events hadn't unfolded the way they did. He probably would've been completely manageable with the right medication. I'm a psychology professor, not a psychiatrist, but I think the way everything happened just sent him to this place that we could never pull him back from."

"I don't understand."

He nodded. "I realize that you don't. And I wish I didn't have to be the one to tell you. But he trusted me with this, so now I'm giving it to you."

I took the folder and opened it. There was a photo of a man inside who looked vaguely familiar. Like I *should* know him, but I didn't. "Who is this? I feel like I've seen him before."

Phillip rolled his shoulders. "Jessa, your father… Yes, he was ill, but perhaps not as ill as you've been led to believe."

I glared at him. "What do you mean?"

"His obsession that someone was going to take you away from him… It was rooted in fact."

I sat there and stared. I said nothing, just waited for him to speak because he was saying the truth that I'd suspected the last several weeks. Since the break-in. That little seed of doubt that maybe my father hadn't been completely out of it. That maybe there was truth to what he was saying all along. Then the mugging happened, and it had seemed like I should've been listening to him my whole life.

Phillip continued. "Your mother met someone when they were having problems."

That knot in my gut tightened, and I could feel bile churning in my stomach.

"I don't know the specifics, but I know that she was planning to leave your father. She was in love, but something happened, and maybe things with your father improved. But once she found out she was having you, she cut it off with the other man. She chose to be with your father because she wanted that life and she loved him.

"There was always a part of him that suspected you might not be his. But he didn't know for certain until you were fifteen."

I was going to throw up. "The kidney transplant?"

Phillip nodded. "Yes. They wanted blood that was a match on hand."

"I was young. I insisted that I wanted to donate something. I knew I was too young to donate a kidney, but they wouldn't even take my blood. They said I was too young. I had to be sixteen."

"Yeah. Since you were close to sixteen you were tested. But the blood type wasn't a match. Which can happen."

"But they found a match for him. He was fine after that."

Phillip nodded. "Yes, he was. But, as you were a minor, he had access to your medical records. You not being a match made him curious. That was how he discovered that you weren't his biological child."

"No. He is my father."

Phillip's voice went soft. "Yes, he was in all the ways that matter."

"He never said anything."

"I think a part of him had always known. But he protected you all the same. You were his child in his heart, but not biologically."

Tears streamed down my face. How had everything become like this? Who was I? "Oh my God."

Phillip placed his hand over mine. "I know this is a shock. I'm so sorry. I begged him to tell you himself. And he said he would. But he told me on the off chance that he didn't get to, that he needed me to do it, and I hated that he put me in that position. Honestly, it is what caused the rift between us and why I hadn't seen him in so long. He refused to tell you that he'd adopted you and that he wasn't your father."

"Oh my God. I can't do this."

Phillip gripped my hand harder. "I'm so sorry, but you need to hear the rest. What I didn't know until later, until I saw him, is that before you were born, some men tried to take your mother. Take her somewhere safe they said. Away from him. She tried to convince him that it was a misunderstanding, a mugging gone wrong. But he'd always suspected that something was off with that scenario. And then more men came when he was in the hospital. It seemed your birth father, or people connected to him, wanted to take you away under the guise of protecting you."

Oh God, I was gonna be ill. My stomach roiled and bubbled. I inhaled deeply, long, deep breaths, trying to still everything in my body. "How could he not tell me?"

"I don't know. But the men, the ones who came for you, all but one of them had this tattoo."

Bile rose in my throat. "Did he know who my real father was?"

Phillip frowned. "He was your *real* father. He took care of you and kept you safe as long as he could."

I swallowed hard. "My birth father. Who was he?"

He pointed at the file. "This first picture. This man. That is King Cassius Winston of the Winston Isles. He was your father. He died two years ago, maybe three. I don't know the timeline." He set the picture aside. "This is his son, Sebastian. He's king now. He had another son out of wedlock. It came out last year that he was the lost prince. He's since been coronated. Lucas Winston. There have been rumors that there is a lost princess. That's you."

My breathing became shallow. My heart boomed against my ribs even as the pace increased, threatening to crack every rib that I had. Oh God, I could feel the sweat seeping from my pores as my mind tried to process what was completely unfathomable.

Oh God. Oh God. I kept hearing the words *princess* and *king* and *taking* and *father*, and none of it made sense. None of the pieces fit together. Phillip was still talking, but I was staring at the photos. At the man who was supposed to have been my father and the men who were my brothers.

But more importantly, I was staring at the second photo he'd shown me. The one with the new king. Next to him was a face I knew well. A body I had spent hours exploring. A smile I had fallen in love with.

Oh God, I wasn't going make it out of the café without vomiting. I stood, shoving the chair back with a loud clatter. Tripping over my feet, I launched myself at the nearest garbage pail, and up came breakfast. The breakfast the man in the photo had cooked for me. Roone. He'd been sent by these people. I'd been busy falling in love and he'd been… well, I didn't know what he'd been doing.

He's been lying. That's what he's been doing.

As my stomach emptied and my brain clouded, the dark

gray on the edges of my vision crowded in around me until I couldn't see. All I felt were strong arms around me and a low voice crooning, "You'll be okay. Just have a seat you'll be okay."

And then everything went black.

Roone...

THE KNOCK on my back door was unexpected. I knew Ariel was off tonight. I assumed she'd still be in Sussex trying to talk to Evan's ex. We'd had the auxiliary team on Jessa all day. They'd been reporting back to me every ten minutes since she'd met with Winchester.

My last update was thirty minutes ago. So where the fuck were they?

I anchored the door open. "You're back already?"

She nodded. "Yeah. And we have problems."

"Tell me about it. We have real problems. The kid from the first night, the one that worked for Jessa? He's dead."

Ariel's face crumbled. "Fuck a duck. How?"

"Murdered. The Detective Inspector wasn't giving any clues as to how, but there was evidence pointing at him stalking the princess." I handed her a beer.

Ariel shook her head. "No thanks. And that makes no sense. He was clean. Dumb, but clean."

"I know. It *has* to be Evan. My money says he's been watching her place just as closely as we have. He suspects something is up with me, but it doesn't make sense that he'd off the kid."

Ariel paced as she ran her hands through her hair. "After what I learned, anything is possible." She stopped and checked her phone. "Wait, when was the last team update? By my check, I haven't had one in thirty minutes."

"You'd be right about that. I was just about to call in. First tell me what you found."

Ariel visibly sagged at the question. "I met with Willow. She's this little slip of a girl. Terrified to talk to anyone. She did tell me what we suspected. Millston is unstable."

"Fuck. We need to pull her out of that situation."

"I know. The stuff she told me was insidious and diabolical. He systematically makes women depend on him, then cuts them off from people who would care about them. Full of rage. He's everywhere, from the gym to the... just everywhere. We have to get her out of here. I'm worried about her. If he's on to us, then he'll know she talked to me."

Fuck. "We need to cover her too."

Ariel ran her hands through her hair. "Jessa's our priority. I'll see if we can do some rotating shifts, but we're short-handed."

I sighed. "We're at the point we need to tell Jessa the truth. We're not serving her well, and her life is spiraling. To give her maximum coverage, she needs to know. Even you have to see that now."

"I agree, which is why I made a call home."

I lifted my brows. "What do you mean you 'made a call home?'"

"Look, we've tried this the hard way. Undercover, surveillance, it's not working. And given how you feel about her, you're working yourself overtime trying to keep her safe, which I completely understand."

"So, you're reprimanding me? You were the one who said I should let go and feel things."

She rolled her eyes. " I think it's great you feel something. I think it's amazing that you have Jessa. I'm happy for you. But trying to protect her while killing yourself and doing extra shifts, not sleeping, it's not good or healthy. So, I got you permission to do the one thing you've been trying to do since we got here."

I perked up. "We can disclose?"

"Yeah. Sebastian's approved it. You can tell her."

Relief flooded my veins. "Are you fucking serious right now?"

"Yeah, I'm fucking serious."

"Jesus fucking Christ, I could kiss you."

She wrinkled her nose. "Why don't you save the kisses for the one who wants them. Just remember, she might not be so enthused about the truth, so be ready for her to try to run. In the meantime, let me get out of here. I want to make sure we have a proper tail on Evan. I don't trust him or what he might do. I need you to watch your six, okay?"

"Of course." I walked her to the door. "I don't even know what to say. Thank you hardly seems appropriate."

"Thank you is *always* appropriate. Especially when I'm awesome."

I chuckled low. "You just changed everything."

"Oh shit, are you gonna get all sappy on me? I think I preferred you when you were on team conceal don't feel."

"Yeah well, my boss insisted I express my emotions."

Ariel laughed, "You should fire your boss."

"I tried to several times, but she keeps sticking."

She flipped me off as she let herself out.

33

Jessa…

MY HANDS WERE STILL SHAKING. NOT ONLY HAD I realized my whole life was a lie, I'd also fainted in public. Only for a moment, but long enough for me to embarrass myself and have a medic called.

The consensus was that I was fine, but I needed rest. As if I was ever going to rest now. After Toby, then the news about my father, I needed a week in bed.

But you aren't getting a week. You know what has to happen now.

I did know, but it didn't mean I was ready. It was like I was walking through numb grayness. How could I have been so wrong? How did I miss everything?

You can worry about that later. Right now, it's time to go.

I moved my bookshelf with some effort and shoved it out of the way. Sweat started to pop on my brow from the exertion.

And then I found the panel my father and I had drywalled over. At the time, I'd thought I was giving in to his delusions.

But he insisted he would put the hole in the wall himself if I didn't.

I'd listened.

It was slightly uneven, but it hadn't mattered at the time. Thanks to the mismatched paint, I found the right angle, placed my elbow, and struck. Pain radiated up my arm, and I cried out.

Shit. Shit, shit, shit. That really hurt. "Jesus Christ."

I held my wounded arm, but as the feeling began to return, I reached into the wall cavity and pulled out a bag.

I'd always told my father he was completely nutters. Who in their right mind kept a go bag? Why had he insisted I'd need one someday? But now, I was glad I'd indulged him.

He'd been well prepared. Inside, I had cash, passports, a couple of changes of clothes, and weapons. Then a knock at the door made me freeze.

Shit. Who was that? I didn't want to take the chance it was Evan or DI Spencer. Or worst of all, Roone. Now forever to be known as Lying Shitface.

I grabbed my duffle and ran into the bedroom to change. Quickly I pulled on a pair of jeans, a long-sleeved T-shirt, and a hoodie. I grabbed my denim jacket and slipped my feet into running shoes. I was really doing this. I was running. Just like my father. Just like all those years of midnight wake-ups followed by hushed whispers of, "Time to go baby. Time to move."

All this time establishing who I was, letting my roots grow, and I was throwing that way.

It was never yours to begin with.

Maybe it didn't have to be permanent. But I did need to buy myself some time. Time to come up with a plan. Where the hell was I going to go? Who was I going to for help?

Think this through. You are smart. Safety first, then thinking time. Right. First thing, I needed to get away from Roone. I wasn't safe with him. The same people my father had run from, he knew. So that meant getting out of my flat.

I heard more insistent banging at the door. Shit. My unit didn't have a back door, so it was either out the window or I had to wait out whoever was banging on the other side of the door.

Turned out they didn't feel like waiting.

The door handle rattled.

I reached into my bag. There were guns and ammo. My father had been deadly serious.

It doesn't matter now, because you're going to have to show what you're made of.

Eventually the door finally gave in.

"Jessa, you're here. Are you okay?"

Roone.

I glared at him.

"Are you okay? There's something I need to tell you. I—" He stopped abruptly when his gaze darted to the wall. "What happened?"

I didn't answer him. I was too busy doing the calculations on if I could get past him.

He approached slowly. "I need to tell you something. It's been—"

I raised my weapon. "No. If you don't mind, I'm not listening to you anymore."

His hands went up. "Fuck. Jessa."

"No. If you're going to open your mouth and tell me how much you care about me, how you're falling for me, how all you want to do is keep me safe, then I can do without the lies."

"Those aren't lies. Look, I haven't been entirely honest but I just—"

"Sorry, you're out of time."

"Princess…"

"Goodbye, Roone," was the whisper on my lips as I pulled the trigger.

To Be Continued in Teasing the Princess…

⚜

Thank you for reading ROYAL TEASE, book 1 in the Royals United Duet! Find out what happens to Roone in the epic conclusion and see who's behind the conspiracy.

She's gone. Someone took her from him. He knew he wasn't supposed to fall in love. But he did it anyway. And now it might have cost his princess - the princess - her life.

Order Teasing the Princess now so you don't miss it!

Read the STUNNING EDGE of your SEAT romance, that Sierra Simone calls, "…A delicious story of **secrets and revenge.**"

*It began with **betrayal.***
*And ended in **murder.***

She was never supposed to cross my path.
*She was never supposed to know about the **Currency of Secrets** or the **Oaths of Blood.***

My so-called brothers killed my friend. *I intend to make them pay. And before it's over, I'll bend all the rules of morality, decency and legality. I will borrow and steal to set the scales right.*

My name is Ben Covington and I know my sins.

Read BIG BEN now!

"...*a dramatic, suspenseful and amazing read* that you just can't put down. I loved it!"
—————**Goodreads Reviewer**

Meet a cocky, billionaire prince that goes undercover in **Cheeky Royal** He's a prince with a secret to protect. The last distraction he can afford is his gorgeous as sin new neighbor. His secrets could get them killed, but still, he can't stay away...

Read Cheeky Royal for FREE now!

Turn the page for an excerpt from Cheeky Royal...

UPCOMING BOOKS

East End
East Bound
Fall of East

ALSO FROM NANA MALONE

CHEEKY ROYAL

"You make a really good model. I'm sure dozens of artists have volunteered to paint you before."
He shook his head. "Not that I can recall. Why? Are you offering?"

I grinned. "I usually do nudes." Why did I say that? It wasn't true. Because you're hoping he'll volunteer as tribute.

He shrugged then reached behind his back and pulled his shirt up, tugged it free, and tossed it aside. "How is this for nude?"

Fuck. Me. I stared for a moment, mouth open and looking like an idiot. Then, well, I snapped a picture. Okay fine, I snapped several. "Uh, that's a start."

He ran a hand through his hair and tussled it, so I snapped several of that. These were romance-cover gold. Getting into it, he started posing for me, making silly faces. I got closer to him, snapping more close-ups of his face. That incredible face.

Then suddenly he went deadly serious again, the intensity in his eyes going harder somehow, sharper. Like a razor. "You look nervous. I thought you said you were used to nudes."

I swallowed around the lump in my throat. "Yeah, at school whenever we had a model, they were always nude. I got used to it."

He narrowed his gaze. "Are you sure about that?"
Shit. He could tell. "Yeah, I am. It's just a human form. Male. Female. No big deal."

His lopsided grin flashed, and my stomach flipped. Stupid traitorous body...and damn him for being so damn good looking. I tried to keep the lens centered on his face, but I had to get several of his abs, for you know...research.
But when his hand rubbed over his stomach and then slid to the button on his jeans, I gasped, "What are you doing?"
"Well, you said you were used doing nudes. Will that make you more comfortable as a photographer?"

I swallowed again, unable to answer, wanting to know what he was doing, how far he would go. And how far would I go?

The button popped, and I swallowed the sawdust in my mouth. I snapped a picture of his hands.

Well yeah, and his abs. So sue me. He popped another button, giving me a hint of the forbidden thing I couldn't have. I kept snapping away. We were locked in this odd, intimate game of chicken. I swung the lens up to capture his face. His gaze was slightly hooded. His lips parted...turned on. I stepped back a step to capture all of him. His jeans loose, his feet bare. Sitting on the stool, leaning back slightly and giving me the sex face, because that's what it was—God's honest truth—the sex face. And I was a total goner.

"You're not taking pictures, Len." His voice was barely above a whisper.

"Oh, sorry." I snapped several in succession. Full body shots, face shots, torso shots. There were several torso shots. I wanted to fully capture what was happening.
He unbuttoned another button, taunting me, tantalizing me. Then he reached into his jeans, and my gaze snapped to meet his. I wanted to say something. Intervene in some way…help maybe… ask him what he was doing. But I couldn't. We were locked in a game that I couldn't break free from. Now I wanted more. I wanted to know just how far he would go.

Would he go nude? Or would he stay in this half-undressed state, teasing me, tempting me to do the thing that I shouldn't do?

I snapped more photos, but this time I was close. I was looking down on him with the camera, angling so I could see his perfectly sculpted abs as they flexed. His hand was inside his jeans. From the bulge, I knew he was touching himself. And then I snapped my gaze up to his face.
Sebastian licked his lip, and I captured the moment that tongue met flesh.

Heat flooded my body, and I pressed my thighs together to abate the ache. At that point, I was just snapping photos, completely in the zone, wanting to see what he might do next.

"Len…"

"Sebastian." My voice was so breathy I could barely get it past my lips.

"Do you want to come closer?"

"I--I think maybe I'm close enough?"

His teeth grazed his bottom lip. "Are you sure about that? I have another question for you."

I snapped several more images, ranging from face shots to shoulders, to torso. Yeah, I also went back to the hand-around-his-dick thing because…wow. "Yeah? Go ahead."

"Why didn't you tell me about your boyfriend 'til now?"

Oh shit. "I—I'm not sure. I didn't think it mattered. It sort of feels like we're supposed to be friends." Lies all lies.

He stood, his big body crowding me. "Yeah, friends…"

I swallowed hard. I couldn't bloody think with him so close. His scent assaulted me, sandalwood and something that was pure Sebastian wrapped around me, making me weak. Making me tingle as I inhaled his scent. Heat throbbed between my thighs, even as my knees went weak. "Sebastian, wh—what are you doing?"

"

Proving to you that we're not friends. Will you let me?"

He was asking my permission. I knew what I wanted to say. I understood what was at stake. But then he raised his hand and traced his knuckles over my cheek, and a whimper escaped.

His voice went softer, so low when he spoke, his words were more like a rumble than anything intelligible. "Is that you telling me to stop?"

Seriously, there were supposed to be words. There were. But somehow I couldn't manage them, so like an idiot I shook my head.

His hand slid into my curls as he gently angled my head. When he leaned down, his lips a whisper from mine, he whispered, "This is all I've been thinking about."

Read Cheeky Royal for FREE now!

NANA MALONE READING LIST

Looking for a few Good Books? Look no Further

FREE
Shameless
Before Sin
Cheeky Royal
Protecting the Heiress

Royals
Royals Undercover

Cheeky Royal
Cheeky King

Royals Undone
Royal Bastard
Bastard Prince

Royals United
Royal Tease

Teasing the Princess

Royal Elite

The Heiress Duet
Protecting the Heiress
Tempting the Heiress

The Prince Duet
Return of the Prince
To Love a Prince

The Bodyguard Duet
Billionaire to the Bodyguard
The Billionaire's Secret

London Royals

London Royal Duet
London Royal
London Soul

Playboy Royal Duet
Royal Playboy
Playboy's Heart

London Lords
See No Evil
Big Ben
The Benefactor
For Her Benefit

Hear No Evil
East End

East Bound
Fall of East

Speak No Evil
London Bridge
Bridge of Lies
Broken Bridge

The Donovans Series
Come Home Again (Nate & Delilah)
Love Reality (Ryan & Mia)
Race For Love (Derek & Kisima)
Love in Plain Sight (Dylan and Serafina)
Eye of the Beholder – (Logan & Jezzie)
Love Struck (Zephyr & Malia)

London Billionaires Standalones
Mr. Trouble (Jarred & Kinsley)
Mr. Big (Zach & Emma)
Mr. Dirty(Nathan & Sophie)

The Shameless World

Shameless
Shameless
Shameful
Unashamed

Force
Enforce

Deep
Deeper

Before Sin
Sin
Sinful

Brazen
Still Brazen

The Player
Bryce
Dax
Echo
Fox
Ransom
Gage

The In Stilettos Series
Sexy in Stilettos (Alec & Jaya)
Sultry in Stilettos (Beckett & Ricca)
Sassy in Stilettos (Caleb & Micha)
Strollers & Stilettos (Alec & Jaya & Alexa)
Seductive in Stilettos (Shane & Tristia)
Stunning in Stilettos (Bryan & Kyra)

~~~

In Stilettos Spin off
Tempting in Stilettos (Serena & Tyson)
Teasing in Stilettos (Cara & Tate)
Tantalizing in Stilettos (Jaggar & Griffin)

Love Match Series
*Game Set Match (Jason & Izzy)
Mismatch (Eli & Jessica)

Don't want to miss a single release? Click here!

Printed in Great Britain
by Amazon